LORD HUMPHREY

Sons of the Marquess
Book 2

A Regency Romance

by Mary Kingswood

D1267788

Lord Humphrey: Sons of the Marquess Book 2

Published by Sutors Publishing

ISBN: 978-1-912167-06-7 (paperback)

Cover design by: Shayne Rutherford of Darkmoon Graphics

Lord Humphrey: Sons of the Marquess Book 2

About this book:

Lord Humphrey Marford has a way with cards, dice and gambling of all forms. He'd love to start his own gaming house, but that takes a lot of money, far more than he or his brothers can come up with. His only solution is to marry an heiress, and he can't be too choosy.

Miss Hortensia Blythe seems perfect - pretty, charming and very, very rich, she's just home from India where her father made a fortune and left her every penny of it. But even as he courts the ladylike but rather dull Miss Blythe, Humphrey is drawn to her companion, who isn't nearly so ladylike, and isn't the slightest bit dull. Unfortunately, she's not rich, either. Whatever is he to do?

Book 2 of the 5-book Sons of the Marquess series, each a complete story with a HEA, but read all of them to find out all the secrets of the Marford family!

About Sons of the Marquess: *the Ninth Marquess of Carrbridge is happily married to the former Miss Constance Allamont, he has an heir and a spare in the nursery, and all seems set fair for a life of perfect bliss. His five younger brothers are a bit of a handful, but young men like to spread their wings a bit. If only they weren't so expensive! And whatever happened to that huge income his father used to boast about? It seems to have vanished in a generation. And now there's the unknown son of his father's who claims to be the legitimate heir to the Marquessate. It's a bit much for a Marquess to deal with. Fortunately, his wife has some ideas about recovering their position...*

Book 0: The Earl of Deveron (a novella, free to mailing list subscribers)
Book 1: Lord Reginald
Book 2: Lord Humphrey
Book 3: Lord Augustus
Book 4: Lord Montague
Book 5: Lord Gilbert

Table of Contents

1: A Tea Party

Lord Humphrey Marford could not recall ever being so nervous before. At the age of seven and twenty, and brother to the Marquess of Carrbridge, he was at ease moving through the saloons and ballrooms of the upper echelons of English society. He could converse with dowagers and debutantes, he could dance the quadrille with elegance, he could discuss the vagaries of the royal family in the clubs and he could play any game from chess to whist or backgammon, and win at most of them. He drove his curricle with style and was a fearsome rider to hounds. He knew the best tailors and bootmakers, and attired himself with panache. He was the complete gentleman, never at a loss.

But he had never before had to choose himself a bride.

Now that the moment had come, he was having second thoughts. It had seemed like such a good idea at the time — to marry a woman of independent wealth, and use those funds to establish his own gaming house. And his sister-in-law Connie, good soul that she was, had organised everything for him. Ten of the richest unmarried women she could find, invited to a modest tea party at Marford House, the family's London home, and he could meet them and make his choice.

He was not much in the petticoat line, it had to be said. A dance or two at a ball, for the sake of politeness, and then he usually took himself off to the card room for a few rubbers of whist and a glass or two of brandy. He had no objection to having a smartly-dressed lady beside him if he chose to drive his curricle around Hyde Park. He might even, if pressed and no better entertainment offered, join a party attending the theatre. But a room full of ladies was a challenge to his fortitude.

The difficulty was that these were not women of quality, the daughters of the aristocracy, with whom he had been familiar since infancy. No, the sort of money he needed could only be found amongst the men of trade. He had never mingled with such people before, had never even noticed them, except when one was pointed out to him at the theatre. Would the women be plain and ill-dressed? Would they be loud, with rough manners? Might they even have dreadful accents? He shuddered. And how would he manage to live with such a person, and entrust his children to her? It was not at all what he was used to. Then he laughed at himself. They were no different from anyone else, these rich women. The ones he had seen had been as fashionably dressed and as pretty as their aristocratic counterparts. No doubt they learnt the same accomplishments and know how to conduct themselves. What foolishness to be so afraid of them!

But still he loitered upstairs, listening to the doorbell ringing, and female voices wafting up from the hall below. Ten times the door opened to admit another young lady, with her chaperon. Twenty pairs of feet tripped across the tiled floor behind the butler and disappeared into the depths of the house. The hall fell silent. Now was the moment when he was supposed to present himself, as if by chance, expressing surprise to find so many charming guests in the house. He sincerely hoped they would be charming.

He could not delay the moment any longer. With a deep breath... then another... he trod slowly down the stairs, and through the house to the Chinese saloon. He opened the door to a cacophony of female chatter, like a cage full of birds, twittering away. At his entrance, the noise dropped away and twenty pairs of eyes turned towards him.

Twenty one pairs, for there was Connie, rising smoothly from her chair. Connie, he reminded himself, had not been born to the nobility. A provincial gentleman's daughter, although a very pretty and charming one, she had caught his oldest brother's eye, and now she was the Marchioness of Carrbridge, and as well-liked by the *ton* as any duke's daughter could be. No one looking at her elegant gown and fashionably short hair would guess her origins. His spirits lifted.

"Humphrey! How delightful! You are not rushing away, I hope. Do come in and meet my guests. We have tea and cake," she added coaxingly.

"So many ladies and not one gentleman," he said, as Connie had coached him to say. "I should be horribly in the way, I believe."

"Not at all," she said. "Lord Carrbridge will be here presently. Do stay for a while."

"If you are sure I shall not inconvenience the talk of gowns, I should be delighted."

And so, with their little performance out of the way, and the visitors, he hoped, convinced that he arrived by mere chance, he moved into the room, and Connie began the introductions.

They were not ill-dressed, that was his first impression. The young ladies were simply attired in pale muslins and fetching bonnets, their mamas in satin of blue or purple or brown, with feathers in their hats. They sipped their tea, and nibbled their cake, and eyed him with curiosity. When he talked to them, the debutantes simpered and their mamas chided them good-humouredly and responded on their behalf. He moved smoothly round the room, talking to everyone for a few minutes, then moving on, distributing his company evenly to all.

One young lady was different. Miss Hortensia Blythe was startlingly beautiful, with fair hair that fell into natural curls, wide blue eyes, and a pleasingly fine figure. When he addressed her, she answered composedly and sensibly, without blushing or simpering. He asked where she was from. She told him that she had arrived from India but days before, so she had not yet decided where to settle. Which county did he recommend, she wanted to know. He told her of his home in the wilds of Yorkshire and how much he loved to gallop across the moors. He wondered if she liked to ride. Yes, she did, and hoped to ride in Hyde Park as soon as she had worked out how to obtain a horse. He talked at length about the best places to rent a mount, and how to set up her stable if she planned to make a prolonged stay in London. Connie had to remind him to move on.

Humphrey dutifully worked his way around the room and then made an excuse to leave. Connie found him in the book room later.

"Well? What did you think? There were some very promising ones, I thought. Did you like the look of any of them?"

"The pretty blonde in the pink gown with the dark red spencer."

"Oh — Miss Blythe?" Her tone was surprised. "She is quite young, only eighteen or so."

"But rich?"

"Very. Two hundred thousand, if hearsay is to be believed, and it usually is. Miss Blythe's father was a nabob, and she is his only relative, so when he died he left her everything, without any conditions. She is only just out of mourning, which is why we have not seen her anywhere before. I believe she spent some years with her mother in England before joining her father in India a few years ago. Is she a firm favourite? You have settled on her already?"

"She was the only one capable of stringing together a coherent sentence. I could not conceivably marry a woman who does nothing but simper and blush."

"That is what I like about you, Humphrey — you are so very decisive."

"It is the gambler in me," he said smiling. "Weigh up the cards at a glance, and make your play with no dithering."

She laughed and patted his cheek. "Whatever the cause, it makes everything easy. I shall invite her to Drummoor over the summer, then, and you may get to know her better. But Humphrey… do not be swayed by blue eyes and a large fortune. Remember that if you marry her, you will spend the rest of your life together, so you must be very sure of your affection for her. If she does not suit, there are plenty more."

Humphrey smiled. "Connie, you are such a romantic! I am not marrying for love, and I shall not expect it of my wife. I need a fortune, and she will gain entry to a marquess's family and will move in the first circles. It will be a business arrangement, nothing more. The most important consideration is that she knows how to conduct herself in society, and will not bring shame on me or the family. Love has nothing to do with it."

She tipped her head to one side and looked at him appraisingly. "Well, you know your own mind best, I daresay, but love has a way of creeping up on one whether one wishes it or not. Look at Reggie — he began in exactly that way, determined to make a pragmatic match, and ended up head over heels in love. Be careful the same does not happen with you and Miss Blythe."

"I am quite safe," Humphrey said with a smile. "I have mixed with the cream of the *ton* these ten years past, and it is not boasting to say that I have had innumerable caps thrown at me in vain. A Miss Hortensia Blythe of no family and no settled home is not likely to touch my heart, you may be sure."

~~~~~

The said Miss Hortensia Blythe and her friend and companion Miss Rosemary Quayle, also of no family and no settled home, leaned back against the squabs of the carriage as it moved at a stately pace through the streets of London, taking them away from Marford House.

"Well, what did you think?" Hortensia said.

Rosemary turned wide eyes to her. "Such elegance! Such a magnificent domed roof! And the chimney piece is as fine as any I saw anywhere."

"Ah, the famous Chinese saloon. Yes, it is very fine, and displays the marchioness's eye for colour to perfection. But what did you think of the company?"

"Lady Carrbridge is delightful. No one could have been more attentive. And Lord Carrbridge is delightful too. So charming and condescending."

"And Lord Humphrey? Is he delightful as well? And oh so *very* condescending, to throw a tea party at the end of the season for all the daughters of cits and nabobs, who would never be invited to a ball at Marford House, you may be sure. Honestly, Rosemary, your wits have gone a-begging if you are dazzled by these people. The only difference between them and us is that some ancestor of Lord Carrbridge's proved of service to a long-dead king. Henry the something, most likely. There were a great many Henrys at one time."

"And Edwards," Rosemary said. "Plenty of Edwards in the middle ages, too. Now it is all Georges. You would think, would you not, that they would want some variety, if only for convenience. Think how tedious it must be to call out for George and have two or three of them come running." She turned wide, innocent eyes on her friend.

"There, that is better," Hortensia said, laughing. "I knew your quickness would reassert itself. But these aristocrats have no imagination. In Lord Carrbridge's family, for instance, the eldest son is always Francis and the next is Reginald. I looked them up in Debrett's. Long lines of men called Francis, and the occasional Reginald. But then, the present marquess's father was a Charles. The third son, you see. No imagination. We are better off without the society of these people. Shall we go to Brighton? It is much more suited to vulgar people like us, for the Prince of Wales goes there."

"You are too cynical," Rosemary said thoughtfully. "I liked Lord and Lady Carrbridge very much, and Lord Humphrey, too. Their manners were excellent, and they made *me* feel very welcome. And the cake was the best I have had since we left Madras, so on those grounds alone I count them among the finest of our acquaintance."

Their laughter lasted the remainder of the journey home, and they talked no more of Lord Humphrey. But if Hortensia said nothing, her thoughts were full of a tall, golden-haired man with shoulders so broad his well-fitted coat needed no padding.

~~~~~

With the season over, Drummoor was a very dreary prospect. Of Humphrey's five brothers, Reggie was off in the depths of the Fens paying court to his betrothed, Gus was at Tattersall's looking for work with horses, Monty was in York being turned into a clergyman, and Gil was in uniform, having joined the King's Own Regiment of

Hussars. Even Harriet had gone off to Brighton with friends. Only Carrbridge and Lady Carrbridge would be there, and the usual array of elderly aunts and uncles and cousins, who ate the marquess's beef and drank his wine and filled the saloons after dinner with their card games, but hardly counted as company for a restless young man of twenty seven.

The long journey north was tedious in the extreme, the weather too uncertain for Humphrey to drive his curricle or even to ride. He sat in the carriage with Carrbridge and Connie for hour after endless hour, until he thought he would go mad if he had to sit still for a single minute longer. As soon as the carriage rolled into the yard of their overnight inn, followed by the servants' carriage and two luggage wagons, Humphrey would leap down and stride off down the street of whatever nondescript little town he found himself in, heedless of the rain. An hour or two of brisk activity was just enough to sustain him through the long, dull hours after dinner.

Reaching Drummoor was a relief, and Humphrey was aback a horse and away across the park before the last of the wagons had been unloaded. He rode at an easy canter at first, for this was Reggie's horse, his own not being in the stables. Away to the village to be shod, he supposed, or else being exercised by one of the grooms. Once he was sure of the horse's footing, he gave it its head and tore across the furthest quarter of the park, flying over the wall and then over three or four fields before slowing with a shout of pure delight. Ah, the freedom, the speed, the thrill of a fast ride! This one was not the equal of his own splendid Ganymede, but it was well enough. He cantered past Wester Drum farm, waving to a group hay making in the distance, then trotted through Drum Woods and on upwards to the open moors.

The ground was too uneven just there to give the horse his head, so he rode at an easy canter along the track for some miles, until he spotted another rider heading towards him rather fast. He slowed his pace to await the inevitable meeting, but long before it occurred, he had identified both rider and horse. The rider was the marquess's agent, Mr Sharp, and the horse was his own, the very horse he had hoped to ride. Its absence had forced him to take Reggie's. He bit back his annoyance — it was impudent, for Sharp had several perfectly good horses at his disposal, and need not have taken a creature as fine as Ganymede, although he could hardly blame him for wanting to. But when he saw the horse lathered and labouring, all his ire flared up in an instant.

"What are you doing to my horse, sir?" he cried, before Sharp was well within earshot.

The agent trotted nearer and pulled up, the horse breathing heavily.

"Good day, my lord, good day!" he said, doffing his old-fashioned tricorn hat, and bowing so low that his nose almost touched the horse's mane. "And a fine one now that the rain has stopped. I was not aware you were expected today, my lord."

"Evidently, or you would not have dared to take Ganymede, or to use him so ill."

"I must humbly beg your pardon, my lord, the fault was entirely mine. He had not been out of the stable for some days, seeming restless to my unskilled eye, and it seemed a good plan to give the animal the exercise he craved. However, I discovered that he was a little too fresh for my meagre abilities and, to my shame, he got away from me rather before I could rein him in."

"How far have you ridden him?" Humphrey said.

"Not far, my lord. Not far at all. I have just been over to Great Mellingham — a small problem with the chimneys, very easily rectified."

Humphrey was too angry to care about chimneys. "I will ride back with you to Drummoor to see Ganymede attended to. We will walk or trot, nothing faster."

"Of course, my lord," Sharp said, doffing his hat again and bowing even lower. "I can only repeat my sincere apologies, and humbly beg your indulgence for any offence, my lord. It was by no means my intent."

They rode back a great deal more slowly, Humphrey seething all the way, although he could see that the horse was already recovering. At the stables, Sharp would have attended to Ganymede himself, but Humphrey impatiently dismissed him. He left Reggie's horse to the care of one of the grooms, and himself began to unsaddle and clean up Ganymede. The horse whickered happily at him.

"Ah, you remember me, you good fellow, for all I have been gone for months. But look at the state of you!"

"Want me to take over, milord?" Humphrey peered over the horse's back to see the familiar grinning face of his groom.

"Ah, there you are, Tom. No, but you can give me a hand, if you wish."

"Lord, where's you been with him, milord? He's covered in burrs."

"So he is. And this one is no ordinary burr. This is a whole teasel. Where *has* Sharp taken you, old fellow?" he said thoughtfully, rubbing the horse's flank.

"Mr Sharp took him out?" Tom said, frowning. "He didn't ought to have done that!"

"On that point we are agreed," Humphrey said acidly.

"But there's no teasels round here," Tom said.

"Indeed. I know of only one place within thirty miles where such things grow. And why did Sharp want to go *there*?"

2: *To And From Drummoor*

Leaving Tom to attend to Ganymede, Humphrey went into the house, striding through the twisting corridors and across courtyards to the principal rooms surrounding Drummoor's main entrance. It took some time but eventually he tracked down Daniel Merton, secretary to the marquess. The two had their heads together over the desk in the ship room, so named for the paintings of ships on the walls, which the marquess used as both office and refuge.

Carrbridge's face bore the pained expression that meant he was being asked to deal with what he called *'papers'* — complaints from his tenants, letters from his lawyers, bills and other pestilences. There were also disputes between neighbours, who naturally turned to him for his opinion as the local landlord and magistrate. For all the residents of farms and villages and mills and small towns this side of York, the Marquess of Carrbridge was the law, a role he found difficult to carry out when all he really asked from life was that everyone should get along together, as befitted friends and neighbours.

Merton's arrival had been a blessing, for he made such matters easy. He had been brought in to evaluate the state of the marquess's finances, and had found so many deficiencies and generally made himself indispensable, that he was now employed as secretary, trying to bring order to the marquess's vast array of properties, holdings and leases. He, if anyone, would be able to answer Humphrey's question.

"There you are, Humphrey," Carrbridge exclaimed, looking up in obvious relief as his brother strode across the room. "Lord, have you been out riding already? I wish *I* could do so, but Merton keeps me chained to my desk dealing with papers, as you can see."

"The obligations of rank, brother," Humphrey said impatiently. "You get the title and the money, but you get to deal with the tedious legal business as well."

"But it is so *difficult*," Carrbridge said. "If I did not have Merton, I should not know what to do at all."

"How fortunate that you have him, then," Humphrey said. "Good day to you, Merton. You have had a pleasant time of it while we have been gallivanting in London, I daresay."

"Very quiet, Lord Humphrey, very quiet." Merton made a respectful bow. "Nothing untoward to report." Merton was not a handsome man, for his face was too thin for good looks, and his hair too straight for fashion, but he was very clever and methodical, qualities which Humphrey held in high regard.

"Is Lady Hardy still here?"

Merton's smile lit up his thin face. "Her ladyship was required at Brinford Manor for a month or so to help with the new baronet's children, but she returned here a few days ago, and is hard at work cataloguing the books in the library most mornings. I believe she is reading to Lady Hester just now."

"Excellent," Humphrey said, with a little smile. "And your house? Are the renovations completed yet?"

"Almost, my lord," Merton said. "The kitchen and principal rooms are completed, and mostly furnished. I moved in two weeks ago, although I am still taking my dinners here, until I have engaged a cook."

"I hope you will always eat with us, Merton," Carrbridge said at once. "I do not like to think of you eating all alone in Lake Cottage."

"Besides, who else will play chess against Lady Hardy in the evenings?" Humphrey said, and was amused to see Merton look conscious. He had long suspected a budding romance between the two, since Lady Hardy had been widowed the previous winter.

"You are very kind, my lord," Merton said. "However, there is little point in renting a house for myself if I make no use of it. Lady Hardy and Lady Carrbridge are to help me interview a possible cook tomorrow. Lord Humphrey, you arrived in such haste, and direct from the stables, that I do not believe you are here to enquire after my domestic arrangements. I shall leave you to talk to Lord Carrbridge now."

"Actually, you are the very person I have been seeking," Humphrey said. "Where exactly is Great Mellingham estate? It is east of here, is it not? Do you go there by way of Drum Woods?"

"That is one possible route, my lord, turning east just past the woods, although it is very exposed. Or you could go south of here and pick up the turnpike — that is a better way in inclement weather. Do you have business there, my lord? There is no one in residence at the moment, with the renovations going on. I was there about ten days ago, and all was in order then."

"Was there some problem with the chimneys?" Humphrey said.

"Chimneys? Not that I heard, my lord."

"Hmm." Humphrey frowned. "That is as I thought. Do we have an estate over by the fulling mill?"

"Silsby Milton? Not to my knowledge, but I have not yet established a complete picture of all his lordship's properties. I have a map in the writing room, if you would be interested."

Humphrey would indeed be very interested, so the three of them made their way there. The writing room had been the office of the eighth marquess, Humphrey's and Carrbridge's father. Merton had been given the task of sorting the vast number of documents and letters filed away in the many large cabinets therein. On one wall he had nailed two maps, one of the local area and one of the whole of Great Britain, each marked with pins with strips of ribbon in various colours.

"The red pins are properties for which the lawyers in London hold the titles," Merton said, "and the blue are those for which the title is in the safe here. The green ones are those which are mentioned in papers, but the title cannot be located, and these yellow ones… well, I *suspect* the marquess owns it, but I cannot be sure."

"Good God!" Humphrey said. "Wales! And Cornwall! And so many greens and yellows. What a mess! I suppose some of these have been sold, and that is why there is no traceable title?"

"Sold or lost at the faro table," Merton said with a wry smile. "Very likely."

"Have you asked Sharp?" Humphrey said. "He claims to know everything, although he says he keeps all the information in his head."

"If he knows anything about these properties, he will not divulge it to me," Merton said.

"He will divulge it to me," Carrbridge said abruptly. "I will not have my *agent* withholding information from my *secretary*, as if you were enemies. You both work on my behalf, and Sharp will be helpful or find himself dismissed. I do not understand maps at all," he added plaintively, tipping his head first one way and then the other. "What are all these squiggly lines? And where are we in all this jumble of colours, Merton?"

"This black square is Drummoor, my lord. And here is York, and London is down there. The squiggly lines are either roads or rivers. This is the moor road to York and this is the turnpike."

"It is all very confusing," Carrbridge grumbled.

"So there is nothing anywhere near Silsby Milton?" Humphrey said. "That is curious, for I met Sharp up on the moors, just here." He stabbed a finger at the local map. "He *said* he had been to Great Mellingham to see about the chimneys but his horse — or rather, *my* horse, for he had taken Ganymede, the impudent fellow — had teasels in his mane. That can only have come from near the fulling mill at Silsby Milton, which is away up here."

"That is strange," Merton said, frowning. "It is quite the wrong direction."

"Well, let us ask him," Carrbridge said. "I do not like mysteries of this nature, nor secrecy. We shall go there at once and have an explanation from him."

But when they made their way to Sharp's cottage, they found no one there but his timid wife, who could tell them nothing except that he had eaten his dinner and gone out again, and she had no idea where.

"As soon as he returns, send him to me," the marquess said. "At once, mind!"

They returned to the house in a very disgruntled frame of mind.

~~~~~

Hortensia squeaked with astonishment.

"Whatever is the matter?" Rosemary said, her eyes wide with alarm. "Not bad news, I hope?"

"It is from the Marchioness of Carrbridge, and we are invited to stay at Drummoor for a month."

Rosemary's knife clattered to her plate. They were sitting at the breakfast table, drinking chocolate and eating ham and toast. Hortensia had paid to receive an early delivery of mail, but they had seen little benefit from it, their correspondence being mainly polite bills and inducements to spend even more money from their mantua maker, milliner and haberdasher. They had few acquaintance in town, and now that the season was all but over, invitations of any sort were thin on the ground.

This particular invitation was unexpected, and the two women stared at each other.

"But why?" Rosemary said, her eyes wide.

"Now that is a very good question," Hortensia said crisply. "Why, indeed? It cannot be for the pleasure of our company, for we have barely exchanged three sentences with any of them. Nor are we of sufficiently high rank to expect to mingle with such people. So it must be the money, and one of the unmarried sons will lower himself to charm the vulgar daughter of a nabob. Lord Humphrey, of course. Do you remember that tea party at Marford House?"

"Oh yes! The Chinese saloon!"

"And Lord Humphrey, with all the cits' heiresses lined up for him to inspect and make his choice, I daresay."

"You make it sound so cold and calculating," Rosemary said. "It is done all the time — a title and vouchers to Almacks in exchange for a fortune. Younger sons have very little to live on, so they must trade on their wits and charm. And he *was* charming, I thought, and handsome too, if a little large. Did you not like him?"

"He was well enough, I daresay," Hortensia said nonchalantly, with an indifferent lift of one shoulder. Yet instantly her mind was filled with the vision of a tall, broad-shouldered man, in a well-cut coat. It was a vision that had troubled her dreams rather. How foolish of her to mope over a man who had undoubtedly never even noticed her.

"He was very tall, with a flamboyant style of dress," Rosemary said. "Rather overpowering."

"A typical aristocrat, then."

"Oh. So you will decline the invitation?"

"Not at all! The moors! And fast horses! Oh, think of the freedom, Rosemary! Think of being able to ride properly again, as I have not since we left Madras. A gentle canter around Hyde Park is not at all the same. I remember every word Lord Humphrey said about his horses and the country around Drummoor. I should dearly like to go there to see it for myself, if I can. And oh, the pleasure of escaping the city — the noise, the bustle, the smells! I can hardly breathe here. I am sure there is good, clean air aplenty in Yorkshire. So yes, let us go, by all means, unless you dislike the idea excessively, dear?"

"Oh, no, not at all! I never did like the thought of Brighton or Bath, for they sound just like London, only smaller and stuffier. We should still know no one, and would have to walk about without anyone to escort us and attend only subscription events and try to pretend we are enjoying ourselves."

"Poor Rosemary, have you disliked London as much as I have?"

"Indeed not, for it has been most interesting. I enjoyed the Tower of London very much, and I do not mind the crowds in the least. However, there is no denying that it is much more comfortable to *know* people and have friends to chat to. I shall like to go to Drummoor, for Lord and Lady Carrbridge were quite delightful, and an intimate house party is so very agreeable, is it not?"

And so to Drummoor they were to go.

~~~~~

After missing Sharp the previous evening, Carrbridge, Humphrey and Merton went to Sharp's cottage before breakfast the following day.

Again, Mrs Sharp's timid face peered round the door at them. She was neatly dressed, but her gown was old-fashioned and patched, and her hair was covered by a cap grey with age. "Begging your pardon, milord, but he ain't here."

"My good woman," the marquess said in exasperated tones, "I gave you a very clear instruction — your husband was to present himself to me the instant he returned home."

"Begging your pardon, milord, but he hasn't been home," she said. "Never come back last night."

"Well, where is he?"

"Begging your pardon, milord, but I don't know. He never said."

"I suppose he never said when he would be back, either?" She shook her head. "This is not good enough," the marquess said, and the hapless Mrs Sharp quailed at his peremptory tone. "We have important questions to be answered, which only Sharp can address. What are we supposed to do now?" Mrs Sharp bowed her head, one hand convulsively grasping and releasing a corner of her apron.

"If I may make a suggestion, my lord," Merton said.

"Pray do so."

"The legal documents to the properties in question will no doubt be safely locked away in Mr Sharp's office. If we can find them, we need not trouble Mr Sharp at all."

"Oh." The marquess seemed surprised. "That is a very simple solution, and they are *my* documents, after all, are they not?"

"Indubitably, my lord."

"Very well. Mrs Sharp, pray admit us to Sharp's office."

She swallowed several times, and the grasping and releasing of the apron became more rapid. "Begging your pardon, milord..." She stopped, heaved a great breath and then went on in a rush. "Can't do it, milord, so help me, it's the gospel truth, but I can't."

"Of course you can, madam," Carrbridge said gently. "I will explain it to Sharp, you know, so no blame will attach to you."

"No, no! Really can't, milord. It's locked, see, and only Mr Sharp has the key. Keeps it in his waistcoat, see, never lets go of it, so you see—"

"Nonsense. He keeps the front parlour as his office, does he not? Well, then, admit us at once, madam."

She retreated into the house immediately, and they all trooped in to the narrow hall. The first door on the right was the office, and it was, as Mrs Sharp had said, locked.

"I shall not be denied access to my own papers," Carrbridge said haughtily. "We shall break down the door. Ready, Humphrey?"

Humphrey laughed. "Carrbridge, I am as willing as the next man to break down a door, but shall we not try Bill Carpenter first? He got the Whittleton children out when they locked themselves in the stable court attics two years ago, remember? He is very competent with locks."

So Bill Carpenter was sent for, a wizened little man who grinned from ear to ear when his task was explained to him. He produced a collection of strangely shaped metal implements, and set to work on the door's lock. Within two or three minutes a satisfying clunk announced his success. He threw open the door, while Mrs Sharp moaned a little in distress.

Carrbridge strode into the room, then stopped dead. "Good God!"

Humphrey peered over his brother's shoulder. The room was furnished with a desk, several chairs and an array of cabinets and shelves, but it was hard to see them as every inch of available surface was covered in papers and letters and documents with official seals. More papers littered the floor in great heaps.

"I had heard Sharp is not too meticulous about filing," Humphrey murmured. Behind him, Mrs Sharp could be heard softly moaning.

"This is unacceptable!" Carrbridge said, spinning round and brushing past Humphrey. "Merton, get some men here and pack up all these papers. Get them over to the writing room. They are yours, now. Mrs Sharp, when your husband returns, tell him that I am deeply disappointed in him." He took one last look at the devastation, then, with an exclamation of disgust, he strode off, with Bill Carpenter scampering after him.

Mrs Sharp whimpered, and ran off into the back area of the house, leaving Merton and Humphrey gazing at each other in surprise.

"Well, that was interesting," Humphrey said.

"The state of the office? I had heard rumours—"

"No, no. I meant Carrbridge. When he gets in high dudgeon like that, he looks exactly like Father. Quite unnerving."

3: Silsby Vale

The entire day was taken up with packing the multitude of papers into old travelling boxes and conveying them to the house. Because they might be confidential, Merton and Humphrey undertook all the packing themselves, and left the grooms and footmen only the task of carrying the boxes. But eventually it was done, every drawer and shelf of Sharp's office cleared, and the boxes safely locked away in the writing room, awaiting the gargantuan effort of sorting the papers into some kind of order.

"As if you did not have enough to do already, dealing with all Father's letters," Humphrey said to Merton that evening, as they sat over their port after dinner. "And there is Carrbridge's correspondence, too."

Merton gave a deprecating shrug. "I had sooner have too much to do than too little, my lord, although it might speed the process to engage someone to help me, if Lord Carrbridge agrees."

"Lady Hardy, perhaps?" Humphrey said slyly.

Merton became a little flushed, but answered with his usual composure. "No, my lord. Some of the late marquess's letters are... not quite suitable for a lady's eyes."

"Not even when the lady in question is married?" Humphrey said, amused.

"Even then," Merton said calmly. "As for Sharp's papers, you saw for yourself how many were personal correspondence."

"Of Father's?" Carrbridge said. "Why then does Sharp have them?"

"That I could not answer," Merton said. "I daresay over the years Mr Sharp has acted as secretary as well as agent, since there was no appointed secretary."

"I did have a secretary, rather briefly," Carrbridge said. "Poor Penicuik! He was the chaplain here before his tragedy."

"So I have heard. Whatever happened to him?" Merton said.

"We never talk about it," Carrbridge said with a shudder. "It was all too horrible for words. So who shall you engage to assist you, Merton?"

"I thought Mr Julius Whittleton, my lord, since he is family, and I daresay he would appreciate a little extra money. I shall pay him out of my own pocket, of course."

"No need to do that," Carrbridge said. "I do not pay you such a high salary as all that, and you have your house to furnish and so forth."

"I have some money of my own," Merton said. "When I had the management of Sir Osborne Hardy's financial affairs, I was able to arrange some of his investments to greater advantage. In gratitude, he was so kind as to leave me a small bequest in his will, enough to give me an independence."

"He was a very warm man, Sir Osborne," Humphrey said thoughtfully. "I daresay he left Lady Hardy well provided for, too."

"Her settlement was most generous," Merton said.

"Although I suppose it reverts to the estate if she remarries?"

"No, it is hers without conditions. There were also some substantial pieces of jewellery."

"What is this sudden interest in Lady Hardy's fortune, Humphrey?" Carrbridge said. "Should I expect an announcement from you very soon?"

Humphrey laughed. "Well, I have nothing but my allowance from you and the use of one of the hunting lodges, so a wealthy widow is an appealing prospect. Besides, she is a very handsome woman, would you not agree, Merton?"

"Very handsome, my lord," Merton said, with a smile that lit his dour face. "Her income is twelve hundred and fifty pounds a year, if you should wish to try your luck with her."

"I am not so sure," Humphrey said solemnly. "The income is an attraction, certainly, but Lady Hardy's skill at the chessboard would be a problem. She is an excellent card player, too. Imagine the disappointment of a wife who constantly defeats one. It would be more than a man's esteem could bear, and I do have my reputation as a skilled gamester to consider. *You* are the only man who can defeat her at chess, I believe, Merton. I daresay Miss Blythe would suit me better. She looks as if she would let me win at everything. Connie has invited her, I take it?"

"She has, although there has been no reply as yet," Carrbridge said. "But Humphrey, you should be cautious. You know nothing of this girl or her family."

"She is rich," Humphrey said, with an indifferent shrug. "What more needs to be said?"

"No one in London knows anything about her or her family."

"Her father lived in India for years. I daresay they have no acquaintance in England at all," Humphrey said. "If it ever comes to a betrothal, I shall make stringent enquiries of her lawyers and financial advisers, you may be sure. But I do not care who her family is, Carrbridge."

"Nevertheless, I shall write to Mrs Mallory, I believe. Beatrice married into the Stoner family, if you recall, and they are — or were — nabobs. Made their whole fortune in India. Mr Stoner may know something of Miss Blythe and her father. And by all means engage Julius Whittleton, Merton. He is a handsome fellow and very much admired by the ladies, but he is not interesting company and he has such a prodigious appetite. It will do him good to earn his beef."

~~~~~

The following day, the weather was favourable enough to tempt Humphrey on a longer than usual ride. Since he was curious about how Ganymede had acquired a teasel in his mane and Sharp had not yet returned, Humphrey followed the same route as his previous ride. Having stretched Ganymede's legs and burnt off his first burst of energy by galloping across the park and fields, he rode more circumspectly through the woods and up to the moor.

He half expected to meet Sharp again, but he saw no sign of any other rider, and cantered on along the broad track at an easy pace. The track forked at a small copse, where once had stood an inn. One way led to Great Mellingham, but Humphrey rode to the west, past a few small hamlets, crossing the York road at the Old Cross Inn, before plunging down into the cool woodlands of Silsby Vale. At the bottom of the descent where the valley opened out was the fulling mill, its cluster of outbuildings and cottages around it. To one side was the field of teasels, grown for their usefulness in the fulling process.

Here Humphrey halted. The road from the inn ran straight on down the valley to the village of Silsby Vale, but there was a narrow track leading through the teasels. He had never been that way before, but clearly Ganymede had, for in no other way could he have acquired teasels in his mane. So Humphrey nudged the horse in that direction, and Ganymede started forward with energy, ears pricked.

The track ran straight through the field, so that the heads of the teasels pressed close, reaching as high as Humphrey's shoulder. The new year's growth fell away as the horse pushed through it, but the older growth, with last year's dried heads still clinging to the stems, snapped easily, leaving spiky burrs attached to Ganymede's mane and coat.

Emerging from the teasel field, the track ran into a narrow valley of smallholdings, busy with chickens, men hoeing, and women draping laundry over bushes, small children at their heels. They all stopped and stared as Humphrey passed by, before turning back to their work.

At the bottom of the valley, the track met a larger lane, but Humphrey had no need to wonder which way to turn, for Ganymede pushed on eagerly, knowing the way. Before too long, palings appeared to one side of the lane and then a gate, standing invitingly open. Humphrey slackened the reins, and the horse turned in at the gate without hesitation.

Humphrey found himself in front of the entrance to a house. It was a gentleman's house, of that there was no doubt. The size, the well-maintained grounds, with a couple of gardeners hard at work, and the tracks of carriage wheels proclaimed it so. He had no idea where he was, but the horse did, that much was clear.

Dismounting gracefully, Humphrey stepped aside to look about him, and at once the horse trotted off and turned a corner of the house with a whicker of pleasure, as if he had arrived home. With an exclamation of annoyance, Humphrey strode after him. As expected, there were the stables tucked away behind the house, and a man had come out to attend to the horse.

"Well, Ganymede, what are you doing back so soon?" the groom said, catching hold of the horse's bridle. Then he saw Humphrey. "Hoy! Who are you?" The groom, a man of forty or so, glared at him.

Humphrey made his way along the side of the house to the stables without haste. "I am Lord Humphrey Marford of Drummoor, brother to the Marquess of Carrbridge."

"Ho, are you now?" the groom said. "And I'm the Prince of Wales."

"Your Royal Highness," Humphrey said, executing a deep bow. "What an unexpected pleasure. I had thought you to be at Brighton."

"Ha," the groom said humourlessly. "You think you're very funny, I daresay."

"Oh, no more than mildly amusing. Your name, my fine prince?"

The groom gave a bark of laughter. "Robert," he said, lifting his chin. "Been groom and coachman here, man and boy, for more'n twenty years."

"That is commendable," Humphrey said, politely. "But tell me, Robert, what is this place?"

"Why, 'tis Silsby Vale House, did you not know?"

"I did not. My horse turned in here and—"

"Your horse? Where is your horse?"

"You are holding him," Humphrey said, bewildered.

The groom laughed. "This ain't *your* horse. This is the master's horse, Ganymede."

"I assure you, Ganymede is *my* horse. I bought him from Tattersall's three years ago, and I can recount his sires and dams for almost as many generations as my own. Who is your master, Robert, and who owns this place?"

"Why, Mr Sharp is master and owns the house, same as he owns this here horse."

This was not entirely a surprise. Humphrey sighed. "We can resolve this very easily. Is Sharp at home? He will vouch for my name and also my ownership of the horse."

"He ain't here, and you can just go about your business, you horse thief, you. Think yourself lucky I don't set the constables on you. Go on, get out of here."

"Is anyone else at home?"

"Not to the likes of you," the groom said stoutly.

The groom's obstinacy was becoming tedious. By this time, a junior groom had emerged from the stable and the two gardeners were loitering interestedly, scythes in hand. Humphrey enjoyed a good mill as much as the next man, and usually won them, too, but four against one made for challenging odds, and he had no wish to start a fracas around so valuable an animal as Ganymede. He raised his hands and backed away.

But as soon as he had rounded the corner of the house again and was out of sight of the stable and the suspicious eye of Robert, he bounced up the steps to the front door and rang the doorbell. The door was answered by a sour-faced housekeeper of similar age to the groom.

"Yes?"

"Good morning... or is it afternoon? I beg pardon for disturbing you, but I have lost my horse, and would appreciate some assistance. Is anyone at home?"

"No."

"No one? Who lives here, then?"

"Mistress lives here, but she don't receive casual callers."

"And your mistress's name?" Humphrey said patiently.

The housekeeper stared at him, obviously debating whether to answer or not, but whether his expensive riding clothes or his accent convinced her that he was a gentleman, at length she said, "This is the home of Mrs Cecil Andrews, sir."

"Would you give my card to your mistress and ask if she would be so good as to receive me?"

The housekeeper's eyes widened as she read his name on the card. She disappeared inside, shutting the door. Humphrey waited without impatience on the step until the door creaked open again.

"Mistress will see you." The surprise in her tone made it clear that this was a rare honour.

Humphrey was shown into a pretty little drawing room, furnished more to comfort and practicality than fashion. Mrs Andrews was alone, a woman approaching fifty, but with her looks intact, and her gown designed to flatter a rather fine figure.

"Oh, do come in, my lord. Oh yes, I see the likeness now. Your father had fair hair, too."

"You knew my father?"

"Many years ago. Pray be seated. Mildred, bring some tea."

Humphrey declined the tea, but sat on a well-cushioned sofa, while the lady of the house perched on its twin.

"How very kind in you to call, for I am so out of the way here that I have few visitors, as you may imagine," she trilled, her cheeks flushed and her eyes bright. "Such a treat for me! But I daresay you bring me a message from Mr Sharp?"

"No, not at all," Humphrey said. "I had no knowledge of Sharp's connection to this place until five minutes ago."

"Oh!" Her face registered first bewilderment and then alarm. "Oh, but I thought… since you are from Drummoor, I assumed—"

"That Sharp had sent me? No. He… *owns* this house, I think the groom said?"

She stared at him, then nodded very slowly.

"How interesting. But not relevant at the moment. My problem, Mrs Andrews, is that your groom, Robert, is claiming that Sharp also owns my horse, Ganymede, and is refusing to release him to me. This is, as you may imagine, rather inconvenient. Please tell your servant to return my horse to me, and then I shall leave you all in peace."

"Ganymede is yours?" she said faintly.

"He is. Sharp had no business to take him out. So if you would be so good—"

"I can't!" she said, hand to mouth. "I just can't! Ambrose would flay me alive if I interfere with his horses. The house… I may do as I please, but the stables are his domain. One of the gardeners rode one of the carriage horses once, and—" She broke off, shuddering, and two great tears rolled down her cheeks. She was one of those rare women who still look pretty while in tears, and Humphrey guessed it was a stratagem she had used for effect many times in the past. He was not influenced by her tears, but it was clear that Sharp was a firm master here, and he had no hope that she would relent.

He rose to his feet. "Is there a village nearby where I might hire a horse?" She shook her head. "An inn, perhaps?"

"The… the Old Cross. At the top of the vale."

"On the York road?" He sighed. He had a long walk ahead of him.

4: *The Old Cross Inn*

Humphrey went back round to the stables first, to check that Ganymede was being properly cared for, but his enquiries of the groom elicited the same response that he'd had from Mrs Andrews — the nearest inn was on the York road. There was nothing for it but to climb back up the vale, past the fulling mill and upwards through the trees until he reached the moors again. A few miles, no more — perhaps an hour, or maybe two, and then he could hire a horse. He would be late for dinner, but Connie would forgive him.

As he walked steadily up the vale past the farmers, he mulled over the odd situation at Silsby Vale House. Was it feasible that Sharp really owned the property? He spent nothing on himself or his wife, so perhaps it was possible. But what then was his relationship to Mrs Andrews? If she were no more than a tenant, there would be no need for Sharp to visit more than once each quarter, or perhaps only on Lady Day. Yet Ganymede was familiar enough with the house to find his own way to the stables — that was not the result of quarterly visits.

Well, it would not be the first time a man kept a mistress hidden away, yet the cost of such an establishment must be large. Even if the gardeners came in now and again from one of the farms, there were still the two manservants — Robert the coachman, and a younger man to act as both groom and footman. Adding in several female servants indoors, and it could not be sustained on much under a thousand pounds a year, he suspected. No matter how he looked at it, he could not reconcile such an expenditure with Sharp, who spent nothing at all on himself or his wife, not even the price of a new coat or gown once a year. He shook his head and walked on.

It was only when it seemed to take an unconscionable length of time to reach the mill that he began to wonder about his timing. He was not a slow walker, but the sun was already well down the sky before he made his way through the teasel field and past the fulling mill. Then there was a seemingly endless climb through the woods. Humphrey had eaten nothing since breakfast, and now rather regretted turning down the offer of tea and perhaps cake.

He was beginning to wonder if he had gone astray, although there had been few branches away from the track, when, quite abruptly, he came out into open country. Now there was no more than a mile or so to reach the inn. He saw it on the horizon long before he reached it, its walls painted red by the dying sun. Beside it, the silhouette of the leaning cross that gave the place its name.

The inn was not one popular with the coach trade, being largely a cheap place for wagons to pass the night. Often, the wagon drivers did not even bother with a room, spending the evening in the tap room and then bedding down for the night on their own wagons. But there were stables and hot food and plenty of ale, and Humphrey was known there, so he was not greeted by facetiousness when he gave his name.

Tommy, the innkeeper, was appropriately deferential, but he regretted to inform his noble patron that there were no horses to be had. He kept three or four spares as a rule, but by ill fortune all were elsewhere, and he had nothing suitable to offer.

"Nothing I'd want to ride across the moors at night, any road," Tommy said. "Not with no moon, and riding alone and all, milord.

Why, if you was to fall and break your neck, think how badly I'd feel."

"I should not feel too cheerful about it myself," Humphrey said. "You are right, it is too dark now to ride. May I take advantage of your hospitality, Tommy?"

"Course, my lord. Tilda, light a fire in the best bedroom for his lordship. And you'll be wanting a parlour, I daresay?"

"No need for that. The taproom will serve me well enough. I hope Meg has something edible left in the kitchen?"

Humphrey was soon provided with a jug of ale and another of something Tommy assured him was wine, together with a bowl of brown liquid with unidentifiable lumps floating in it. He felt that opinions might differ on whether this concoction was actually edible or not, but he made a valiant attempt to find out. At least the bread was not too stale. He wondered what delights he was missing at Drummoor — goose, perhaps, or a tasty pigeon pie, with the first peas and strawberries from the vegetable garden, and a syllabub to follow, washed down with a decent drop of claret. He sighed, and pushed aside the bowl. There was nothing for it but to go to bed.

Here again the standards of the establishment left something to be desired. Humphrey was used to the best inns on the London to York route, with everything of superior quality. He had never stayed at the Old Cross Inn before, but he could see at a glance that the bedrooms were most definitely not of superior quality. The bedding was rough, and he suspected the mattress to be stuffed with heather. There was no other furniture in the room apart from a small table, a rickety chair and a stained rag rug. There was no bar for the door, and nothing more to secure it than a metal latch that rotated into a hook, but Humphrey had nothing with him apart from the clothes he was wearing, a small purse of coins and a thin dagger tucked into one boot. His pistols were back at Drummoor.

He sat down on the bed, and realised with a rueful smile that he had no way to remove his tightly-fitted riding boots, a task normally left to his valet. He sighed, toying with the idea of summoning a boy to wrestle them off, but then reminded himself of the consequences if his boots were inappropriately handled or even, perish the thought, damaged, and decided not to attempt it. Billings would sulk for a month! Never was a valet so proud of his way with boots. Humphrey himself cared little for such matters, but it never did to upset one's valet. He would just have to sleep in his boots, indeed, in all his clothes, for he had the strongest apprehension of bed bugs. He lay down, his head on his folded coat, snuffed his candle and closed his eyes, but somehow sleep eluded him. For hours, it seemed, he turned this way and that, half-dozing before some horrid dream jerked him awake again.

But then something else woke him, a sound just on the edge of hearing.

He strained his ears, but all was silent. The room was no longer night-black, the dawn not far off. He turned over for the fortieth time, and closed his eyes. Still time for another two or three hours of sleep.

Scratch, scratch. His eyes flew open. Rats? But then a slight metallic clink, that was caused by no rat. Silently, he reached into his boot for the dagger and drew it forth. Even as he watched, the metal latch inside the door was lifted by some device from without — a knife, perhaps? The door opened silently on well-greased hinges. But Humphrey now had no apprehension that he would be murdered in his bed. The odd little latch, so easy to open from the outside, the greased hinges — all spoke of a regular type of thievery, perhaps even with the connivance of Tommy. This was one of the ostlers or taproom boys, looking to steal a coin or two from unwary travellers.

But Humphrey was by no means unwary. He lay still, the dagger hidden beneath him, pretending to sleep, but listening intently to the stealthy movements. The intruder crept into the room — Humphrey could hear him breathing — then stopped, no doubt looking about assessingly. But there was nothing to assess — no boxes or saddle-bags, not even a coat cast carelessly over a chair. There was nothing in the room but Humphrey, seemingly asleep on the bed, his coat under his head.

A sensible thief would judge the pickings thin and possibly risky, and make his exit at this point, but clearly this was not a sensible thief. He came nearer to the bed, his location betrayed by his heavy breathing and a certain horsey odour. One of the ostlers, then. Humphrey lay, eyes almost closed but not quite, as the would-be thief leaned over him and them stretched out a hand to investigate under the coat.

Humphrey's eyes shot open and in one smooth movement he sat up and grasped the intruder by the neck. The man gasped, widening eyes just visible beneath a well-wrapped scarf. Definitely an inn employee, then, hiding his identity. Humphrey was on his feet, dragging the intruder across the room, before he had time for more than a squeak of alarm. Slamming him against the wall, he hissed in the man's face, "Want something, my fine fellow? You are lucky I did not stick you with this." He waved the dagger under the man's nose.

"Sorry! Sorry! Please, I meant no harm! Just... just lookin' about!"

"Just stealing," Humphrey said. "You know the penalty for that, I assume."

"Please, I've took nothing, mister, honest. I was just lookin'. Don't send me to the magistrate, please!"

Humphrey realised too late that the fellow was right — he had as yet stolen nothing. His only crime was to enter a guest's bedchamber, and if he were truly an inn employee, he could claim he was checking the fire or some such excuse. With an exclamation of disgust, Humphrey released him.

"Thank you, sir, thank you! You'll not report me? I've done nothing wrong, I swear! I'll leave you to sleep now, sir."

"As if I could sleep a wink," Humphrey said. "Even before you decided to pay me a visit, there was no possibility of sleep in this wretched place. It is not what I am accustomed to."

"Aye — you're a gent, sir," the intruder said, grinning. "I could tell as soon as you opened your mouth. That's no local accent." And to Humphrey's astonishment, he repeated his words with the exact intonation. "'*Even before you decided to pay me a visit, there was no possibility of sleep in this wretched place.*' That's a real gent's accent, that is."

Humphrey laughed. "That is very clever. Who are you, my fine mimic?"

He reached for the scarf, but the man danced aside. "No need for that, sir. Just passing through, you wouldn't know me."

"Nonsense," Humphrey said. "You work here, I am certain of it. You know your way around too well. Besides, you smell of the stables, so you must be an ostler here. I can get Tommy to find out who you are easily enough."

"No, please, sir! I need this job, sir."

But when Humphrey reached for the scarf, he stood still and allowed it to be unwound, revealing a mop of untidy blond hair and a surprisingly handsome face.

"Well, now," Humphrey said, staring at him in astonishment. "What is your name, my good thief?"

"*Not* a thief," he said sullenly. "I'm Charlie, sir."

Humphrey laughed. "Charlie! Of course you are. Do you like your work here, Charlie? Do you like horses?"

"Aye, sir, I do. Horses don't judge like people do. If you treat them right, they behave themselves and respect you and they're glad to see you when you bring them hay or a carrot."

"And people do not?" Humphrey said gently, sitting down on the bed and tucking the dagger away in his boot again.

"People see a poor man, a man with no money or learning, and they treat him like dirt, just cause he's got less money than they have. See, if you was to take me to the magistrate and say I'd broke into your room, he'd send me to Australia without a second thought, even though I took nothing. Whereas if *you* was to stand before the magistrate, he'd waggle his finger and tell you not to do it again. And he'd probably have dinner with you after, and you'd be the best of friends."

"That is very likely true," Humphrey said thoughtfully. "But the world is an odd place, Charlie. Sometimes unexpected things happen. Now, if I were just another traveller passing through on my way to or from York, I might be so annoyed by a petty thief like you that I would haul you off to the magistrate, and there you would be, taking ship for Australia. But I am *not* just another traveller passing through. I am Lord Humphrey Marford from Drummoor, and I find you most interesting."

"Me, sir?" His face was a picture of apprehension.

"Not for any sinister reason, I assure you," Humphrey said. "In fact, it may prove to be materially to your advantage. I wish to know you a little better, Charlie. Would you like to be a groom at Drummoor? There is just one condition, however. You will have to give up your nocturnal wanderings and live a blameless life henceforth. What do you say?"

For a moment, Humphrey thought Charlie had been struck by some seizure or other, for he froze, his mouth hanging open, and his cheeks aflame.

"Charlie? Does the idea appeal to you?"

Charlie's mouth flapped open once or twice, but no words emerged.

Humphrey laughed. "Might I assume that your silence signifies agreement?"

Poor Charlie was too much overcome to speak, but he nodded vigorously at this.

"Excellent. Then your first task as my employee is to get these wretched boots off, before my feet expire altogether."

~~~~~

After an indifferent breakfast, Humphrey and his new groom found a lift from a wagon driver heading towards Drummoor, and began the slow ride home. They had not gone far, however, when they were hailed by a gaggle of riders with dogs, heading in the opposite direction.

"Good day to you," called a familiar voice. "Have you seen any sign of a fine black horse, or perhaps a rider without a horse? For my brother is missing and he came this way yesterday, and we are concerned for his safety."

"Carrbridge!" Humphrey cried, jumping from the back of the wagon before it had properly stopped moving. "I am safe and well, as you can see."

Carrbridge leapt down from his horse and flung his arms around his brother. "Whatever happened to you? When you did not come home— Where is Ganymede? He did not fall?"

"No, no, he is fine, but... it is a long story. Thank you for coming to my rescue. It was not necessary in this instance, but I am glad of it, nevertheless." He looked about at the assembled search party. Merton was there, and Reggie, who must only have arrived the day before, a couple of the Whittleton cousins, as well as several grooms. And Ben Gartmore was there with the dogs. He was a recently discovered natural son of their father, the eighth marquess, now employed as an under-gamekeeper.

That reminded Humphrey of his newest employee. "I would have you all meet my new groom. This is Charlie. Get down here, Charlie. Let everyone see you."

Slowly, reluctantly, Charlie climbed down from the wagon. There was a collective gasp of surprise.

"Good God!" Carrbridge said. "How is that even possible?"

Merton laughed. "His name is Charlie, my lord. I daresay he was named for his father, would you not think?"

"It must be so," Carrbridge said. "But it is extraordinary, nevertheless."

Charlie looked from one to the other, bewilderment plain on his features. "What do you know of my father?" he said, lifting his chin. "Even *I* don't know nothing about my father."

Carrbridge gazed at him, then at Humphrey. "He does not know?"

"There has been no opportunity to discuss it. When we get to Drummoor—"

"No, now!" Charlie cried. "If you know something about my father, you'd best tell me right now, whoever you are!"

Humphrey and Carrbridge exchanged glances, then Carrbridge nodded. "Now, Charlie," he said, "I am the Marquess of Carrbridge — the ninth of that line. And you — I will say this plainly, so that there is no misunderstanding, for your name and your looks all tell the same tale. You are the natural son of my father, the eighth Marquess of Carrbridge. You are, in fact, my half brother."

"What?" Charlie said. "You mean I'm a bastard? Well, stone me! And my mother told me my father was a soldier what died in France. Women! Can't trust a word they say!" And he spat disgustedly on the ground.

5: Reflections

"There!" Humphrey said. "Can you see the likeness now?"

Charlie stared into the looking glass on the wall outside the servants' hall. "Lord love us! We could be brothers!"

Humphrey laughed. "Almost certainly we *are* brothers, or half-brothers, at least. The nose... that is a true Marford nose you have there, Charlie, and Father was blond like that, once, although all the portraits show him either powdered or grey-haired. You must be a little younger than I am, though. I am seven and twenty. Do you know how old you are?"

"Not sure."

"I would guess you are about Monty's age — three and twenty. You are a bit shorter and thinner than I am, but with a haircut and a shave and some decent clothes you could pass for me anywhere. In fact, if I teach you the quadrille and the proper way to a bow to a lady, I could send you to all the most boring balls of the season in my place."

Charlie grinned. "That'd be fun — pretending to be you. And I can do the accent right enough. *'If I teach you the quadrille and the proper way to bow to a lady, I could send you to all the most boring balls of the season.'* See?"

Humphrey laughed. "That is a neat trick. But it astonishes me that no one commented on the likeness. I am well-known at the Old Cross, and surely someone would have noticed."

"Aye, the ostlers used to tease me about it when I first went there. You was never mentioned by name, but they said I looked like a toff, and asked if I knew who me father was. But only one of them called me a bastard to me face, and he's still got the scars to show for it. They shut up about it after that. Never occurred to me there was anything in it. I always believed what me mother told me. Ha! That were a mistake."

"Where is your mother?" Humphrey said.

"Still down the vale — Silsby Vale House, where she's always been. I were born there. She's the cook there now."

"Now that is *very* interesting," Humphrey said thoughtfully.

"Don't see why," Charlie said sullenly. "Don't see why you care about any of this. Even if it's true that your father planted one on me mother, what does that matter to anyone? Happens all the time. Why did you bring me here anyway? Do you really want me to be a groom?"

"As to that, it is up to you. When my father died, he charged my brother to look after his sons — *all* his sons. We did not understand him at the time, but it seems he left more than one natural son behind, and he wanted us to ensure they were looked after and given careers. It is probably too late for you to train as a lawyer, Charlie, but we will give you work here and make sure you never have to worry about finding your next meal. After all, you may have been born outside of wedlock, but you are still the son of a marquess."

Charlie's eyes widened. "Lord! Me, the son of a marquess — who'd have thought it?" And he grinned widely at Humphrey.

~~~~~

Carrbridge, Humphrey, Reggie and Merton had retreated to the ship room, leaving Charlie to the care of old John Coachman, who already accommodated Ben Gartmore and was very glad to extend his household to include another of the late marquess's by-blows. Humphrey had told his brothers all that had occurred at Silsby Vale House.

"So Sharp keeps a mistress down the Silsby Vale," Lord Carrbridge said thoughtfully.

"As to that, it may be so, who can say?" Humphrey said. "I should not like to malign the lady without greater knowledge of the situation. But what is certain is that Sharp goes there regularly — on *my* horse, if you please — and is regarded as the master there. Both the groom and Mrs Andrews herself told me that he owns the place, and perhaps it may be so, for ought I know."

"He could have inherited it, I suppose," Merton said, but his tone was dubious. "But the expense of a house such as you describe would be beyond his means, unless he has other income. I know his salary to the penny. Although perhaps the lady pays the expenses. It is very much a mystery. All I can tell you for certain is that I have not encountered any reference to Silsby Vale House in the accounts or paperwork so far. Mrs Andrews... I might take another look at the accounts, to see if there is any mention of such a person, or her husband, perhaps. I do not like mysteries, and there are far too many surrounding Mr Sharp, as well as your late father, my lord, if I may be permitted to say so."

"You may say what you like about him," Carrbridge said. "I am beginning to feel as though I did not know him at all. This is the second of his little mishaps we have discovered, and who knows how many more there may be? But this one is your responsibility, Humphrey. The boy has had no education, so we cannot train him up for a worthwhile career."

"He will do very well in the stables," Humphrey said. "That is what he has been doing at the inn, after all. Tom will look after him, and show him how we do things here."

"But what about Ganymede?" Reggie said. "Shall we all go over there and retrieve him? These people cannot deny Carrbridge, after all."

Humphrey pondered the possibility. There would be some satisfaction in riding over there like a platoon of hussars to rescue the horse, which was legally his, after all, and it was always amusing to see his oldest brother in his full peer of the realm glory. But there were other ways to deal with the problem, which might be even more amusing. However, one aspect of the situation made him uncomfortable. "These people are terrified of Sharp and I do not like to expose them to his anger. Besides, I am certain Ganymede is being well cared for. When Sharp returns, I shall send him to fetch the horse."

Reggie snorted with laughter. "Oh yes, send Sharp! An excellent notion. Although I should like to know how he explains the matter to his mistress, or whatever she is. Do you know, I used to like Sharp very well, but the more I discover about him, the less I like him. Where is he, by the way?"

"No one knows," Merton said. "No one ever knows where he goes to, not even his wife. Whenever I have asked him, he merely says that he is about the marquess's business. But I have been tracking his comings and goings for months, and I can tell you that he is away five days out of seven. Sometimes it is only one night, but more often four or five."

"That is ridiculous!" Carrbridge said. "Surely he does not need to travel so much? Wherever can he go to?"

"We have found one of his destinations — Silsby Vale House," Merton said. "But there must be others. Shall I set someone to follow him on his travels, my lord? It is a little devious, but…"

"Hmm, would that be a good plan?" the marquess said. "Humphrey, what do you think?"

"It would certainly be amusing, but I cannot see the necessity. Sharp is your employee, and must answer to you in all matters. Ask him where he goes — *precisely* where he goes, and what he does when he gets there. If he refuses to answer or is evasive, then tell him he is not to go anywhere without your explicit authority. We have every piece of his paperwork, after all, so it is perfectly reasonable to expect him to wait until Merton has sorted through it all."

"Very well," Carrbridge said. "I shall ask him to explain himself."

"Just make sure I am here when you do it," Humphrey said. "I have never much liked the man, and I should like to see his face so that I may judge whether he lies or not. I do not care if he keeps a mistress or not, for that is between him and his conscience, but using Ganymede without my permission is beyond anything. And if you do not object greatly, Carrbridge, I should like my horse back safely before you start leaning on Sharp."

The marquess laughed and agreed to it, and Humphrey reflected on how genial and easy-going his brother had become since he had married. He had inherited the title at the early age of one and twenty, and he had floundered for a few years until chance had thrown Miss Constance Allamont in his way. Despite her provincial background it had proved to be a perfect match. Carrbridge was not a deep thinker, so he was happy to defer to her authority in all domestic matters, and since her understanding was excellent, the outcome was beneficial to all.

Humphrey envied them their happiness, but wondered if he would ever find a wife who suited him quite so well. Not one he would defer to, that much was certain! He liked Connie very much, but he could never see himself tamely led by his wife as Carrbridge was. Now, Reggie's betrothed, Miss Chamberlain, was a pleasant enough girl, but dreadfully conventional, and Humphrey was not sure that would suit him either. She was currently visiting Drummoor with her parents, who were just as conventional as she was, and although this made them pleasant enough company, they were not, to Humphrey's mind, the least bit interesting.

And that led his thoughts to Miss Blythe, who would arrive in a few days with her two hundred thousand pounds and her curled hair and blue eyes. She reminded him of a china doll Harriet had once had, which had survived Harriet's robust style of play for a surprisingly long time. Perhaps Miss Blythe, too, would turn out to be more resilient than her delicate appearance suggested, and would match him stride for stride on the hunting field, or at least play a decent hand of whist. He sighed, wondering for the hundredth time if this was such a clever idea. Well, he was not committed to Miss Blythe yet. She was to stay for a month, as part of Connie's summer attempt to fill Drummoor to its crenellated roof with guests. If she and Humphrey found they did not suit, she would leave again and no harm done. With such a fortune, she would have no trouble finding a husband to her taste, after all. But then where would Humphrey find the money for his gaming house? He would have to begin his search for a rich wife all over again.

He had not long to wait before Sharp returned from his wanderings. Humphrey was in the stables, mulling over the possible mounts for his morning ride, and finding himself unenthusiastic about all of them, when a clatter of hooves echoed around the high ceiling.

"Ah, Sharp, there you are!"

"Good morning, my lord."

"No, do not dismount, Sharp. I have an urgent task for you."

"I am entirely at your disposal, naturally, my lord. Always happy to oblige any of his lordship's family, as you know. Might I be permitted to call at home first, my lord, to change my clothing?"

"No, you may not. You are to ride directly to Silsby Vale House, and tell that fool of a groom of yours to release Ganymede. Then you will bring my horse directly back to Drummoor. You will not need to ride hard to be back in time for your dinner. Which is more than I was last night, for I had to walk home, and a long step it is on foot, let me tell you. I was obliged to spend an uncomfortable night at the Old Cross Inn, which is not an experience I wish to repeat soon — or ever, now that I think on it. I am seriously displeased, Sharp, so I suggest you leave this instant, if you wish to avoid my wrath."

Sharp's face was such a ludicrous mixture of fear and dismay that Humphrey was almost tempted to laugh. But that would never do. He jumped up to sit on a cross-rail to bring himself to the same height as the mounted agent, and folded his arms with a haughty glare, his bearing every inch the aristocrat.

Sharp licked his lips. His eyes skittered left and right, as if he looked for aid, or perhaps an escape route. "Silsby Vale House, my lord?" he croaked. Then, more strongly, "I did not know your lordship had any connection there."

"Nor did I, Sharp, nor did I, until I went that way on Ganymede and he seemed pleased to be there, and the groom addressed him by name. The lady who lives there — Mrs Andrews, is it? — was most affable. She is a good friend of yours, I take it?" He paused, but Sharp seemed incapable of speech just then, his mouth opening and closing ineffectually. "Mrs Andrews told me that you owned the house, Sharp. I must congratulate you. It is a fine property indeed."

Now the man's eyes were wide, and the horse tossed its head restlessly, sensing some tension in the rider. Then, clearly making a decision, Sharp turned the horse. "I will fetch Ganymede at once, my lord."

And with that he was gone.

Humphrey smiled grimly. "Very good, Sharp, so you do not want to explain now. So be it. But you will explain it later, if I have to thrash it out of you."

He jumped down from the rail, and at once a familiar face popped up from one of the empty stalls. "That Mrs Andrews?" Charlie said, grinning at Humphrey, the likeness with his own reflection disconcerting Humphrey all over again. "She ain't no lady, that's for sure. She's got some devious ways to pay the bills, that one."

"That is enough!" Humphrey said, although he smiled a little too. "Do not go around repeating servants' hall gossip about your betters, Charlie. And remember that your mother still works there. You do not want to set Sharp against her. And you should not eavesdrop. It is very bad manners, and liable to get you cast off without a reference."

But Charlie just grinned even more. Humphrey began to wonder if he had made a huge mistake in bringing the fellow to Drummoor, son of the marquess or not.

6: *Cards And Horses*

Hortensia delighted in the long journey north to Drummoor. She had equipped herself with a comfortable travelling carriage, a coachman, a groom and two footmen, together with a luggage wagon and driver. She had no lady's maid, but as she would travel with her governess and companion, Miss Quayle, would need no further chaperonage. Lady Carrbridge had answered by return, with a long list of inns which she might safely patronise, and precise details of the route and journey times. There was nothing, therefore, to be done except to gaze at the English scenery passing the windows like an endless series of water colour paintings, each more ravishingly beautiful than the last.

"Is it not magnificent?" she said to Rosemary. "Look at that castle — so dramatic with the lowering sky behind it."

"It looks like rain," Rosemary said, pulling her tippet closer about her shoulders and burying her hands in her muff. "The road will be churned to mud, I daresay. Are we stopping soon? For I should like another hot stone for my feet."

"Poor dear! How you do feel the cold! And this is summer, so I dare not contemplate how chilled you will be in winter. Just think of it — ice and snow and frost and all sorts of magical things. But you will not be able to enjoy them unless you accustom yourself to the cold, dearest."

"It is all very well for you," Rosemary said. "You grew up in England, but I have known nothing but India and heat and wonderful spicy food. The sauces here are so dull. Like the weather."

Hortensia laughed, and turned her head to gaze out of the window again. "Such charming stone cottages, and the gardens so pretty with all those pale colours. And green! I had forgotten England possessed so many shades of green! Oh look, such a delightful little church with a spire. Do look, dear."

But Rosemary had closed her eyes, and was leaning back against the squabs.

Eventually they turned off the main road onto a smaller one, and then another even smaller, deeply rutted, so that the carriage swayed about a great deal, to Rosemary's alarm. They came in time to the village of Mishcombe, the road shining with a recently-passed rainstorm, water still streaming into ditches filled with wildflowers. Many of the inhabitants of the village were out and about, the women neat in their cloaks and bonnets, the men dark-coated, striding about importantly. All turned to stare as the impressive entourage passed by, taking in the array of impassive postilions and coachmen, and then curtsying deeply at the glimpse of Hortensia's feather-trimmed bonnet peeping from the carriage window. A small child waved cheerfully to her, and delightedly she waved back.

Then they were through the village and back into trees and two miles of rain-dampened gloom before they turned under the crenellated archway that marked the entrance to Drummoor. Another two miles of winding driveway gave but brief glimpses of the house, then a small hill, the house again, a lake and finally, in all its glory, Drummoor itself. If Hortensia had ever imagined the perfect English nobleman's house, Drummoor fitted the image precisely. From the latticed windows to the battlemented roof and the gargoyles adorning every wall, it was enchanting. And beyond it, acre upon acre of smoothly turfed parkland, absolutely begging to be galloped over.

"Oh!" she breathed. "This... this is a place I could enjoy. Oh, if only I could live here!"

Rosemary peered over her shoulder. "I wonder if it has ghosts?"

Hortensia laughed. "Almost certainly, my dear. Well, here we are. We have arrived."

~~~~~

Humphrey was relieved to discover that Miss Blythe was every bit as pretty as memory had made her. Her creamy-white skin, wide blue eyes framed with yellow curls and enchanting dimples when she smiled made his murmured expression of pleasure as he made his bow entirely genuine.

"How delightful to see you again, Miss Blythe. I trust your journey was not too trying."

"How do you do, Lord Humphrey," she answered composedly. "It was as trying as such journeys generally are, but we had no great difficulties or set-backs to trouble us, and every inn that Lady Carrbridge so kindly recommended looked after us perfectly. Indeed, we were so well informed about every possible contingency that we never had the least thing to worry us. Nevertheless, I am very glad to have arrived."

And that easy composure was exactly why he had chosen her, he reminded himself, not her beauty. He had never had much time for tongue-tied debutantes, and here was one who, even at the young age of eighteen, was an easy conversationalist.

"Do you remember my companion, Miss Quayle?" she went on.

He had not taken much notice of the companion at the tea party, having some vague memory of a severe-faced older woman who had not spoken. Surely she must be quite old, as companions customarily were. He was surprised to find himself faced with a woman of much his own age, and almost as tall. A severe cambric cap covered an abundance of dark hair coiled neatly under her bonnet, with only a single soft curl falling over each ear. She was thin and wiry, not especially pretty but a pair of huge brown eyes gave her face a great deal of intelligence. The eyes were sparkling in amusement at that moment, their owner understanding perfectly his confusion.

"Lord Humphrey." She curtsied, head lowered demurely, but when she lifted her head again, her lips were curved into a little smile.

"Miss Quayle. Welcome to Drummoor."

That evening was a pleasant one. Humphrey was too well-bred to devote all his attention to Miss Blythe, but there were snatches of conversation with her as he moved around the room before dinner, and he was pleased to see that she was well situated during the meal between Carrbridge and Mr Chamberlain. The house was already alive with guests who had fallen into Connie's orbit in London, as well as numerous Marford relations and the impoverished Whittleton cousins, and it did not surprise him to see Julius Whittleton make straight for Miss Blythe after dinner, having now discovered the extent of her fortune.

While they drank their tea, some of the young ladies performed on the pianoforte, and Humphrey had the pleasure of discovering that while Miss Blythe was no more than tolerably competent on the instrument, she had a lovely singing voice. When once this was discovered, a duet with Julius Whittleton was called for, and Humphrey had to admit that they made a striking pair, two handsome young people with the voices of angels.

After the music, the company settled down to play cards. The older guests played whist while the younger ones set up a large, noisy game of speculation. Humphrey joined this group, largely because Miss Blythe was part of it, although the simplicity of the game soon palled, and there was no possibility of rational conversation in the shrieks of delight or groans of disappointment after each play.

Looking about the room in boredom, he noticed Miss Quayle sitting quietly on her own. She had some sewing resting in her lap, but she was not paying it much attention, being engaged in looking about her with great interest. Her eyes met Humphrey's and she smiled before turning back to her neglected stitchery. Excusing himself from the game, he made his way across to her.

"May I sit with you for a while?" he said.

"I beg your pardon, Lord Humphrey," she said, shaking her head so that the two curls danced on either side of her face. "I did not mean to distract you from the play."

"Believe me when I say that I am very ready to be distracted," he said. "But do you not wish to play yourself? Or should you like to join Mrs Chamberlain, Mrs Graham and Mrs Ambleside over by the fire?"

"Oh no, for they are talking about weddings and babies and other matters of the utmost interest to mothers. I should have nothing at all to contribute to such a conversation. As to the games, the whist tables are all filled and I do not much enjoy speculation. There is but little skill to it. Please be assured that I am perfectly content to sit here and watch everyone else. I am nothing but a paid companion, Lord Humphrey. I do not expect to be included in every social occasion."

He smiled at that. "Even companions may play cards, Miss Quayle. If you wish to play whist, I can find two more players in a moment. Or chess may be played with two. Cribbage, perhaps? Or piquet?"

"You are very good." She eyed him speculatively. "I should by no means wish you to take pity on me if your charity takes you away from better play or better company."

At that moment the speculation table burst into great whoops of delight.

Humphrey leaned forward to whisper, "The company is quieter and more sensible here, I warrant, and I do not enjoy speculation any more than you do, Miss Quayle. It would please me greatly to play something a little more challenging. What shall it be?"

She smiled at him, a wide smile that lit her eyes so that they shone with brilliance. "I have never played piquet, and it would interest me to learn."

"Piquet it is, then."

He found a small table a little distance from the noisy speculation table, and prepared the cards. He had only to explain the rules once for her to grasp the essence of it, and she was soon playing with some competence.

"There, you see?" he said with glee, as she took a game in handsome style. "I am very well rewarded for my good deed in taking pity on you, Miss Quayle. I should not have enjoyed half so entertaining an evening elsewhere. You are already an excellent player."

She laughed. "Why, thank you, Lord Humphrey. You play quite well yourself."

"I am accounted a tolerably good player," he said, amused, as he deftly shuffled and dealt. "Is this your first visit to England?"

"Why, no, I—" She paused and was that a blush on her cheeks? "Yes, it is, but I have heard so much of it, and read so many books telling of the most minute details of English life that I feel as if I have been here before. So much is familiar. Do you not find it so? Have you ever been abroad, Lord Humphrey?"

He answered her easily, and forbore to press her further, but he was intrigued, all the same. Such a simple question, yet she had stumbled over it. He could not help wondering why.

~~~~~

"So what do you think of him?" Hortensia said as she unwound the coils of Rosemary's hair and began to brush them out.

"Mr Whittleton?" Rosemary said, turning innocent eyes on her. "Why, he sings divinely."

"And is perfectly well aware of it," Hortensia said impatiently. "I hope we may look a little higher than Mr Julius Whittleton, dear. Besides, he has not a feather to fly with, Lady Patience informed me, so we must not be taken in by his beautiful face. No, I meant Lord Humphrey, for that is why we have been invited here, is it not?"

"And how many feathers has he to fly with?" Rosemary asked.

It was an excellent question, and one with which Hortensia had been much exercised. "He has the title, but it is only a courtesy one, and his chances of inheriting are very slim."

"Hortensia!" Rosemary stared at her friend. "That is... very calculating."

"And is it not calculating in Lord and Lady Carrbridge to invite *us* here to stay?" she retorted. "Let us be honest, marriage at this level of society is always a matter of contracts and settlements and dowries and estates, and however much one might hope to be swept away by romantic love, one must always be practical. It is best to ensure that one is swept away by love for a gentleman of rank if one can possibly contrive it. It is a business arrangement, no more than that. We have two hundred thousand pounds on the table, so we must weigh that against the gentleman's assets. Let me enumerate them. He has a courtesy title, probably an allowance from his brother and very little else, apart from his own charms. He *is* rather charming, it must be said."

"Do you think so?" Rosemary said doubtfully. "He frightens me a little, for he is so tall and strikingly attired and... and *powerful*. Such a *masculine* man, if you understand me."

"He frightens you? But he is so gentle and well-bred, and although his clothes may seem outlandish at first sight, they are all of the first stare of fashion, I do assure you."

"Oh yes, indeed! But so large! It is all very well for you, Hortensia, for you are a great tall creature yourself, and I daresay he seems less imposing to you. But I have one asset to add to his catalogue, for I overheard some of the ladies talking of it in the retiring room. He is a very great card player, most expert, and indeed increases his income somewhat by his skill at the tables. And he wishes to set up a gaming house, but the cost is beyond his means and that is why he is looking for a rich wife, I daresay."

"Well now, that is very interesting," Hortensia said thoughtfully. "Most interesting."

~~~~~

The following day, Lady Carrbridge decided that the weather was settled enough to permit a riding of the bounds, as she liked to describe it. This procedure involved assembling as many of the company as could be persuaded to it to ride a complete circuit of the park, a distance of some twelve miles. It was an easy ride, and always drew a great crowd, all to be provided with mounts, so that the grooms were in a frenzy of anxious activity. The stables were always augmented at this time of year by a number of hired horses from Sagborough and York, but even with this assistance, there were never enough.

Humphrey's role in the business was to ensure that every participant was supplied with a suitable horse, and this was no easy task to accomplish. If one asked a lady what sort of horse she would find most amenable, she was apt to demur and say that she was but a timid rider, and could a very gentle mount be found? Whereas a gentleman would always require *'something with spirit'*. And yet, often it would turn out to be the case that some gentlemen were hard put to control their spirited beasts, and the ladies grew frustrated with their sluggish mounts. It was a matter of the utmost delicacy to determine which riders were truly able to cope with a lively mount, and which could not, and which would be most mortified by a wrong assignation.

And every time, in Humphrey's experience, a gentleman would take a liking to one of Gus's ill-tempered beasts and want to try his hand, and how could Humphrey refuse? On this occasion, it was Julius Whittleton who fancied his skills adequate to the task.

"I do not recommend it, Julius," Humphrey said, with more forcefulness than usual. "Masterful is a hard animal to control, even for Gus. I would not take him out in a mixed group myself. Why not try Lucifer or Fast Demon, if you must have something challenging?"

"Do you think I cannot manage him, Humphrey?" Julius said disdainfully. "I assure you I am more than capable, even if you have reservations yourself."

There was no arguing with such wilful self-delusion, so Humphrey bowed and gave the orders. For Miss Blythe he chose one of the hired hacks, which he knew to be well-behaved. If she complained of its slowness, then he could find her something more spirited for next time.

Some twenty riders ventured forth into pleasant sunshine, with no sign of rain. They rode at an easy trot down the drive to the boundary woods, and there turned to follow the perimeter, passing first along the northern edge of the village. Some of the faster horses had already disappeared into the distance, including Harriet, but the other ladies and slower riders set a more gentle pace. Humphrey was amused to see Julius try to keep his frisky mount alongside Miss Blythe, but the horse was wild to be less restrained, and after a while the amusement palled as Humphrey saw that Masterful's energy was afflicting Miss Blythe's more docile horse, and she was becoming distressed.

Humphrey manoeuvred Ganymede alongside Miss Blythe, and took a firm hold of the horse's bridle. "Julius, will you not give Masterful his head? He is disturbing Rose Garden."

"I can control him," Julius muttered distractedly. But as if to disprove his words, the horse kicked up his heels and set off at a gallop through the woods, Julius pulling ineffectually at the reins.

"Thank you so much, my lord!" Miss Blythe said, turning her blue eyes on him, as her horse immediately settled down. "I was so frightened, for I had thought Rose Garden such a pleasant horse, so quiet and well-behaved, and yet for a moment I thought she was going to bolt with me. I have the greatest terror of being aboard a bolting horse, you cannot imagine."

"It is rather unnerving when a horse runs away with one, is it not?" Humphrey said sympathetically.

"Oh, I have no such experience on which to found my terror, my lord," she said. "It is more the idea of the event than anything else. I can imagine it, and that is almost as bad as experiencing it, would you not agree? I do so enjoy riding at this gentle pace, but anything faster — no, I must leave that to those braver than I." She visibly shuddered at the thought.

And Humphrey, who could not imagine any pleasure in never riding above a walking speed, was forced to smile and nod politely, and bite his tongue.

That evening, Humphrey found himself seated next to Miss Blythe at dinner. It was not his intent, for he had no wish to make his attentions obvious at too early a stage, but Julius had seized the seat on one side of her, and Humphrey felt in all conscience that he ought to do what he could to relieve the lady of the burden of too heavy a dose of Mr Whittleton. At first it looked as if even this charitable plan was doomed to failure, for Julius seemed determined to monopolise her entirely, but luckily a dispute further down the table on the relative merits of pheasant and partridge distracted him and Humphrey was able to gain the lady's attention.

"Did you enjoy the boundary ride today, Miss Blythe?" was his conventional opening play.

"Oh yes!" she cried, her blue eyes widening. "It was delightful, and everything planned to perfection. It did not rain at all, nor was the wind excessive, and the picnic Lady Carrbridge had arranged beside the waterfall was quite charming. There is something so pleasing about a meal taken in the open air, do you not agree? The company is in the highest of spirits, and one may move about and converse with everyone in turn, which is most agreeable." She lowered her voice somewhat. "I must thank you again for the most welcome service you provided, my lord. The occasion was so frightening to me, but once you took charge of the situation, I had not the least cause for alarm. *So* reassuring."

Humphrey had almost forgotten the incident, but he smiled and accepted her gratitude with the proper degree of demurral, and the conversation moved on to other subjects. But his heart was heavy. Could he truly respect a woman who was so timid on horseback? He was very much afraid he could not. But then he reminded himself that Miss Blythe was pretty and charming and inoffensive, and even if she might not be a bruising rider, was comfortable in society, and a woman who could with confidence be left to manage the domestic sphere. He need not have very much to do with her at all. Yes, she would do very well.

So he smiled and said all that was proper, and then talked to her about India for half an hour, which brought her to a very pleasing degree of animation. But then Julius remembered her and turned his attention back in her direction, and when he asked if he might be permitted the privilege of hearing her sing again, she grew even more animated.

"Oh, yes, if you will join me, Mr Whittleton! For you have the most splendid voice, and I should so enjoy hearing it again."

Humphrey began to wonder for the first time if Julius might be a serious rival for her hand. Well, he might not sing as beautifully as Julius — who could, after all? Still, he could be attentive to a lady if he chose to be. The gambler in him rose to the fore. Time to raise the stakes and snatch his two hundred thousand pounds out of Julius's avaricious grasp.

And yet his conscience whispered that he was every bit as avaricious as Julius, for what could be more mercenary than to choose a wife purely on the size of her fortune? He sat in uneasy silence.

7: Whist And Piquet

After dinner, Humphrey drifted back to the drawing room before the other gentlemen. He accepted his tea from Connie, and went to sit alone in a far corner of the room where he could ponder his sudden outbreak of conscience, and consider how he might overcome it, or whether perhaps he should abandon the charming Miss Blythe after all. Now that he was newly awakened to the awkwardness of marrying for money, he could see the disadvantages of the match that had never struck him before. She was so young, for one thing, no more than eighteen, and he was almost ten years older than her. That in itself was no great obstacle, for many men waited until they reached thirty or more before looking for a wife, and then made their choice from that season's debutantes. There was nothing at all wrong with that, if all one wanted was a wife who would be presentable in society and run a reasonably orderly home.

Yet now that he thought about it, Humphrey realised that he had always assumed that his wife, should he be lucky enough to marry, would be more of an equal to him, as both friend and lover. A timid milk-and-water wife was not at all what he had expected or hoped for. When he had considered the matter at all, he had had an image of a wife who rode as hard as he did, and who could at least play a decent game of whist. That was something he did not know about Miss Blythe. Perhaps she was not much of a rider, but was a deep thinker at the card table. He knew how he could find out.

So when the music was finished and the card tables were forming, seeing Julius occupied in receiving the plaudits of the listeners, he stepped forward quickly to claim her.

"Shall you play whist tonight, Miss Blythe? I should be very happy to partner you, if so."

"Why, thank you, my lord. I should be honoured, for I know you to be a formidable card player, and I enjoy whist of all things."

Well, that was promising. Humphrey secured the Amblesides as opponents and found them a table, and so the game began. It took him but five minutes to discover that Miss Blythe's enjoyment in the game stemmed largely in the conversation to be had while play was underway. She chatted to Mrs Ambleside very freely, until Ambleside rather tersely pointed out that the ladies had lost three tricks owing to their inattention. After that, all conversation was restricted to the gaps between games when the men totted up the scores and dealt the cards. When supper was announced, Humphrey was more than ready to abandon the game, and he saw that Ambleside was equally so.

After supper, he saw Miss Blythe claimed by the ever-opportunistic Julius Whittleton to join a large game of vingt-et-un, which was a much better match for her sociable inclinations. He was about to join the group himself, to keep a watchful eye on Julius, when his gaze fell on his pupil of the previous night. There she was, tucked self-effacingly in a corner of the grand saloon, which was difficult for a woman of her commanding height, and again her needlework sat neglected in her lap as she looked about her eagerly. So interested in the other guests and yet so reluctant to mix with them!

Her wandering eyes caught sight of his amused gaze, and she promptly bent her head to her work. Did she blush? He could not be sure. A stitch... another... and a third, before she peeped up at him under her lashes. This time she definitely blushed. He lost interest in the vingt-et-un game, seeing the prospect of far more entertaining play before him. Unhurriedly he crossed the room to stand before her.

"Miss Quayle, would you be interested in continuing our piquet lessons?"

"Thank you, my lord, but as you see I am being a conscientious needlewoman tonight."

He smiled, but said, "Your diligence is commendable, but I am persuaded that you would enjoy piquet rather more, and I assure you it would bring me the greatest pleasure."

She set down her needlework and looked at him appraisingly, head tilted at a slight angle. "It is kind of you to offer, Lord Humphrey, but I have discovered that you are a player of exceptional quickness. It would be impertinent in me to monopolise your attention with my beginner's stumbles when you will have much more enjoyable play elsewhere."

"You may be assured that I receive just as much enjoyment in teaching an interested beginner as in playing any other game here tonight."

But she shook her head, the two curls bouncing. "You are all generosity, but I beg you will not waste your time on me. I am perfectly happy to watch the company from here."

"Then I shall watch the company with you," he said firmly. Pulling forward a gilt-framed chair, he placed it next to hers and sat down, legs stretched out and crossed neatly at the ankles, arms folded. "And see how I am rewarded already by following your example, Miss Quayle. I can see the top of Lady Carrbridge's head almost entirely from this vantage point. Such a charming comb above her left ear. And look, the lower legs of Lord Carrbridge and Mr Graham are perfectly visible through that chair. And if I merely lean at an angle to the left, I may peer around that urn and immediately two — no, two and a half of the vingt-et-un players are revealed to me. Well, almost revealed, at any rate. I fear I should only be able to see them in their entirety by leaning at such a precipitous angle as to risk a humiliating tumble to the floor."

She laughed and shook her head. "Such absurdity! Of course I can see very little, hidden away as I am, but you see I am being a good little companion and keeping out of the way while the tables are being formed. As soon as everyone is settled, I shall creep a little nearer so that I may enjoy the conversations without the necessity for joining in myself."

"In other words, you are determined to remain invisible. Is that how paid companions are expected to behave, in your opinion, Miss Quayle? Or is this a certain timidity in your nature which suggests this degree of invisibility?"

"Timidity? Oh, quite the reverse," she said, smiling so suddenly that he was taken quite by surprise. Why, her countenance was not at all plain when she looked so mischievous, and those eyes! So expressive and full of life. "If I join in, I should be sure to express my opinions forcefully and dominate the conversation in a manner most disagreeable, not to mention inappropriate for my station. In a setting like this, and in such elevated company, it is difficult to remember that I am—"

"—just a paid companion," he said, making her laugh outright. "Then play piquet with me, Miss Quayle, and you may dominate the conversation as much as you choose — or rather, as much as you *can*, for you will have to contend with my own tendency to dominate."

She laughed even harder at that. "How can I resist such a challenge? Well then, let us see which of us will succeed in out-conversing the other. Shall we have a few guineas on the outcome?"

He regarded her quizzically, then said neutrally, "Companions must be paid very well to afford wagers at such a level." She bit her lip, but before she could reply, he went on, "But you are safe from me, Miss Quayle. I am not minded for high play tonight. Let us play for fish, instead. Shall we ask Timothy to set out a table for us?"

She nodded her assent, and he signalled to the footman, offering Miss Quayle his arm as they made their way to where the table was being placed. There was an unexpected pleasure in walking with so tall a woman, for her steps matched his perfectly. For once he had no need to moderate his stride. "Will this position suit you? There is a reasonable view of the whist players from here, although, alas, we can no longer see the vingt-et-un players."

She laughed merrily at this, but answered seriously, "Lord Humphrey, are you quite sure this will not be too dull an exercise for you?"

"It is never dull to teach an apt pupil, as you must have found yourself," he said as he shuffled. "Miss Blythe is a credit to your instruction."

"Oh yes! She was always a most attentive pupil, and worked so hard to learn everything I taught her. My efforts were not always entirely successful, for her number work was never above the commonplace, and she had little understanding of logic or philosophy. Her performance on the pianoforte is a trifle haphazard, perhaps, but so long as she sings, no one notices that. But her embroidery, her dancing and deportment, her manners, her painting, her recitation of poetry, her conversation — no one could fault her, and it is to the credit of her own aptitude and application, and not at all to my instruction, I assure you."

Humphrey smiled at this effusive summary of Miss Blythe's perfections, and Miss Quayle's manner was so perfectly sincere and artless that he was obliged to acquit her of any attempt to encourage a match between Miss Blythe and himself. He wondered what the two of them made of this invitation to Drummoor? Miss Quayle, at least, was so quick-minded that she must have deduced the intention at once. Of course, that did not preclude a successful outcome. It was for him to win Miss Blythe's hand by securing her affections towards him.

"Now then," he said, as he deftly dealt the cards, "you have a good grasp of the basics of piquet, Miss Quayle, so we shall come to the interesting part—"

"Strategy!" she cried, her face alight with enthusiasm.

"Exactly so. Piquet is superficially a simple game, but there are great subtleties in the manner of play, especially in the discard. Tonight I shall lay out my cards on the table after each deal, and explain to you which cards I plan to discard, and why. You need not show your cards—"

"But you will have a fair idea of them."

"I will indeed," he said, delighted with her quick mind. "However, there is still room for chance as well as skill. Now, let us begin…"

That hour Humphrey reckoned one of the pleasantest he had ever spent in that room. His pupil was so swift to learn that he had constantly to scramble for new techniques to teach her. Within three hands she was guessing his own discards with great accuracy, and within six it became clear that her memory for cards was every bit the equal of his own. Had she not been so new to the game and therefore still prone to mistakes, he must have feared his reputation as a consummate player to be in some danger.

The time passed so quickly that he was shocked when Miss Blythe appeared beside them.

"I beg pardon for disturbing you, my lord," she said, timidly. "I merely wished to tell... my friend that I am going upstairs now."

"Oh, has your game finished already?" Miss Quayle said, looking up in surprise.

"Some time ago, dearest. But there is no need for you to abandon yours, if his lordship wishes to play on."

"Indeed, the fault is entirely mine," Humphrey said gallantly. "I was kept so well entertained by your friend, Miss Blythe, that I had no notion I was keeping her up so late. A thousand apologies, Miss Quayle. Perhaps we may continue the lessons on another occasion?"

She smiled and agreed to it, and bade him good night, and as the two women walked away, Humphrey watched them speculatively. One was sweet and pretty and rich, a perfect match for the younger son of a marquess, but he had as yet found nothing in her to capture his interest. The other was lively and as sharp as a needle, but poor — and yet she interested him greatly.

His determination to court Miss Blythe and her fortune was undimmed, but there was something mysterious and intriguing about Miss Quayle and he very much wanted to find it out.

~~~~~

Hortensia walked up the stairs a little ahead of her friend.

"Dearest," came Rosemary's voice from behind her, a little hesitantly. "I am not very comfortable with this."

"Come now, are you not enjoying yourself?" Hortensia stopped and waited for her, then linked arms companionably.

"Oh yes! Very much, but... I am uncomfortable with our situation"

"You are not developing a *tendre* for Lord Humphrey, are you? For that would never do."

"Oh, no, nothing of the sort. He is very attentive, as are several of the gentlemen, which is very pleasant, naturally, but none are such as to tempt me. But it does not seem quite right."

"Perhaps not," Hortensia said pensively. "Still, it is only for a month and then we shall be gone from here. We will settle in Bath or Harrogate or some other dull but respectable place, and live very quiet for the rest of our lives."

"Oh." Rosemary sounded very downcast, and Hortensia had to admit that the prospect did not appeal so much as it once had. It was all very difficult.

~~~~~

Sharp had been notified that Lord Carrbridge required his attendance to explain some irregularities in the management of the estates. On Merton's advice, several days had elapsed to allow Sharp to dissipate his ire over the seizure of all his papers, but he presented himself at the ship room at the precise hour with his usual equanimity.

"Your lordship wished to speak with me?" he said, smiling in his oily way, with the excessively deferential bow that always irritated Humphrey. The man was, after all, the estate's agent, so there was no need for him to be so obsequious. His clothes were another irritant, so obtrusively old-fashioned as to suggest that his master kept him in poverty.

Carrbridge had insisted that Reggie and Humphrey be there for family unity, and Merton, too. Julius Whittleton had been left in charge of the writing room, since he was now deemed competent to open and sort all the marquess's newly arrived letters. Humphrey was amused to see that Sharp's bows to the rest of them were very finely judged — respectfully low to Reggie, somewhat less so to his rival Merton and almost insultingly slight to Humphrey himself, who had clearly not been forgiven for reclaiming Ganymede and discovering the secrets of Silsby Vale House.

Carrbridge sat behind the desk, with Sharp standing on the other side of it. Merton was seated at the end of the desk, his pen poised to record any items of note. Reggie sat on the window seat, keeping himself out of the way, only present because the brothers wished to present a united face. Humphrey decided that he might be best employed as an oppressive presence, so he leaned casually against the mantelpiece, his height allowing him to loom over Sharp.

"Now, Sharp, this will not do," Carrbridge said, in his most imperious manner. "I have asked Mr Merton to discover the full extent of the estate's holdings, information which should have been at your fingertips, and you have not been at all helpful, even when you have been here. And that is another matter, all this jauntering about."

"As agent, I must keep an eye on all your lordship's holdings," Sharp said, with undented calmness. "You would not wish me to neglect my duties, my lord, I'm sure."

"No, of course not, but still—"

"As to Mr Merton, he's your lordship's secretary, who writes letters and so forth. I was not aware he had any responsibility towards your lordship's estates. Or perhaps I'm mistaken on that point, and he's your lordship's agent now?"

"Not at all, but—"

"Perhaps you have some complaint to make of me, my lord? Some matter left unattended to? A task not performed to your satisfaction?"

"No, but—"

Humphrey shifted restlessly. "Tell us about Silsby Vale House, Sharp."

"Of course, my lord. What is your lordship wishful to know?"

"What is your interest there?"

"The lady who lives there is a friend of mine, my lord."

"A friend. Very well. Let us say no more on that score, for your private affairs are no concern of ours," Humphrey said disdainfully. "But who owns it?"

"Why, his lordship, naturally."

"Really?" Humphrey said, startled. "Then why was I told by those who live there that *you* owned it?"

"As to that, I couldn't say, my lord," Sharp said, his smile undiminished.

"May I ask how this property came to be in the marquess's possession?" Merton said.

"The late marquess won the property at faro from Mr Cecil Andrews," Sharp said easily. "From Christian charity he allowed the gentleman to continue to live there free of rent, and when Mr Andrews died shortly thereafter, the gentleman's widow continued on the same terms."

"And where is the title to the property?"

"Now that is an interesting question," Sharp said, his smile never faltering. "Were I in my own office, with all my papers as I left them, I daresay I could have set my hand to the relevant document in no time at all. But since your lordship has seen fit to remove everything—"

"Yes, yes, you have not the least idea, I suppose," Carrbridge said testily.

"All the papers were labelled as they were boxed up," Merton said smoothly. "If you can tell me roughly where in the room the title was located, I should be able to find it very easily."

For the first time, Sharp's smile slipped a little. "It is just possible," he said, "that the title is... elsewhere. I cannot say for sure. I know where it *ought* to be, you understand, but as to whether it is *actually* there..."

"If it is amongst your papers, we will find it," Humphrey said. "If it is not, we will be returning to you with more questions, you may be sure."

Sharp licked his lips, and for the first time seemed discomfited. Humphrey caught Merton's eye, knowing that the secretary would be just as pleased as he was to have dented Sharp's armour for once. At least they knew now why there was no record in the accounts of rental payments from Silsby Vale House. But it was unsatisfactory, all the same, for how many other properties might fall into the same nebulous position? What else was Sharp hiding?

8: A Ride On The Moors

The weather turned wet for several days, and Connie kept her guests entertained with charades, readings of poetry and Shakespeare, musical recitals, and lessons in the waltz, the scandalous new dance sweeping Europe which was not yet publicly performed but which most of the *ton* had already experimented with in private. Humphrey's presence was required at all these events, and being a dutiful brother-in-law he was happy to oblige the lady of the house, especially since it threw him constantly into Miss Blythe's company. He could not say that he was making much progress with her. She received his attentions with complaisance, but she behaved just the same towards every young man who paid court to her. It was not very encouraging.

So much time indoors made Humphrey restless, and when the sun finally appeared and Connie bore the ladies off triumphantly in a great procession of carriages to the shops in Sagborough, he took the opportunity to hasten to the stables and relieve his pent-up energy in a fast ride.

He found an unexpected figure there, chatting quietly to Ganymede and stroking the horse's nose as she did so.

"Why, Miss Quayle! Are you not enticed by the prospect of several hours looking at ribbons and gloves? There is to be a cold collation at Lady Hawthorn's house, I understand, and a stroll along her peacock walk is not entirely out of the question. How can you possibly resist?"

She laughed. "The peacock walk is a temptation, naturally, Lord Humphrey, and a cold collation — I can barely contain my excitement. But as a mere companion, I must make the attempt. My friend is very well chaperoned, so my attendance is not needed, and I may follow my own inclinations for once. The stables here are magnificent — this great high ceiling and the decorated columns make it seem like a cathedral to the worship of horseflesh, which is entirely appropriate with such a splendid collection of animals as you have here."

"Not all of them belonging to the family, of course. Our many guests' horses have filled a great number of the stalls."

"Oh yes," she said, "but the visiting horses are easy enough to determine. The stolid carriage horses, the docile grooms' mounts, the pretty ladies' mares, the showy gentlemen's hacks. But everything on this side of the stables is splendid. The Marford family has impeccable taste in horseflesh."

"I had not realised you were so expert a judge," Humphrey said, trying not to smile at this all too accurate assessment. "Do you ride, Miss Quayle?"

"Oh yes!"

"Yet you did not venture forth with Lady Carrbridge's expedition around the boundary."

"No." She looked conscious, then said primly, "As a mere companion, I do not like to put myself forward on social occasions, as you know." Then she quite spoilt the effect by looking under her lashes at him mischievously and adding, "Besides, it sounded very tame."

He laughed out loud at this honesty. "So it was, so it was. If you had a completely free choice, which horse would you ride for your own pleasure?"

To his delight, she took the question seriously, her eyes roving across the various Marford riding horses and lingering on several in silent assessment. Eventually, she patted Ganymede's nose. "This fellow, I think. He looks fast enough to be enjoyable, but without the evil temper I see on some of these. He is yours, Tom told me — did you choose him yourself, or did Lord Augustus advise you?"

It was interesting that she had been loitering in the stables long enough to know the names of the grooms, and to have picked up their gossip. "Gus is very much the expert where horses are concerned, so naturally I took him along to approve my choice. Do you have a riding habit with you?"

"Of course, but— oh!" She turned her expressive eyes on him, and he could read the hope, the yearning in them as clearly as if she had spoken.

"Go and get changed, then, and I will have him saddled for you. He is used to Lady Harriet, so he will carry you quite happily."

A hesitation, and doubt clouded her face. "But will you let me ride him *properly*? At a gallop?"

He smiled at her. "At a gallop, and jumping every obstacle, if that is your wish."

"Oh! Oh, *yes*!" And without another word, she spun on one booted heel and raced away.

Humphrey flushed Tom out from the saddle room. "A lady's saddle on Ganymede, Tom, and I shall take Titan. Saddle something for yourself."

Tom's eyebrows lifted. "Ganymede? For Miss Blythe?"

"For Miss Quayle. She wishes to gallop, Tom."

The eyebrows lifted even further, but he set to work without further comment.

She was quick, that much was certain. Not twenty minutes after rushing away, Miss Quayle arrived back at a run, her face alight with expectation, like a child in anticipation of some great treat. And maybe it was, at that. She had not been interested in shopping expeditions or decorous rides around the park, but the chance of a gallop drew her out of her self-imposed decision not to put herself forward, and into her riding habit. And what a riding habit it was! Humphrey was no judge of female finery, but the splendid green velvet with its rows of military-style frogging, full skirt and matching hat with a very jaunty feather were not, he suspected, suitable attire for a mere companion. Nor was the outfit likely to be one of Miss Blythe's, for she was much shorter than her friend, yet the habit was a perfect fit.

With a quick skip of her long legs, she jumped onto the mounting block, and settled herself on Ganymede's back. Humphrey swung himself onto Titan, and then led the way out into the stable court.

"Now, Miss Quayle, some things you should know. Ganymede is a sweet-tempered horse, and will allow you to set his pace most willingly, but once you give him his head you should be prepared to let him run, and also to jump, if he wishes to. If you try to halt him or turn him before he is ready, he will take it badly."

"I understand," she said, eyes glittering with excitement.

"Follow me, and keep to my pace."

He trotted through the stable court and out onto the track that skirted the pleasure grounds, first at a walk, then a trot, and finally, when they escaped the bounds of the shrubbery and the way ahead was clear, at a canter. Miss Quayle rode almost alongside him, close enough that he could see that she rode easily, without any tension in her hands. When they came to the open park, he halted.

"Here is where you have a choice, Miss Quayle. If you are happy to jump, then point Ganymede directly at that gate in the wall down there. He will jump the wall just to the right. The ground drops away on the other side, but he is very familiar with it and you may trust his instincts. After that he will want to cross the fields beyond, jumping the gates until the far hill slows him. However, if you do not want to jump him—"

But the sentence remained unfinished, for she had kicked Ganymede into motion and was away already, head low to his neck, allowing him his head, aiming straight for the gate.

"There's a lady with pluck!" Tom said. "Never seen anyone but Lady Harriet do that! Better get after her, my lord."

Humphrey agreed, and set off in pursuit, his heart in his mouth as he watched the pair race across the park at frightening speed. Titan was fast enough but he had no hope of catching Ganymede. All Humphrey could do was watch in terror as the horse closed on the wall, quite determined to take it in his usual way. Would his rider trust him enough, or would she try to pull him up? Closer, closer, closer… and now there was no option but to jump. And Ganymede adjusted his stride a touch, she shifted her hands a touch, and they were up… up in the air… flying over the wall… the lady's shriek audible even from some distance away. Was that piercing cry excitement or sudden terror?

He almost closed his eyes, hardly able to watch. Would they make it? For an instant they were both out of sight and he feared… Oh God, where were they? *There!* They were away across the field, not even looking back. He yelled in sheer delight, and then there was no time to watch them, for Titan was approaching the gate, about to jump it and it took all Humphrey's concentration to get himself and the unfamiliar mount over in reasonable style.

At the far side of the fourth field, he caught up with them, Miss Quayle laughing in glee, her face aglow, her eyes great shining orbs. How had he ever thought her plain? It was inconceivable.

"You are magnificent!" he cried, then hastily added, "... a magnificent rider!"

She laughed again, as their two horses danced around each other, still energised from the fast ride. "Ganymede is the magnificent one. I just gave him his head, and hung on while he did as he pleased. That was absolutely splendid, Lord Humphrey! Thank you so much for entrusting him to me. But look, he wants to go off again! Where to next?"

"First we wait for Tom to catch up, for his horse is a slug and he must open every gate to pass through," he said, laughing too, from the exhilaration of the ride and her own infectious enthusiasm. "Then we may pass through Wester Drum farmyard and back into the park to the boundary ride. Or else we may skirt the farm on this side, and through the woods onto the moor."

"Oh, the moor, please! I have so longed to see it, ever since you spoke of it with such feeling at the tea party at Marford House."

"Did I? I do not remember what I said then. But the moor it shall be then."

When Tom reached them at his slower pace, they set off at an easy canter around the hayfields, and through the woods, cool on their heated faces, the leaves rustling overhead, sunlight shimmering far above as the breeze parted the canopy. Ganymede, knowing the way, pulled ahead and Humphrey let him go, happy to admire the elegant rear view of Miss Quayle. They made their way up and up, until the trees fell away and all around was open country, wild and windswept, an empty vista of tussocky grass, bog and heather, with here and there a rocky crag.

Miss Quayle pulled up and gazed around her. "Oh, this is *wonderful!* Your description did not exaggerate the beauty of this place in the slightest. The air is so fresh and pure here. I was very happy in India, but I have so missed this English air." She took deep gulps of it, filling her lungs. "Ah, how glorious the moor is!"

"I love it here too," Humphrey said, watching her face enchantedly. Such an expressive face, with those lustrous eyes, and that wide mouth, ripe for kissing... And she exuded such energy and life, so unlike the mouse-like character of the companion that she assumed in company. But she was not for him. However much he admired Miss Quayle, he could not afford to marry a woman so poor.

She laughed aloud. "Oh, but who could not love it? Such a place must speak to the heart of anyone with the least amount of sensibility. Such wildness, and yet such freedom. It is possible to see for mile upon mile, and nothing to prevent one from wandering wherever the spirit desires. Perhaps I should buy an estate nearby, for I should love to live up here, where no one could cage me and hedge me around with arbitrary strictures."

Humphrey made no comment on the matter of a companion buying an estate, but he noted it as another piece in the puzzle that was Miss Rosemary Quayle. Instead, he said neutrally, "Do you feel caged?"

"Every moment! Women are caged every moment of their lives, Lord Humphrey. Society expects them to behave in certain ways, and punishes them severely for any transgression, and the options are so limited — daughter, wife, mother... Cages, every one of them. Oh, they might be very comfortable cages, but cages nevertheless."

"I do not think men have an easier time of it," Humphrey said quietly. "We are every bit as constrained by the expectations of society. We cannot do just as we please."

"No, but you may choose what to do with your lives, whether to have a career or not, whether to marry or not. A man who remains a bachelor is still a person of standing in the community, and well respected by all, whereas a spinster is an object of ridicule. What is more pitiful than an old maid? And what employment is open to a woman? Governess or courtesan."

"Or companion," Humphrey reminded her mildly. "And your employer is kind, and treats you as a friend, I think, so the work is not arduous. The same is true of many marriages, where the husband is fond of his wife. Lady Carrbridge is not caged, I think. As for careers, we have few choices, too. Carrbridge came into his honours when he was but one and twenty, and finds it a great burden, for all his apparent wealth and position in society. I know he feels it to be a cage about him, sometimes. As for the rest of us, the unwanted younger sons of a marquess, each with only a courtesy title and no fortune, what options are available to us? We cannot take up honest hard work like candle making or tailoring, and even respectable occupations such as physician or banker would be frowned upon. Only the church, the army, the law or the fringes of politics will do — and if none of those appeal, we must marry an heiress and live the idle lives of gentlemen. I should love to set up my own business, but I cannot afford it. I nurture my winnings at the card table, but at the present rate it will take me thirty years to accumulate the necessary sum."

She looked at him with sudden interest. "You speak as though you have a business in mind."

"I do. I should like to establish a gaming house, an honest and respectable one where gentlemen, and ladies too, may play for whatever stakes they can afford, and know that the house will not cheat them. But it will take close to a hundred thousand pounds to start with, if I am to attract the highest players, and where am I to find such a sum? Carrbridge cannot afford to invest in such a risky venture, and who else has such an amount?"

"An heiress?" she said, her lips quirked into a smile, and those speaking eyes told him that she understood his position very well.

He laughed and acknowledged the hit. "The thought has crossed my mind, certainly. Connie has been busily finding likely candidates for each of us, for she fancies herself as a matchmaker. Reggie was so obliging as to fall in love with his heiress, and she with him. But without a degree of mutual affection, I cannot imagine there would be much comfort in such a marriage, on either side." It was the first time he had expressed this idea, or even thought it, but the truth of it struck him very hard. How could he marry Miss Blythe without love, or at least a degree of respect and esteem? It would be intolerable. Could he sit down every night to play whist with a woman who chattered constantly? Many men married wives they did not love, he knew, and some were happy anyway. Yet more were not, and took mistresses or were away from home a great deal or drank or gambled away their unhappiness.

"You do not have to marry your investor, surely, Lord Humphrey? Might you not look for a wealthy supporter? Or perhaps ten less wealthy would serve the purpose."

"That is true, but there would be complications — contracts and other legal matters, the sharing of profits, and how to deal with differences of opinion."

"Whereas with a wife, her money would be yours to do with as you please," she said, without rancour. "She would have no say in the matter."

"Essentially, that is the way the law has it, Miss Quayle, although in practice it would not be so rigid, I am sure. It is difficult, and I have not yet found the ideal solution to my dilemma. Shall we ride on, now that Tom has rested his horse a little? Take great care on this rough track, for there are many hidden dips and bumps. We may gallop again when we reach the road. If we turn this way, we will go past Great Mellingham, which is to be given to Reggie and Miss Chamberlain as a wedding gift."

"Generous indeed," she said, smiling again. "Most couples are happy to receive silverware, or a dinner service."

He smiled too, for it was impossible not to respond to her good humour. "The house has been empty for some years since the last tenant died, and Miss Chamberlain's fortune is paying for the new furnishings and wallpapers, so the cost to Carrbridge is small, fortunately."

"I have heard the Marquess of Carrbridge spoken of as one of the richest men in England," she said with a frown.

"The seventh Marquess was certainly so, and my father *seemed* so, but the huge estates he held have long gone — lost in the wars, given away or gambled at the faro table, or just mismanaged. Now there is hardly any money coming in at all."

"So Lord Carrbridge is down to his last ten thousand a year, I suppose," she said, teasingly.

"Less than that," he answered sombrely. "Much less than that. We are all having to rethink how we live."

The rest of the ride passed in near silence, both of them thoughtful. Humphrey had spoken openly, for it was not in his nature to employ deceit in his dealings with a lady, and Miss Quayle would relay the details faithfully to her friend. If he were to court Miss Blythe in good earnest, then he wanted her to know his circumstances, and the family's circumstances, too. It would not matter to her, perhaps, that the Marfords were so impoverished, for she had a vast fortune of her own, but he did not want her to be under any illusions. Was he trying to put her off? He could not be sure. He was no longer entirely certain that he wished to marry her, despite the fortune. But he would have to make a decision soon, for her visit was more than half gone.

These thoughts absorbed him all the way back to the stables, but as they clattered into the stable court, they were greeted by the sound of shouting. A noisy group of grooms and gardeners surrounded one person, angrily berating him. One rather familiar person.

"Oh, Charlie," Humphrey murmured. "Now what have you done?"

9: *Theft And Deception*

Humphrey slid from his horse, and strode across to the group. "Harris, Frank, Williamson, Brenson... stand aside, if you please. Now, which of you has a complaint against Charlie?"

"Almost all of us, milord," Harris, the head gardener, said indignantly. "We've all lost odd sums since he arrived, but now Brenson's caught him with his hand in his pocket. It's not right, milord, and so I tell you. We're honest folk here, and none of us so rich we can afford to lose even a penny or two, and it's not right for him to steal like that, whatever he may have done before."

"Indeed, it is not right," Humphrey said. "Frank, Tom... and where is Lester? Ah, there you are. Tell me, all of you, how does Charlie do his work? Is he industrious, punctual, tidy?"

"Aye, milord," Lester, the head groom, said. "He's a good hard worker, and sharp, you know? Only have to tell him once. If it weren't for the thieving, I'd be right glad to have him." The other grooms nodded their agreement, as Charlie watched warily.

"That is a glowing testimony indeed," Humphrey said. "I am reluctant to turn off a good worker, just because he has not yet set aside some bad habits. Everyone should be given a chance to learn to do better. You say you only have to tell him something once, so let us put that to the test. Charlie, I am going to ask you to explain yourself to me, but be warned — if you lie to me or refuse to answer, then I will be forced to take you to the constable so that the magistrate can examine your case more thoroughly. However, if you are willing to confess to everything you have done and make full recompense, and promise never to steal from anyone ever again, then you may keep your job here, and all will go on as before."

Charlie's head lifted, and he said sullenly, "You've already made your mind up that I'm guilty, then."

"I have, because I have known most of these men around you for years. Harris was working here before I was even born. Lester lifted me onto my first pony when I was two or three years old. Brenson started work here the day my youngest brother was born, and if he says he caught you with your hand in his pocket, then I believe him. You will not convince me of your innocence — remember how I met you, after all. But if you admit to your crimes openly and honestly, and swear never to do such a thing again, I will allow you to keep your job here."

Charlie licked his lips, and looked at Humphrey and then at the hostile faces around him. Straightening his back, he said, "I did steal, it's true. Only small amounts, honest. I never meant no harm by it, milord, truly. It's just a habit, I suppose. I'm really sorry."

"It is not I to whom your apology should be addressed."

Charlie hung his head again. "I'm sorry, really sorry," he muttered to the assembled grooms and gardeners. "I'm just not used to working with decent folk, and... and I wanted to buy ale for some of you at the Hare And Hounds, cos you've been kind to me, and I had no money."

There was a stunned silence, then Lester burst out laughing. "You stole our own money to buy us ale? Oh, that's priceless, Charlie. You're an idiot, you know that?" He clapped Charlie on the shoulder, and the others laughed and shook their heads.

Humphrey said, "Lester, Harris, let me have a full reckoning of all that has been taken, and I shall see that it is repaid from Charlie's salary. He will not be buying anyone ale for a while, I fear. Go on, get back to work, all of you."

He turned to see Miss Quayle still standing in the yard, watching events with great interest.

"Let me escort you to your room," he said. "I shall show you the quickest way to and from the stables. Ganymede is yours to ride whenever you wish for the duration of your stay."

"Lord Humphrey, you are too generous! But I am far too selfish a creature to refuse such a magnificent offer. Thank you! A thousand times thank you!"

"I know you will take great care of him," he said, smiling at her enthusiasm. "But promise me you will always take one of the grooms with you. They know the best routes, and also the hidden dangers that might catch you out. There are gullies and hidden streams on the moors where an unwary rider could come to grief, and I would hate you to break Ganymede's neck. Or your neck, either."

She laughed out loud at his impudence. "I shall take the greatest care of Ganymede, you may be sure of that, and I will try very hard not to break any necks." She followed him into the house and up the stable stairs. After a pause, she added, "He is very like you. Indeed, you might almost be brothers."

"Charlie? The likeness is remarkable, and you can guess the reason, I suppose. Our new under gamekeeper is another of Father's little surprises."

"Every family has such surprises," she said equably. "It is no great matter, after all. You met him when he picked *your* pocket, I gather."

"Something like that," he said, with a little laugh. "He is not a very good thief, but he is clever in other ways. He can imitate my voice perfectly, even the accent. Now that he has shaved and cut his hair, if he were dressed in my clothes he could pass himself off as me in a moment."

"And could you pass yourself off as him?" she said, with an amused smile.

Humphrey cleared his throat. *'Aye, reckon I could do that right enough. T'Yorkshire speech ain't so 'ard.'*

She laughed. "Too much! His accent is not so strong. But a good effort. You are right about Charlie, though — he *is* clever. After all of your dreadful warnings, he did not, in the end, make any promises for the future."

Humphrey stopped dead. "Good God! You are quite right. What a sneaky little fellow he is! I must remember to talk to him again, and extract his solemn promise, and perhaps I should get him to swear on the Bible."

"I should say his word was enough," she said. "You do not trust him, and yet you keep him here and even excuse his bad behaviour."

He shrugged. "He is family. Despite his origins, he is my brother and think how embarrassing it would be if he were to be transported or hanged. Carrbridge would feel it greatly."

"He is a gentle soul, the marquess," she said. "We go through this door next, I think."

"You know your way around already," he said, chagrined.

"While... my friend was engaged with her social activities, I have been exploring. I hope you do not mind."

"Not in the least," Humphrey said. "But now I am on my mettle to show you some part of Drummoor that will provide you with a novelty."

"The cellars?" she hazarded. "The servants' quarters? The roof? I have heard Mr Chamberlain describing the Drummoor roof as having something quite exceptional in the way of chimneys, so I expect Lady Carrbridge to order an expedition there forthwith, the aunts to be conveyed in sedan chairs and a picnic provided, with chilled champagne and cold leg of duck."

"What an enchanting idea!" he said, grinning. "I must suggest it to Connie. But for today, how about the attics? If we take this stair just through here, we can reach the play attic. Most of the attics are pretty dull, full of broken furniture and old trunks and the like, but the play attic has all the old toys, and in wet weather we were allowed to have sword fights and hobby-horse races and dress up in embroidered coats and wigs and tricorn hats, pretending to be grown up. Such fun we had up there! Come on."

And without thinking he grabbed her hand and towed her along at a run, up a narrow stair, along a dusty corridor and then through a low door to the attic. She laughed and allowed herself to be towed. He had no idea how long they stayed there, for she spotted an ancient puppet theatre and nothing would do but to find all the puppets and put on an impromptu performance of Punch and Judy. She took the female parts, and he the male, and he could not remember a time when he had laughed so much or enjoyed himself so unreservedly. Not since he was a boy, certainly.

It was only when they heard, very faintly, the dressing gong, that they brushed away the accumulated dust and spiders' webs from their clothes, and rushed away to change for dinner.

Humphrey had thought he was going to be late, but when he reached the pink drawing room, only Connie was there.

"Where is everyone?"

"Still waiting for the footmen to carry hot water upstairs for their baths, I daresay," Connie said. "We were dreadfully late back from Sagborough. Lord Carrbridge was here a moment ago, but he was called away by a visitor."

"Ah, the privileges of rank — taking your share of the hot water before your guests," Humphrey said, bending to kiss her hand. "Was Sagborough interesting? Did the peacock walk live up to expectations?"

"Very much so, you teasing boy! You would have found it dreadfully dull, but the ladies enjoyed it enormously, even the peacock walk. Although I must confess, the peacocks were as untidy as any I have ever seen. Do they moult, do you think? Or perhaps they were suffering from the mange. But one showed his tail to us, so Lady Hawthorn's honour was satisfied. How has your day been? I expect you have been out riding, and not doing your duty visiting our neighbours."

He pulled a face. "Tambray Hall? The Melthwaites are too dull for words. I have been more pleasurably engaged in riding out with Miss Quayle. Tell me, Connie, what do you think of her?"

"Miss Quayle? A little mouse of a thing. She never says a word. Humphrey, it is kind in you to take an interest in the poor creature, and it may help you to fix your interest with her mistress, but do not waste too much time on her, for she has not a penny to her name. You are supposed to be wooing Hortensia Blythe, not Rosemary Quayle."

"I am aware. But what do you think of her gowns?"

"Her gowns?" She stared at him, bemused. "Well, they are very stylish, for a companion. An expensive *modiste*, certainly, but then I suppose Miss Blythe clothes her. She dresses a little drably, which is fitting, but—"

"Exactly! Those greys and violets — they look to me like half-mourning colours."

"So they are," she said. "Or would be, with black gloves. But quite unexceptional, for a companion. Humphrey, what are you thinking?"

But there was no time to discuss the oddities of Miss Quayle further, for Carrbridge entered the drawing room with his visitor, who was to stay for a night or two. Lord Kilbraith was cousin to both Mary, Lady Hardy and also to Connie, and was heir to an earldom in Scotland. Having had business in York, he had impulsively extended his journey to Drummoor. Naturally, Connie was delighted to add him to her roster of house guests, and not merely on account of the family connection. Lord Kilbraith was rich, handsome and amiable, and therefore must be welcome in any company. In addition, he was only a little above thirty and as yet unmarried, which made him of the greatest interest to the ladies.

With the day's visit to Sagborough and the addition of a charming new guest, the dinner-table conversation was as lively as Humphrey could remember. One end of the table was absorbed in the minutiae of lace and boot-buttons and Lady Hawthorn's peacock walk, while the other exchanged family news and compared the children's growth and wondered why they met so seldom.

Yet Humphrey was restless. He knew he ought to intensify his courtship of Miss Blythe if he was to have any hope of winning her, yet his head was full of glowing brown eyes and a lady in a green riding habit, a lady who could put Ganymede over the wall without the least hesitation. She had not a penny to her name, and he could not afford to think of her, yet he could not get her out of his mind. And his foolish hesitation meant that he lost the chance to sit beside either of them. Miss Blythe was claimed by two of the Marford cousins, squabbling for the right to lead her into the dining room, and settling the matter by each offering an arm. And Miss Quayle was led in to dinner by Julius Whittleton.

Now that was an odd thing. Everyone knew that Julius was hanging out for a rich wife, and he never, ever pursued a lady, even in the mildest of flirtations, unless there was a fortune to be gained. He had been pursuing Miss Blythe assiduously ever since he had met her. Yet tonight he was exerting all his considerable charm towards Miss Quayle.

Humphrey sat morosely halfway down the table, too far away to participate in any of the livelier groups, surrounded by uncles and aunts who had nothing original to say, and were far more interested in their food than in him. He did his polite best to engage them in conversation, but it was hard work.

In between these efforts, he watched the two friends covertly. Miss Blythe was as pretty as a summer garden in pale pinks and blues which set off her delicate complexion to perfection. Her gown was simply styled, as became her age, and was both elegant and fashionable, but she wore no jewels and nothing but a ribbon in her hair. She looked charmingly unsophisticated, as she smiled and chatted readily to her dinner companions, without seeming to be especially interested in either.

Miss Quayle's dark hair was even more simply styled, with nothing but a silver comb adorning it, and she, too, wore no jewels, but her lilac gown and sheer over-gown bore the sort of understated embroidery that Humphrey knew was hideously expensive. He was not much of a judge of ladies' attire, but it struck him now that if one were obliged to pick one of the two as the heiress by the quality of her gown alone, then Miss Quayle would certainly be the winner. As he considered this interesting fact, he remembered her remark about buying an estate on the moors, and her confusion over whether she had ever lived in England before. Yet only that day she had said *'I have so missed this English air'*.

Was it possible that they were all mistaken, and Miss Quayle was the heiress, and Miss Blythe the companion? Or had they even taken each other's names? Yes! For they never called each other by name, and talked always of *'my friend'*, to avoid the possibility of a mistake. And Miss Blythe — the real Miss Blythe — was only just out of mourning for her father, and had a wardrobe full of grey and lilac gowns, easy enough to reuse as a companion's attire. Two women, newly arrived from India, with no relatives and no acquaintance in society — how simple to switch identities.

But the real question was — why? What was to be gained by the deceit? Even as he solved one part of the puzzle, another rose to take its place.

He was very satisfied with his deduction, but if any corner of doubt had remained in his mind, one other factor would have convinced him, and that was Julius Whittleton's change of allegiance from Miss Blythe to Miss Quayle. Somehow, he knew about the deception. And then Humphrey remembered that Julius had been helping Merton for some time, and had occasionally been left to open and sort the marquess's mail. Carrbridge had written to someone with connections to India to enquire about Miss Blythe, and it was entirely possible that Julius had read the reply.

Now Humphrey was in a dilemma. He could no longer pursue the lady who called herself Miss Blythe, knowing she had no fortune. Yet equally, it would look very odd in him to abandon his attentions to her altogether. That was not the behaviour of a gentleman. Nor could he act as Julius had, and suddenly pay court to the lady who really had the two hundred thousand pounds. Only an unmitigated fortune hunter would act so.

And yet... the lady with the fortune was also, seemingly, the one who rode as bravely as any man, who learnt a new game in the time it took to explain the rules, who could match him in intellect, in spirit and in physical prowess. His dark-eyed lady who drew his gaze over and over again. Usually when he glanced her way, she was turned away from him, listening politely to one of Julius's monologues. But once, she was looking straight at him, and she lifted her knife and fork and made a little gesture with them, suggestive of Mr Punch being hit over the head. Then she smiled, such an intimate, secretive little smile that his heart turned over.

What was happening to him? He knew so little about her, and yet he was more than halfway to being utterly, irrevocably in love with her.

10: *Mutual Attraction*

When the ladies withdrew and the gentlemen rearranged themselves at one end of the table, Humphrey found himself sitting next to Lord Kilbraith. As soon as the port had passed round, Kilbraith turned to Humphrey and said, "Who is the pretty little thing in the blue and pink? The one with all the blonde curls directly opposite you."

"That would be Miss Hortensia Blythe," Humphrey said, wondering even as he spoke if that was true. "Recently arrived from India."

"Fabulously wealthy," Uncle Joshua put in. "Two hundred thousand, by all accounts, and in her own control, with no restrictions. I imagine *she* will not be husbandless for long." He laughed, a deep, fruity rumble. "Humphrey has his eye on her already. A good match for him, if he can get her, although you could cut him out, I make no doubt, Kilbraith, if you set your mind to it. The chit would like to be the Countess of Strathmorran one day, I daresay. Shall we have a small wager on which of you will win her?"

"I beg you will not," Humphrey said sharply. "It is too bad when a lady is the object of gossip and speculation just because she has a fortune at her command."

"Too bad it may be," said Uncle Joshua, "but it is the way of the world, Humphrey, m'boy. Pretty girl, money by the bucketful —

bound to set folk wondering. Bound to be surrounded by hopeful young men. Only natural. But you had better get a move on, or Kilbraith will snaffle her from under your nose." He chuckled again, and it was fortunate for Humphrey's temper that his uncle was called to intervene in a debate further down the table.

Kilbraith talked for a while on indifferent topics, but later, when the port had circulated more freely and the table was becoming noisy, he said in a low voice to Humphrey, "Tell me truly, Marford, what is your situation with Miss Blythe? For I would not for the world encroach if there is any existing attachment or understanding. But if there is not—"

Humphrey caught his breath. How easy it would be! An agreement between gentlemen. A smile, a nod, a conscious look — and Kilbraith need not trouble him. His own pursuit of Miss Blythe could continue unimpeded, for even Julius had withdrawn, seemingly.

But abruptly everything had changed. If the lady he pursued was not, in fact, Miss Blythe or an heiress, then he could not afford to marry her and his pursuit was very dangerous. What if he offered for her and found himself trapped in a loveless marriage to a penniless woman? Was he right in his supposition? If so, he stood on the brink of disaster if he continued to court the supposed Miss Blythe. If he was wrong — well, there would be other heiresses, no doubt. Or other ways to raise the ready. He was a gambler, and loved a risk, but only when he could afford to lose and here he knew he could not.

So he answered honestly. "There is no such attachment or understanding. I have only known the lady for a little over a month, after all."

"Yet your uncle is in expectation of a match."

Humphrey shrugged. "It is an obvious supposition. A younger son with no prospects, and a wealthy heiress — what could be more natural? And my sister-in-law is a great matchmaker and has been promoting the pairing, and I have dutifully taken an interest in the lady." Dutifully? Even as he spoke the word, he understood the significance of it. Yes, his courtship of Miss Blythe was more duty than desire. "It would be a most convenient thing, were we to make a match of it. But I tell you this — if I had seen any sign of attachment on the lady's side, I should have been ordering my wedding coat by now. As it is, she is as pleasantly affable to me as to anyone else. So if you have an admiration for her, the way is clear."

Kilbraith leaned back in his chair with a smile of satisfaction on his face. Not long after that, he left the gentlemen to rejoin the ladies.

Humphrey sat on, wondering at himself. He had personally selected Miss Blythe, and she had been invited to Drummoor precisely so that he might attempt to win her hand. Ever since her arrival, he had been showing her some not inconsiderable attention, by his own standards, for he was not accustomed to paying court to ladies. On the contrary, he had been very sure never to behave in any way which might give rise to expectations in a young lady's breast. Many had tried to attach him over the years, but all had failed.

Now that he had finally come round to the idea of marriage, he had expended more time and effort on Miss Blythe than in ten years of mingling with the *ton*. It was not his way to be ostentatious in his pursuit, or so he hoped, but to those who knew him, his intentions must have been obvious. And yet, he had as good as handed her over to Kilbraith.

He ought, by rights, to feel — what, precisely? Jealousy? Anger? Sadness? But when he examined his own heart with a dispassionate eye, he realised that it would be a relief if Kilbraith were to whisk Miss Blythe away to Scotland. He liked the lady well enough, but for him it would be a marriage of convenience only. He had no desire to marry her solely for her fortune, to selfishly use her inheritance to fund his gaming house. His heart whispered that perhaps he had another reason to wish Kilbraith well in his endeavours, a reason with dark eyes that turned his insides to jelly. It was a conundrum, and hovered over him like a black cloud of uncertainty. What was he to do?

When Humphrey returned to the drawing room, he found Miss Blythe singing again, and Kilbraith watching her, transfixed. She seemed to have noticed him, too, for from time to time she cast little glances his way, then blushed before turning quickly back to her music sheet.

Before Humphrey had taken three steps into the room, Connie had grabbed his elbow and steered him straight back out again.

"What are you *about*?" she hissed, all concern. "If you do not take care, Cousin Max will have her and all our efforts will have been in vain."

"He will inherit an earldom," Humphrey said with a shrug. "It would be a good match for her, if she takes to him. And why should she not? He is a handsome fellow, and most amiable."

"And so are you, silly boy." Her eyes narrowed. "Do you dislike her? Is that it? Are you losing interest in her? You spend almost as much time with Miss Quayle as with Miss Blythe, which is very good-natured of you, for she is such a quiet little thing, never putting herself forward, but you must not lose sight of where your best interests lie."

"Ah, you must not quiz me, Connie," he said. "I hardly know what I feel just now, and a month is not enough time to settle my confused mind. I fear I cannot oblige you by falling in love with a lady just because she is rich."

"Of course not, dear, and no one wishes you to marry without love. Reggie was delightfully compliant in that respect, but I am not so heartless as to push you if you have quite given up the idea of Miss Blythe."

Humphrey sighed. "That is just the trouble, I have not the least idea what I want, or what she wants either."

"Then, perhaps for my sake, you will be your charming self with her for a little longer so that she may compare you and Max directly? I do not want any gentlemanly nonsense about standing aside and not getting in each other's way. I nearly married Reggie because Lord Carrbridge had agreed not to compete with him, do you remember? It was *you* who insisted that I should be given the choice, and how glad I was of it! Imagine if I had married the wrong brother, and all because I did not know that my dear Francis still loved me. A lady should be allowed to make up her own mind, Humphrey."

He laughed, remembering the occasion well. "You are quite right, and if it should happen that Miss Blythe forms an unshakable attachment to me, then you may be sure that I will marry her. But Connie, promise me you will not be disappointed if she should prefer Kilbraith?"

"I shall do no such thing, for naturally it will be the gravest disappointment if my skills as a matchmaker are found to be so deplorably lacking. Although, since they were introduced under my roof, I may still take the credit for it, may I not? For your sake, I hope you win her, but for mine, Miss Blythe may marry whomever she wishes, with my goodwill."

And so, when the tables were brought out for cards, Humphrey allowed himself to be partnered at whist with Miss Blythe, against

Kilbraith and Miss Quayle. In the space of two minutes, he perceived that if Miss Blythe were to form an unshakable attachment, it should not be towards himself. She talked and played very composedly, but every time Kilbraith addressed her, a blush suffused her cheeks. Once, his hand accidentally brushed against hers, and she instantly went scarlet, and it took ten minutes of the gentlemen determinedly talking about nothing in particular before she had regained her usual colour.

Miss Quayle, meanwhile, was intent upon the game at first, and spoke of nothing outside of it, but when her friend blushed so vividly, she seemed to become aware of Lord Kilbraith for the first time. She fell silent, watching him and Miss Blythe with a serious, almost concerned, expression.

After the supper break, Kilbraith eagerly proposed a resumption of their four, although with the small alteration that he would partner Miss Blythe. Humphrey understood why, for it enabled him to gaze at her directly across the table. She would be constantly in his view, without the least need to turn his head, and it gave him the opportunity to talk to her more frequently. The change meant that Humphrey partnered Miss Quayle, and their combined skills were so great and their opponents so distracted that they took every game and almost every trick.

When the final points were added up, Kilbraith was astonished at the depth of their loss. "I usually acquit myself a little better than that," he said, frowning. "But then to lose to Lord Humphrey Marford is no great blow to my pride. It would be astonishing had you *not* had the victory."

Humphrey bowed at the compliment, but added, "I believe my partner may claim just as much credit for our success."

"Of course. My compliments on your fine play, Miss... erm, Quayle."

She acknowledged the compliment, but he was already turning away to speak to Miss Blythe. With a conspiratorial grin, Miss Quayle whispered to Humphrey, "Just think how we might have thrashed them if we had not been throwing away trumps almost from the start. Why, you cast away the ace, once."

Humphrey laughed. "Even such outrageous moves could not bring them a respectable score when they were so... preoccupied, shall we say. I have never seen such a violent case of love at first sight."

The smile on her face dropped, and she gazed after the pair with anxious eyes. "Indeed. It is not like... my friend to be so smitten on five minutes' acquaintance."

"Whereas he has a history of such sudden starts," Humphrey said. "Did you know that he was once briefly betrothed to Mary, Lady Hardy, after just such an instant attraction?"

She turned her gaze full on him. "No! What happened? Why did they not marry?"

"Oh... family reasons," he said vaguely.

"Was it to do with money?" she said, and there was an intentness in her look that he believed he understood. If Miss Blythe were *not* the heiress, yet Kilbraith believed that she was...

"No, money was not the problem," Humphrey said quickly. "Kilbraith fought in the Peninsula and has made enough there to give him an independent income, as well as being heir to a wealthy earldom. Miss Blythe's fortune will not weigh with him. There was some family history that made the match with Lady Hardy ineligible, that was all."

"Ah." She seemed relieved, and if he had not already worked out the secret, her manner now would have given all away. Naturally, she did not want her impoverished friend to fall for Lord Kilbraith if he was looking out for a rich wife. But Humphrey had misgivings, all the same. Kilbraith may not care one jot whether Miss Blythe be rich or poor, but he might care very much to find himself deceived in the matter.

~~~~~

"Hortensia, this cannot go on! Ow!"

"I beg your pardon." Hortensia laid down the hairbrush and gazed at her friend in the mirror. "This is a tangle, is it not, dearest?"

"My hair or... *us*?" Rosemary said.

For a moment, Hortensia stared at her, then both of them burst out laughing. "Oh, what a mess!" Hortensia said, shaking her dark curls. "And I am *not* talking about your hair. It seemed like such a good idea to switch places. You would get your chance to shine, as you deserve, and would find yourself an adoring husband, and I... I could hide away for a time, and get used to being alone in the world without suitors flitting round me all the while like a cloud of gnats. But we never quite worked out how we would switch back again, and oh, how awkward it is, when everyone thinks you are the rich heiress and I am just your companion. How can we possibly tell people?"

"And everyone has been so agreeable to us," Rosemary said, heaving a sigh. "Lord and Lady Carrbridge have been everything that is kind and generous, and now I feel like a *worm* for deceiving them. And... and, dearest..." She blushed, looking down and pleating the skirt of her gown with her fingers. "Now there is *him*!" she burst out.

"There is indeed *him*," Hortensia said dryly. "If we could but have got through our month here, we might have slunk away to Bath or... or somewhere else we are not known. Then perhaps we could begin again, a little more circumspectly. But Lord Kilbraith is a problem, there is no doubt about it."

"We must tell him," Rosemary said. "He cannot go on believing me to be the rich Miss Blythe."

Hortensia sighed, making no answer.

"And there is Lord Humphrey, too," Rosemary said. "You like him, I know you do, for I have seen how you look when you speak of him, and if he knew how rich you are—"

"I do not think—"

"It would be perfect," Rosemary said, spinning round on the dressing stool to face Hortensia, her face alight with excitement. "If we confess, *you* can marry Lord Humphrey, and *I* can marry Lord Kilbraith, and everyone would be happy."

Hortensia gave a tight little smile. Yes, it would be perfect! But she had scarcely dared to think about such possibilities herself. She had seen the way Lord Humphrey looked at her sometimes, but was that just admiration for her riding skills or her ability at cards, pursuits which he enjoyed too? Surely he could have no admiration for her as a woman, for who could, plain as she was? Could he? Was it possible? Her heart whispered that it must be so, for why else spend so much time in her company, and with such apparent pleasure? Why give her his own horse to ride? That was not mere gentlemanly chivalry. And he knew nothing of her fortune, so his attention must be disinterested. Was it possible that he could love her for herself, not caring about her fortune? But she dared not hope for such joy. She had had such hopes before, and been disappointed.

"I do not think it would work out quite as perfectly as you imagine," Hortensia said. "Here is what we shall do. Let us wait for a few days, to see how things go on with Lord Kilbraith. If matters become serious, then we shall tell him everything, I promise you. If not... no, do not look so distraught, for who knows what may happen? We must consider all possibilities, dearest. If it comes to nothing, then we may leave here at the end of our month undiscovered, and I daresay we shall not meet the Marfords again, so it will not matter."

Rosemary nodded, too used to Hortensia deciding everything to argue with her.

But when Hortensia had seen her friend settled in bed, and had returned to her own room, she sat for a very long time at the window, gazing down into the kitchen court below, a faint scent of honeysuckle and lavender wafting up to her. Her thoughts were not on plants or the beauty of the night sky or even, as might be supposed, on the problem of Rosemary and Lord Kilbraith. Instead her mind was full of a man who let her ride his finest horse, who taught her to play card games to his own level, a man who *noticed* her, as no one else in that crowded house had. And a man who, she had to admit, was charming and handsome and all that she could desire, with a pair of smiling eyes which set her stomach fluttering as if it were full of butterflies. If only she could have him... If only...

~~~~~

Humphrey was far too unsettled to sleep. His thoughts bounced around, without an ounce of sense to any of them. First he wondered about Miss Blythe and Kilbraith — could they really fall in love so abruptly? Would they wake tomorrow to think better of it? And yet — what could be more fitting than that a pretty and accomplished young lady should marry an eligible nobleman? Her poverty — if she were indeed impoverished — only made the possibility the more romantic. Yet Humphrey could not be easy about it, all the same. Kilbraith might fall out of love as easily as he fell into it, especially if he found out that his beloved had deceived him.

Then there was Miss Quayle, whose wealth — if she were indeed wealthy — would resolve Humphrey's difficulties while also bringing him a wife he could truly love. Was he in love with her already? He dared not be, for he could not afford a poor wife, yet nor could he court two seemingly wealthy women in the same month. It was impossible, and the worst of it was that she would suit him admirably. If only he could have her... If only...

11: An Outing Is Planned

Humphrey woke to the sudden realisation that, so long as the two ladies' deception continued, he need make no adjustments to his behaviour. Indeed, it would be thought odd if he were to do so. And if all was revealed, why, then he would make another plan and allow the dice to fall as they may. There was an excitement in it, knowing, or at least suspecting, the secret behind the two ladies and having not the least idea where it would all end up. It was like a good hunting day, following the hounds wherever they went, no matter how high the obstacles to be jumped, and having no greater ambition than not to find oneself head first in the mud. And if it went badly, as was always possible — well, no point thinking about hypothetical futures.

So when he met Connie at the breakfast table, he was in mellow mood.

"Humphrey!" she cried. "Just the person I need. I am planning an outing to Branksford Abbey—"

"Oh no!" he said. "Connie, it always rains, you know that. How many times have you attempted this? And it always rains!"

"It will not rain this year. The weather is set fair, Harris and Lester agree for once. Shall you come? The ladies are all very keen, but I need a few more gentlemen."

"Must I?" he said, pulling a face. "Ruined abbeys are not very appealing."

"It would be a very pleasant outing in your curricle, you must agree."

That certainly made a difference. "Hmm. It is time I stretched the greys' legs a little."

"Quite so," she said, pressing home her advantage. "You might invite Miss Blythe to accompany you. If you take your groom, it would be quite unexceptional."

But Miss Blythe did not come down to breakfast, and by the time Humphrey met up with her again, just before dinner, his invitation was met with blushes and a stammered refusal. Lord Kilbraith, it seemed, had secured the lady's company already, with Lady Hardy and Merton taking the remaining seats in his carriage.

Humphrey accepted this with outward composure, but excitement rushed through him. Now he was free to solicit Miss Quayle instead, as his heart wished. Instantly he sought her out in her accustomed quiet corner of the drawing room.

"Shall you go to Branksford Abbey?" he began, too keen to secure her company to be subtle.

"Oh, I think not."

Relief. At least Julius had not got ahead of him. "It is a very fine ruin. Quite one of the best ruins in Yorkshire, I believe."

She shot him an amused glance. "Very tempting, but I think I must still refuse."

"It is a very pleasant drive in my curricle, and—"

"You are very kind, Lord Humphrey, but—"

"—I am sure you would enjoy driving my greys."

"Oh!" Her squeak of astonishment caused heads to turn. She clapped her hands to her mouth, as if to suppress any further outbreaks, but her eyes were round. "Truly?" she whispered, when she had got her voice under control.

"Truly."

"You do not feel that it would wound your masculine pride to be driven by a woman?"

He laughed at that. "I think it would increase my consequence greatly to be driven about the countryside by a stylish lady who is an excellent whip. I look forward to tooling through the village quite at my ease, bowing and waving to all my acquaintance in the most casual manner, which I cannot do half so well if I am managing reins and whip and trying to avoid the pig farmer's cart. I assume you *are* an excellent whip, Miss Quayle? Having seen your competence on horseback, I am tolerably certain of it."

"In India I was accounted so, yes, but I have not yet tested my skills on English roads. Oh, yes *please!* I should like of all things to drive your greys. You are the most generous of men, Lord Humphrey. I cannot think of anyone else who would hand over their precious cattle to a stranger in this way. Lord Augustus would not, I wager!"

"Absolutely not! No one drives one of Gus's teams but Gus himself. His riding mounts, yes, he is not so close-fisted with those, but never his precious matched pairs. He once called a fellow out who had the temerity merely to *ask* if he might try the bays. Carrbridge would not give you his curricle either — he would be terrified that you would overturn and injure yourself. As for Reggie, it would never occur to him that a lady would ever want to drive, even though his sister does. Now Monty is so sweet-natured that he would let anyone do anything, but he has never in his life owned anything faster than a hedgehog. He will be ideally situated as clergyman, for he will be able to drive everywhere at walking pace in a gig. And Gil—" He stopped, frowning. "Gil would let you do it for a lark, and then provoke the horses until you ended up in a ditch with a broken head. Miss Quayle, you must never, ever go driving with Gil, do you hear me? He is wild beyond all sense, sometimes."

"I am not likely to have the opportunity," she said gently. "Lord Gilbert is not here, and I shall be gone in a few days."

Her words were like an arrow through Humphrey's heart. A few days! He had grown so easy in her company, he had quite forgotten her visit was almost at an end. And then what was he to do? It was unthinkable to lose her now, quite intolerable. And that was the point at which he knew, beyond the faintest shadow of doubt, that his heart was irretrievably lost.

~~~~~

The excursion to Branksford Abbey was just the sort of outing most calculated to bore Humphrey to tears. Thirty-five people were to be assembled, squeezed into an array of equipages and driven at a funereal pace on bad roads. The speed was dictated by Aunt Patience and Aunt Agnes, who agreed that walking pace was the only sensible rate of progress for any conveyance, having due consideration for the comfort, security and rank of the occupants. The two disagreed about almost everything, and if one were to say the air was too hot, the other would be sure to assert that in fact it was too cold. But on this single point, they were of one mind, and therefore the carriages must proceed in stately fashion, so that all might arrive in good order at their destination, and every urchin and farmer might have ample opportunity to ogle them as they passed by.

As if this were not desperate enough for a man for whom anything less than breakneck speed is mere dawdling, there would be hours of sitting about while the ladies worried about the dampness of the grass, and whether it would rain, and the encroaching habits of bees and wasps. On one such occasion, the sighting of a cow caused an outbreak of screaming.

Then there would be the slow procession home, and inevitably one or other of the carriages would break something, or a horse would go lame, and there would be disruption and upset and general inconvenience, and like as not Humphrey would be left at the side of the road to await the arrival of the farrier or wheelwright. It was all too tedious for words.

But this present outing promised Humphrey far better entertainment. Even at the slow pace dictated by the aunts, the pleasure of Miss Quayle's company outweighed every other nuisance. He would have a whole day at her side, and he could scarcely imagine at that moment any greater delight. In a few days, she would be gone from his life for ever, but there was no need at all to think of that yet. He would worry about that in the future, for today he was determined to be happy.

He hummed as he dressed that morning, and made no remonstrance when Billings took several attempts to fix his cravat to the valet's satisfaction. Humphrey chose his clothes with care and liked to appear to advantage, but he normally grew impatient at too much time wasted in front of the looking glass. Today, unaccountably, he wished to look his best, and while Billings fussed over him, Humphrey speculated pleasurably on what sort of carriage dress Miss Quayle might adopt for the occasion. One of her plain companion's gowns, or something as stylish as her riding habit?

Miss Quayle did not appear for the early breakfast enjoyed by most of the gentlemen, so it was not until the excursion party assembled in the entrance hall that Humphrey had his curiosity satisfied. He had positioned himself in a dark corner, half hidden by a Chinese urn, from which station he could watch the ladies descend the stairs, the aunts ponderously and the Miss Whittletons with girlish skips and many giggles. Then Connie and Harriet, laughing at some shared joke, with Carrbridge just behind them. And then—

A hush fell on the assembly. Two pairs of elegant boots appeared on the half landing, turning, stopping, as if to be admired. Two feet were carefully placed on the next stair and then the next, revealing the swirling hems of their gowns. Slowly, ever so slowly, the two ladies descended, Miss Blythe and Miss Quayle, arm in arm, united in friendship and in fashion. For Miss Quayle was, if anything, the more elegantly attired of the two. While Miss Blythe kept to the pale muslin appropriate for her age, Miss Quayle wore a rich ruby pelisse and matching hat of such style that even Humphrey, no expert on female attire, knew it must have cost a fortune. It was the first time she had appeared in company clad as the lady she undoubtedly was, and every head was turned her way.

By the time the pair had reached the level of the hall, Lord Kilbraith had rushed forward to claim Miss Blythe and Julius Whittleton, eyes positively bulging, was offering his arm to Miss Quayle. She smiled, shook her head, demurred. Humphrey knew his cue — stepping out of his hiding place, he crossed the hall to her side.

"Miss Quayle is to drive with me, Julius," he murmured.

Julius spluttered, his mouth opening and closing a few times, before he wisely chose to keep silent, merely bowing and withdrawing with as much dignity as he could muster.

Humphrey had no attention to spare for him, his gaze drawn to those lustrous dark eyes that gleamed with mischief.

"Miss Quayle," he murmured, holding his arm for her. "Shall we go outside to await the carriages?"

"Lord Humphrey," she said, curtsying demurely, then lifting her head to reveal a wide grin. Such inviting lips she had, and despite his height, she was almost near enough to kiss...

Then she lowered her head and took his arm and, mesmerised, he led her past the silently watching throng, past the footmen swinging open the doors, and down the broad steps to the drive. Several carriages waited there already, as well as two barouches and the first of the curricles. The horses tossed their heads impatiently as grooms did their best to hold them steady, while footmen rushed about with hot bricks and rugs, opening doors, unfolding steps, rushing back to assist Uncle Thomas and Aunt Theodosia out of the house and into their carriage.

Just then, Humphrey's curricle bowled round the corner from the stable court with Tom at the reins.

"Ah!" Miss Quayle said. Humphrey thought her smile could not stretch any wider, yet it did.

"Your conveyance, madam," he said, with a little bow. "May I assist you aboard?"

"Thank you, but I can manage." And with that she nimbly climbed up onto the seat and took the reins from Tom, who jumped down to hold the horses' heads. Turning to Humphrey, she said, "Will you join me, my lord?"

That smile again! If she had asked him to dance a reel instead, he suspected he would have obeyed her just as readily. He took his seat beside her, and folded his arms. "We shall have a while to wait, I daresay. It always takes forever to get the aunts settled."

"Must we stay?" She turned those great eyes on him in entreaty. "The horses are fresh and I cannot wait to get onto the road. Would it be a great breach of protocol for us to go on ahead?"

Humphrey did not hesitate. "Yes, but I dare you to do it anyway."

She burst into laughter. "Tom, stand away!" Then with a snick of the whip, she set the curricle into motion, Tom leapt up behind and they were bowling away down the drive, leaving astonishment and pointing fingers in their dust.

~~~~~

Hortensia could not suppress a beaming grin. Worse than that, she was actually laughing in delight. Oh, the pleasure of having two fine horses at her command, and a splendid vehicle to tool about in. The amusement of setting off before any of the others added spice to the day. She would have to do penance for it later, she knew, for here everything revolved around rank. The marquess's carriage should have gone first, and then, no doubt, the guests, the aunts and uncles, and the young people at the back of the long procession. It was not so in India, where a spirited young lady driving her own curricle was permitted a degree of indulgence.

Here, as a mere companion, she should be subservient, know her place, always hang back. Oh, she was so tired of hanging back! So tired of being meek, demure companion Miss Rosemary Quayle, instead of outspoken heiress Miss Hortensia Blythe. How she longed to confess, and yet, how awkward it was to admit to such an outrageous deception. So much easier to drift along and hope for the best, and enjoy the attentions of a man who was gloriously ignorant of her true situation.

They rattled down the drive at a rapid pace, the horses still fresh and pressing to go faster. She held them in check, not sure how far they had to go. Beside her, Lord Humphrey said nothing, but every time she stole a glance at him, she saw him grinning from ear to ear, just as she was. He was so much fun! Not in the least stuffy, not like some of these society people. He never stood on ceremony with her, and treated her with such ease, as if they were equals. So handsome, and that smile... those eyes that looked at her as if she were the only woman in the world... and his voice, when he lowered it to speak confidentially, warmed her to the soles of her feet. How easily she had fallen in love with him, after all these years when she had been quite heart-free. And he loved her, she was sure of it now. She could not mistake the glow of ardour in his eyes! He loved her, thinking her nothing but a companion, loved her solely for herself. Happiness bubbled up inside her, making her want to laugh and cry and sing for joy.

Of course, as long as he believed her penniless, there was no question of marriage, but if he knew her to be wealthy... But she must not let her emotions get the better of her, not today. She must use her head, and think what must be done. But it was so difficult when he looked at her just that way. When she stole a glance at him, his head was turned towards her.

"This is fun, is it not?" His laugh spun itself around her like a web.

"Have I shocked all your relations?" she said, slowing the horses to a walk at the end of the long drive, as two children from the lodge rushed to open the gates for them.

"Oh, I do hope so. Not for driving off in this way, for it is exactly what Harriet used to do, and Gil certainly would if he were here. No, I expect they are horrified to see a mere companion as fashionably dressed as her mistress — and *more* fashionably dressed than the other ladies today. You outshine them all and that is an unforgivable sin in one so lowly."

"Ah, but you see today I am not lowly, nor am I hiding away in a dark corner. I am driving two beautiful steppers in a fine curricle, and it is incumbent upon me to rise to the occasion and do them justice. Today, I am not Miss Quayle, a mere companion. Today I am..." She stopped herself in time.

"Yes?" he said politely. "And who are you?"

"Someone else entirely," she said quickly. She focused her attention on the horses, chiding herself for being so careless. She had almost let her secret slip! It was to be hoped that Lord Humphrey had noticed nothing odd in her manner.

"That will not do." To her relief, his tone was light. "You must have a name. Let me see, to drive a bang-up outfit like this, you must be very rich, I should think. Someone of importance."

This was getting onto dangerous ground. Did he suspect? He was quick-witted, there was no doubt about it. It was very necessary to divert him in a safer direction. "I am a lady," she said. "I think... yes, today I am Lady Anne."

He chuckled. "Very well, Lady Anne it shall be. But you must have a family name, my lady."

"Lady Anne... Dunhiding."

That made him laugh so much she feared he might fall out of the curricle altogether. They came into the village, so for a while she concentrated on managing the greys, avoiding unwary walkers crossing the road as well as other vehicles.

"And your father, my lady?" he said, as soon as they were clear of the village again.

"He is... the Duke of West Riding," she said. "His ancestor came over with the Conqueror—"

"Naturally!"

"—and slew one thousand, three hundred and forty seven Saxons with his own hand. He was rewarded with his dukedom, and since then his descendants have lived a blameless, if idle, life on the proceeds."

Lord Humphrey laughed again. "You have a wonderful imagination, my lady, although I am disappointed at the lack of scandals in your family. All great families have their little secrets. But now I must match you, and not be myself today. Who am I? Let me think... I know! I am Jem, your faithful and devoted retainer. I am the gamekeeper's son—"

"Oh no, that is not near romantic enough." She paused to negotiate at speed past a farmer's cart, while Lord Humphrey exchanged friendly greetings. "I should like to have brought you as a slave from the West Indies to have as my page boy, only to set you free later from compassion, but you are too pale complexioned for that. I have it — you are the chimney-sweep's boy, who became stuck in chimneys at... um, Castle Dunhiding at the age of three. I rescued you from your cruel employer and so you became my faithful retainer."

"The chimneys at Castle Dunhiding must be exceptionally narrow if a three-year-old can become stuck."

"You were very well grown for your age," she responded solemnly.

That brought another chuckle. "I see. So I have been in your employ since I was three, and now I am quite indispensable to you. I accompany you everywhere you go, and have frequently been obliged to see off the most persistent and annoying of your many suitors by drawing their corks."

"Oh, how splendidly chivalrous!" she cried. "But now I feel it would be better for you to be a gentleman, so that you may challenge these scoundrels to duels. Perhaps you are secretly the son of an earl?"

"Do you know, I have always thought a duel the most damnably silly business," Lord Humphrey said. "Meeting at dawn, and trying to kill a man for the most frivolous of reasons, sometimes, and then perhaps having to flee the country afterwards. I had much sooner have a good mill with the fellow on the spot, if it is all the same to you, my lady."

That was so much of a piece with the straightforward nature of the man that she must approve it. "Very well, Jem, you shall not be a gentleman after all. But your accent! I must have been an indulgent employer indeed to have paid for you to attend the finest educational establishments."

"Nay, milady, 'twere not so. I were only taught me letters the t'village school, like."

"That is much better. You must know your place, Jem, and not ape your betters."

"No, milady. Won't 'appen again, milady."

And in this delightfully nonsensical way, they beguiled away the miles to Branksford Abbey.

12: Branksford Abbey

They were so far ahead of the others that they had time for a lengthy detour over the moors. Even so, when Hortensia turned the greys in through the gate of the abbey grounds and brought them slowly to a halt, they were still the first to arrive. The servants' wagons stood nearby, with the horses tethered in the shade. Near the abbey, the pavilion was but half erected, as footmen wrestled with the canvas, and housemaids scurried about with rugs and chairs.

Branksford Abbey was a fine ruin, the walls mostly intact and only the roof missing. It was situated beside a lake and surrounded by meadows sheltered by banks of woodland, and in every particular was ideal for a party of pleasure-bound people to spend a summer's day. It was a lovely, tranquil spot, but all Hortensia could feel at that moment was sorrow that her drive was over, for no doubt Lord Humphrey would want to drive home. She sat, reins in hand, gazing unseeingly at the beauty before her, before turning to Lord Humphrey.

"Thank you!" she said in heartfelt tones.

"Thank you!" he said, at the same moment, so that they both laughed.

"Why are you thanking *me*?" she said, still smiling. "It is I who must thank *you* for the pleasure of driving your magnificent horses.

No matter what the rest of the day brings, I shall always account it one of the most memorable of my life."

"I thank you for the enjoyment of watching such an expert with the whip. If you were a man, I should not hesitate to put you up for the Four-Horse Club. You do drive four-in-hand, I take it? I am sure you do."

His confidence in her skill made her blush. "I do, yes. You pay me such splendid compliments, Lord Humphrey. Most gentlemen content themselves with a comment about a lady's looks or gown or skill upon the pianoforte, but I greatly prefer your flattery."

"It is hardly flattery when it is the absolute truth." His eyes shone so warmly as he spoke, that she blushed again. Why did this man have such an effect on her? She, who never blushed and inwardly despised any man who addressed such flummery to her — yet her heart somersaulted when he talked in that low, intimate tone. Love... love rendered the most sensible person foolish. It certainly made *her* foolish. But she must not be beguiled by him, for it meant nothing. Even if he loved her, he would never offer for her if he believed her penniless. But if he knew the truth, her heart whispered... what then?

To distract herself from such nonsensical thoughts, she said, "Look, the others are arriving now. Although... why are they coming from that direction?"

Across on the far side of the abbey meadow, a slow procession of carriages wended its way through a different gate and drove slowly to a shaded position near the trees. Once she looked closely, Hortensia could see that these were not the Marford carriages at all, for none of them bore a coat of arms on the side.

"Another pleasure party," Lord Humphrey said. "What fun! Let us drive round to introduce ourselves."

There was a rough track around the perimeter of the meadow, so Hortensia set the greys in motion again and they made their way to where the other carriages had stopped. Several of the occupants had descended and were engaged in an agitated discussion. As they drew near, a man of middle years stepped forward with a deep bow. He was respectably dressed, although not in the first style of fashion, his clothes rather plain.

"Your pardon, sir! We had no notion to disrupt your gathering. We intended an informal picnic only, and would not for the world encroach. We will withdraw at once."

"Nonsense, my good sir!" Lord Humphrey said, leaping down from the curricle. "The abbey is for anyone to enjoy. Pray do not leave, for there is room for all of us, would you not agree?"

"You are most obliging, sir. Most obliging." He bowed again. "If you are quite certain that our presence will not spoil your party's pleasure in the occasion, we will be very happy to stay. You may be sure that we will keep well away from you."

Lord Humphrey smiled and Hortensia was struck again by his charm. Some of the nobility were very high in the instep and would have chased away any intruders, but he was all affability. "You are most generous. My brother the Marquess of Carrbridge will be here shortly. Who may I say is enjoying the abbey with us today?"

The man's eyes widened at the mention of the marquess, but he answered readily enough. "I am Mr Percival Stoner, presently of York."

Before Lord Humphrey could speak, a small figure pelted towards him, pelisse and bonnet ribbons flying. "Humphrey? Humphrey! It is you, I swear!"

"Beatrice? Good heavens, what are you doing here?"

She chortled with laughter. "Why, the same as you, I daresay, enjoying an outing! We are all staying in York while the new house is got ready, for my father-in-law is *finally* building his house, and it will be quite splendid, I do assure you! Not like Drummoor, of course, but terribly modern and every possible convenience. Hot water on every floor, and lifting devices so that the housemaids will never have to carry coal upstairs. Well, how funny, to meet you here."

After that, half of Mr Stoner's party came over to greet Lord Humphrey or to be introduced, and Hortensia was introduced too, and there was no more talk of encroaching or leaving or keeping away from each other. By the time they returned to the other side of the meadow, the marquess had arrived, and carriages were streaming through the gate.

"Who is she?" Hortensia said, as she brought the curricle to a halt.

"Beatrice Mallory is a former neighbour," Lord Humphrey said, jumping down. "Used to live in Lake Cottage, the house Merton now has. She and her sister both married into the Stoner family. You can leave Tom to deal with the horses. Come on down."

He held up his arms, and with only the tiniest hesitation she allowed him to put his hands about her waist and effortlessly lift her down. He was so strong! Even through her pelisse, she could feel the solidity and warmth of his hands, and that brought blushes to her cheeks again. He did not notice her discomposure, rushing off to talk to the marquess and leaving her standing, alone and rather forlorn, beside the curricle.

She was not alone for long. Rosemary came to her with a distraught expression on her face. "Dearest, this cannot go on! I know how reluctant you are to speak out, but I fear it must be done. Lord Kilbraith..." She paused, blushing, then gave a little laugh. "He is *so* attentive, and he wishes me — us — to go to Scotland when he returns there. He wants to introduce me to his father."

"Oh, that *is* serious!" Hortensia said.

"But he must be told! And I do not know how I can contrive it. I cannot find a moment to be private with him. Might you tell him?"

"It would be just as awkward for me to be private with him, dearest."

"Then what is to be done? You always know what must be done, dearest Hortensia. Help me, please!"

"Do not be anxious, dear. I shall tell Lord Humphrey, and he shall tell Lord Kilbraith. And then... and then..."

They were both silent. What would happen then? Their futures would be in the hands of the two men they loved.

~~~~~

Although there was some muttering from the aunts, the marquess and marchioness were delighted to see old friends, and within half an hour, the two groups were mingling as readily as if they had set out together. They settled themselves in and around the pavilion, the older ones on chairs, the younger on rugs, while footmen walked around with trays of iced lemonade and ratafia and strawberries. The ranks of the footmen had been swelled by gardeners and grooms, and Humphrey spotted Charlie, rather splendid in his livery, walking round with a tray. The eating and drinking induced a festival atmosphere, the chatter rose to a noisy crescendo, and all was smiling felicity.

Humphrey, however, was not smiling and felt no felicity. It was the worst mischance that threw these two groups together. Of all the people in the world to encounter, why did it have to be Beatrice Mallory? Or Mrs Andrew Stoner, as she now was, and there lay the problem. For her father-in-law Mr Stoner was a nabob who had made his fortune in India, and who might just know something of an heiress by the name of Miss Hortensia Blythe. Humphrey rather thought he must do, for the marquess had applied to Mrs Mallory and Mr Stoner for information, and Julius Whittleton had transferred his attentions to Miss Quayle shortly afterwards.

The two women might now be on the very brink of disaster. If their subterfuge were to be uncovered in this way, it would be of all things the most damaging to their reputations. How much better would it be for them to confess the deceit at once than to have it discovered through another person. And yet, what could Humphrey do? He could hardly force a confession from Miss Quayle or Miss Blythe.

A small voice deep inside Humphrey pointed out that if once Miss Quayle was uncovered as a great heiress, there would be no barrier between them. He could court her openly, exactly as he wished. Not immediately, perhaps, for he would look like the worst kind of fortune hunter if he were to transfer his attentions so readily, but in the future.

As soon as everyone was settled, a process which took an unconscionable amount of time, owing to the nuances of rank that the aunts, at least, considered important, Humphrey looked about him for Miss Quayle. He saw her standing a little apart, but with Julius Whittleton by her side. She looked downcast, and Humphrey could not blame her, for Julius must be the most tedious and persistent man in Christendom. There was no getting rid of him, except by brute force. Well, that was something Humphrey excelled at.

"Miss Quayle!" he cried, striding across to her. "Is this tiresome cub becoming a nuisance? Shall I get rid of him for you?"

She looked up at once, and with such a speaking expression of relief as warmed Humphrey inside.

"I say, Humphrey, doing it rather too brown!" Julius said. "Miss Quayle and I are having a very comfortable coze, and there is no need for you to get so high and mighty."

"Off you go and leave Miss Quayle in peace," Humphrey said amiably. Julius was above average height but Humphrey towered over him, and with his broad shoulders and chest that owed nothing to buckram padding, he knew himself to be an intimidating presence.

Julius, however, was strutting before a lady and therefore not likely to back down. "Really, Humphrey! Do not make such a cake of yourself. If you think—"

Humphrey positioned himself an inch away from Julius, looming over him to such an extent that the poor man was forced to lean away. "Go," Humphrey said, in his quietest tones, and even Julius recognised the finality in his voice. He turned and strode away, red-faced.

Miss Quayle laughed. "Thank you for coming to my rescue! Mr Whittleton's compliments become... a little wearing after a while. My lord... may I talk to you?" Was that guilt on her face? Some emotion that was not very comfortable, at any event.

Humphrey silently offered her his arm, and they walked away from the chattering groups in the pavilion and towards the lake. He said nothing, waiting for her to collect her thoughts and for the noise to recede into the distance so that they could be more private. But when they had walked half way around the lake and were beginning to draw near to the abbey itself, he said, "Miss Quayle, you may speak freely to me. Whatever is troubling you, be assured that I will treat it with the utmost confidence, as your friend. I hope I may consider myself as a friend to you, despite the shortness of our acquaintance?"

"Oh yes!" she said, looking up at him eagerly. "You have been so kind to me, and you cannot imagine how grateful I am. But it is so difficult... I do not know quite how to begin."

Since he had a fair idea at this point what it was that she wished to say to him, he was not discomposed by this ominous beginning. "There is a fallen tree just on the edge of the woods above us, where we may sit and be comfortable, without fear of interruption," he said. "Then you may take your time to tell me whatever you wish."

She agreed to it, and he led her there directly. It was indeed a good spot, for they could look down on the whole meadow, and could also be clearly seen, so there was complete privacy without the least impropriety. And there, head lowered and after several halting starts, she finally came to the point he had been expecting.

"My lord, I am not who you think I am!"

"So you are not, in fact, Lady Anne Dunhiding?" he said gently.

She raised her head at that, but could not quite manage a smile. "If only that were all! But it is far worse than that. I am not Miss Quayle. I am Hortensia Blythe, and my friend is Rosemary Quayle. Oh!" Her eyes widened. "You are not surprised — you knew!"

"I guessed," he admitted. "You slipped up a few times. Once, when I asked if you had been to England before, you said you had, then immediately changed your mind, yet later you said you had missed the English air. And the desire to buy an estate on the moors is not one normally found in a lowly companion."

"Oh, I had forgotten that!" she said, with a rueful smile. "It was so hard to watch every word I said."

"And deceit does not come easily to you," he said, absurdly pleased to realise this about her. "You and Miss... Quayle always called each other *'my friend'*, which sounded odd until I began to suspect the truth, and realised that you were terrified of calling each other by the wrong name."

"Yes, that is exactly it! Oh, I am so glad I have told you, and you are saying nothing of condemnation, although you must think it, for I know it is abominable of us to play such a trick on you — on everyone! The marquess and marchioness! I am so ashamed."

"There might be those who will be condemnatory, but for myself any disapproval would depend on your reasons for acting thus. I do not imagine for one moment the scheme was intended for personal gain."

"Oh *no!* Nothing could have been further from our minds. But a fortune of two hundred thousand pounds... it changes everything. You cannot conceive how humiliating it is."

"Humiliating?" he said, raising his eyebrows, and laughing softly. "To inherit so much money?"

"Oh yes! For ten years after I came out, I was just Geoffrey Blythe's daughter, with no beauty, no drawing room accomplishments, no society manners — and no suitors. We always seemed to have enough money, but no one ever imagined we were rich. And then Papa died and this enormous fortune dropped into my lap, and suddenly I was the most popular girl in the East Indies. Men I had known for years came to tell me how much they had always admired me. Men I had never met turned up on the doorstep. I had offers of marriage arriving in letters almost every day."

"Good heavens!"

"Exactly. It was hideous, and I had not the least idea how to respond to such attentions. There was no longer anything to keep me in India, or Rosemary either, so we decided to come home to England. Well, it was *my* home until I was fourteen. Rosemary had never lived anywhere but India. She came to live with us she was eight, after her mother died, so she is just like a sister to me. I really did teach her, you know. That part was true," she said sadly.

He said nothing, but he remembered her enthusiastic manner in talking of her pupil's aptitude. Her heartfelt sincerity could never have been false.

"Rosemary's father was dead," she went on, "so when my father also died and we were both alone in the world, we booked passage on the next ship to England. But a strange thing happened when we went aboard. Everyone knew, of course, who Miss Hortensia Blythe was, but no one on the ship had ever met me."

"Ah," Humphrey said, taking the point. "Miss… Quayle was assumed to be the heiress?"

"What could be more natural a mistake? The young, beautiful ingenue must be the heiress, and the plain older woman her penniless companion. It suited us perfectly. Rosemary was very well used to deflecting ardent admirers, and the attention that so distressed me bothered her not at all. She could stand in the sunshine while I could hide in the shadows to grieve for my father, and grow accustomed by degrees to my new wealth. However, even the long sea voyage was not sufficient for that purpose. I found myself not yet ready to emerge into the full glare of society's gaze."

"So you continued the deception."

She looked up at him, perhaps catching a hint of disapprobation in his tone. He had not intended it, for his affection for her had grown to the point that he would forgive a great many offences. Still, it was one thing to fall into deception accidentally, and quite another to continue deliberately.

"You blame me, and I cannot wonder at it," she said. "But I had reasons for continuing, both for Rosemary's sake and for my own. Rosemary has no money of her own, and she will take none of mine, yet with her loveliness and good nature, as well as her accomplishments, she deserves a husband worthy of her. It was my intent to give her time to find such a husband. Brighton, or Bath, perhaps... and some eligible young man would fall violently in love with her. You, of course, can see the flaw in my careful plan, which had not occurred to me until Lord Kilbraith arrived and did indeed fall violently in love with her. For one cannot deal so with a man of honour, to tell him once he is well on the way to matrimony that his love is not who he thought she was. It is a despicable way to treat a man, is it not?"

"It is true that one cannot build the necessary trust for marriage by beginning with a lie," he said slowly. "Or at least, it would take an extraordinary amount of good-nature and affection to overcome such a beginning."

"Indeed. He must be told at once! His hints are becoming extremely pointed, and Rosemary is in the greatest distress over it. My lord, would you...? May I ask...?"

"You wish me to inform Kilbraith that the heiress he has fallen in love with is no such thing? It would be much better coming from Miss Quayle herself. She will cry, he will at once wish to console her, he may even be provoked into a declaration on the spot. Whereas he will look on me as an interfering busybody."

"She has been trying for days, but there has been no opportunity. They are never alone, and it is imperative that he knows at once. One gentleman may easily talk privately with another."

He considered that, for it was a good point. "Very well, I shall find him directly. But he is not the only one who must be told. You have been guests of Lord and Lady Carrbridge for three weeks now, under false pretences. Indeed, everyone you have met has been duped by you, and while some will understand, you must be prepared for some censure."

"Must they know just yet?" she said, turning pleading eyes on him. "We will be gone soon. Apart from Lord Kilbraith, need anyone else know?"

"For the sake of honesty, I believe the truth should be told," he said quietly. "Your own conscience must tell you so. But even if you wished to keep your secret a little longer, I do not know if it will be possible. Mr Stoner is from India, and I suspect knows more about you than you would wish. This little game may not survive the end of the day, Miss Blythe."

"Oh." She hung her head, and he wanted so badly to wrap her in his arms and hold her tight that it was the greatest effort to sit still.

"Does it matter so much to you?" he said gently. "You are so strong in spirit, I have every confidence that you will cope admirably with the attentions of your fortune-hunting suitors."

"You are very kind to say so," she said wanly, and it wrung his heart to see her so subdued. "That is not what distresses me, however. You see, ever since I learnt of my inheritance and was surrounded by suitors, I have hoped that one day I would find someone who would love me for myself alone, without consideration of my money. The likelihood was never great, but once all is known, it will be non-existent. I shall never be able to tell if a man is attracted to me or to my money."

She heaved a great sigh, and her eyes glistened with tears.

Humphrey understood. She had lost something precious today, her ability to melt into the background and be quietly ignored. She would never be a nonentity again. But he had lost something precious too, for he had lost that easy friendship they had shared when she was nobody, and there was no certainty he would ever be able to recover it.

13: Confessions

Lord Humphrey was not a man to delay a necessary task. He returned Hortensia promptly to the pavilion, and a seat beside Rosemary. Then he skilfully detached Lord Kilbraith from the group and led him away.

Hortensia watched him go listlessly.

"Well?" Rosemary said.

"I have told him all, and he will explain it to Lord Kilbraith."

"Oh. Oh, that is… a relief." But she did not sound in the least relieved.

"It is better this way," Hortensia said flatly. "We could not go on as we were. Now everyone will know the truth and there will be no more secrets."

"And no more lying awake worrying about being found out," Rosemary said. "This is much the best way." But her face was as white as chalk.

All around them was merriment and excited chatter, but the two were glum-faced, both facing monumental changes. Rosemary stood to lose the man she loved, and Hortensia… Hortensia had already lost hers. All this time she had thought he cared for her, *loved* her, for herself alone, thinking her penniless, and it was not so. He had known for some time that she was the heiress, and had transferred his attentions from Rosemary to herself. He was no better than Mr Whittleton! She had so badly wanted to believe he truly loved her for herself, and now she was filled with grief. How stupid she was! Was it all a sham, and he felt nothing for her? Was he just pretending? She could not tell, for her own hopes and wishes prevented rational thought where Humphrey was concerned. Stupid, stupid, stupid!

She was so lost in her own sorrowful thoughts, that it was a shock when a gentle voice at her ear said, "Miss Blythe? Miss Quayle? Why such sad faces? Is all well with you?"

The two jumped to their feet and curtsied. "Lady Carrbridge, a thousand apologies," Hortensia said. "We are— oh! Where is everyone?"

The pavilion was almost empty, only a few of the oldest aunts and uncles still in their seats, two playing cribbage, and the rest dozing in the sun.

"I have sent them all off to inspect the ruins while the servants lay the tables for our picnic," she said. "Will you join us? Or shall I have someone fetch you a glass of lemonade? Where are Humphrey and Lord Kilbraith?" She scanned the lakeside and spotted them in animated discussion some distance away. "Oh no! They are not...? There is no... *dispute*?" She glanced anxiously at Rosemary's wan face, clearly imagining the two men coming to blows over her.

That made Hortensia smile a little. "No, no! They are not about to break into a fight, if that is what you fear. But..." She hesitated, but it was as good a time as any. "My lady, there is something that you should know."

Rosemary gave a convulsive sob, bowing her head. Lady Carrbridge looked from one to the other, then sat down. "I am listening, my dears."

It was easier the second time. Perhaps that was merely because Hortensia had already rehearsed the story, but more likely because her own emotions were less tangled this time. With Humphrey, she had desperately wanted him to accept the news without anger or censure. With Lady Carrbridge, she knew she ought to care just as much, for if the marchioness were inclined to take offence, they would be leaving Drummoor tomorrow and would never be able to show their faces in good society again. Yet somehow her good opinion meant less than Humphrey's.

But after the first exclamations of astonishment, Lady Carrbridge was all sympathy. "How dreadful for you!" she said many times, and "You poor things!" and, most heartening of all, "I quite understand how it was." At the end of the tale, she said, "Well, perhaps it was not quite right to act so, but I cannot blame you one bit. It is not at all comfortable to be ignored one moment and then fêted the next. My circumstances were not dissimilar, so I feel for you most sincerely, Miss Quayle... Blythe... oh dear!"

Then Lord Carrbridge came looking for his wife, and the tale had to be told again, with many interjections from the marchioness. The marquess's reaction was less sympathetic than his wife's. He said very little, but his face darkened. At the end of the recitation, Hortensia waited, her heart leaden. Lord Carrbridge's response would sink them, she was sure.

He looked from Hortensia to Rosemary and back again. "I do not like being made a fool of." His voice was like ice.

"I do not think they meant any harm, dear," Lady Carrbridge said. "It is very difficult to find oneself surrounded by fortune hunters. Most disagreeable."

"Perhaps, but that does not excuse such behaviour. Where would we be if everyone decided to pretend to be someone they were not? Society would collapse entirely. One cannot shirk the responsibilities thrust upon one, however disagreeable they may be," he added sadly, and Hortensia had an unexpected glimpse into the marquess's life.

"I am so very sorry," she said to him. "We will leave tomorrow."

"Oh, no, surely there is no need—" the marchioness said distressfully. "Do not go! Lord Carrbridge, tell them they need not go. And there is Lord Kilbraith…"

"So there is," the marquess said. "Someone ought to tell him."

"That is all right," Hortensia said quickly. "Humph—Lord Humphrey is telling him now. It was not right to keep him in the dark a moment longer."

"So Humphrey knows?" Lady Carrbridge said in surprise.

"Oh yes. I asked him to tell Lord Kilbraith."

Lady Carrbridge's eyes flew to Humphrey, still conferring with Lord Kilbraith, and then back to Hortensia. "Did you so? How interesting."

Lord Carrbridge sighed. "Very well, Miss Quayle… Blythe… ladies, you may stay, since it would distress Lady Carrbridge if you were to leave abruptly, but everyone must be told the truth and I do not know how it is to be managed," he said. "My dear, what must we do?"

"I think it would be best to announce it when everyone is gathered together, and may hear the news at the same time. Perhaps at the grand dinner three days from now? You can make a joke of it, you know… an amusing little trick, fooled everyone… that sort of thing. You are so good at these speeches, my dear."

The marquess graciously agreed to the plan and so, to Hortensia's amazement, she was to remain Miss Quayle a little longer.

"But I must talk to Kilbraith," the marquess said, and strode away to where Humphrey and Lord Kilbraith were still deep in conversation.

Hortensia watched them conferring anxiously. Even from some distance away, she could see their serious expressions. Lord Kilbraith was the first to return to the pavilion, and it was clear from the smile on his face that he was not in the least displeased by the news. He sat beside Rosemary and talked animatedly to her, so that she blushed and smiled and was soon quite her usual self. Hortensia wished she could be as comfortable, for when Humphrey and Lord Carrbridge returned, there were no smiles.

Lord Kilbraith jumped up at once. "Shall we walk about amongst these ruins?" he said, addressing himself mostly to Rosemary. "I have heard so much about them, and I am anxious to compare them with the many picturesque ruins we have in Scotland, some of the strangest design. There are those in the wild north which are perfectly round, and barely the width of a mill chimney, and how anyone might have lived in such a place is more than I can imagine."

They all rose, and began to drift away from the pavilion in pairs, Lord Kilbraith with Rosemary, then Lord and Lady Carrbridge, with Humphrey and Hortensia at the rear. Humphrey was silent, and when Hortensia dared to steal a glance, his expression was serious and unsmiling. She could not quite understand him. He had known about her deception, so he could not suddenly despise her for it. And whether he truly loved her, or was pretending in order to secure her fortune, the way was now clear for him to make his suit publicly. Nor could he have any concerns about Rosemary and Lord Kilbraith, for their course now seemed set fair. It was, perhaps, too soon to talk of marriage, but this must be the beginning of a very earnest courtship which could only end in the happiness of both.

There was another possibility which she could not bear to consider. Perhaps he had only been amusing himself at her expense, flirting with her while he concentrated his attention on Rosemary. Now that all was revealed, he would withdraw his attentions, for he had no real interest in her. Who could, plain and unattractive as she was? If only she were dainty and pretty and demure, like Rosemary! Then she could have any man she wanted. It was very dispiriting to be so tall.

In such silence, they walked down to the lake and around to the abbey. It was indeed a very fine ruin, and when Hortensia stopped to admire the remains of an arched window, Humphrey at last began to speak, talking of the history of the place, of its days of power and then the dissolution and devastation. He knew no more of the history or the era than she did, but he knew a little of this particular abbey, and pointed out some carvings and knew the names and parts of each of the buildings. Gradually, Hortensia's spirits lifted, for how could she be downcast when Humphrey was with her? Their chaperons had long since disappeared, but it hardly mattered, for they were quite public.

In this way, they walked through the infirmary and dormitories, passing the refectory and kitchen, across the cloister and finally, in respectful silence, into the skeleton of the church, its walls and pillars still towering over their heads. There were few people here, most of the party having returned to the pavilion for refreshments, so their silence remained unbroken. They walked slowly up the nave, passing from sunshine to shade, from warmth to chill, as the fragments of wall and gaping windows allowed. To Hortensia, it seemed all of a piece with her life just then, tossed from one state to another, from exhilaration to despair in a moment, and back again just as quickly. She hardly knew who she was any more, or what she truly felt, still less what Humphrey felt.

She was not sure how she could get through these final days at Drummoor in such uncertainty.

In the side chapel, a fallen block of masonry provided a seat and she flopped onto it gratefully. Humphrey turned to her at once, concern on his face.

"What is it? Are you unwell?" The gentleness in his voice almost brought her to tears.

"I am quite well, but perhaps... a little tired."

"Of course. We will sit here until you are quite rested." He sat beside her, and even with her head lowered and the sides of her bonnet hiding him from her, she was acutely aware of his presence, his solidly reassuring masculinity and some indefinable bond between them that surely was no mere product of her imagination?

He gave a little laugh, rather self-consciously, it seemed to her. "I do not know what I am to call you now."

'Hortensia', she wanted to say, *'or darling, or my dear one, or my love.'* If only she could speak so to him! Instead, she sighed. "I am to remain Miss Quayle for a few days longer."

"I see." Nothing to be read in his tone, and she dared not look at his face. Instead she gazed steadily downwards at the handle of her parasol. "Connie will be disappointed," he went on, and this time there was an edge of amusement in his voice. "She had very high hopes that Miss... *Blythe* and I would make a match of it." He chuckled. "But we should never have suited. She will do much better with Kilbraith."

Hortensia could scarcely breathe. She would not have dared to raise the subject herself, but now that he had... she had to try. It was not in her nature to baulk at the jump when it was immediately before her. So she lifted her head and tried to keep her voice steady.

"I believe that Lady Carrbridge still nurtures hopes that you and *Miss Blythe* will make a match of it."

She looked directly at him, and saw his eyes widen — indeed, he could not mistake her meaning! But the dismay in his face cut her to the quick. He did not want her! Even with her fortune, he did not want her! Was she right, then — she meant nothing to him, and all his attentions had been nothing but *flirtation?* Was that how it was? Her breath caught in her throat, and she dropped her gaze.

"Oh, if only it were so simple," he said, his voice so soft that she was not sure she heard him correctly. Her head shot up, and he was looking at her with such... such *regret* that she gave a little gasp.

"Is it not?" she said before she could stop herself.

"Miss Quayle." He took one of her hands and held it in both of his, and this time he was the one who looked down, gently stroking her gloved fingers. "Let us consider a situation... purely hypothetical, you understand. Imagine, if you will, a young man of impeccable family, but a younger son, without fortune or an independence. If he should happen to meet a young lady of wealth, and he should happen to attach himself to her, why then society will smile upon both of them. *'How happy they will be,'* society will say, and declare it a love match, heedless of the actual circumstances. *'How convenient that that impoverished young man should happen to fall in love with that rich young lady, and she with him.'* Society, in short, will give such a match its blessing."

She said nothing, guessing how the story would end, but mesmerised by the warmth of his hands, and the softness of his voice! Ah, his voice! What would she not do for a man who spoke to her in such a way, a voice as mellow and warm and soothing as chocolate.

"But imagine now," he went on, "if that young man should discover that the object of his attentions is not, in fact, rich at all, but poor. Were he now to divert all his attention to another young lady, a *rich* young lady, what will society make of him now? He will be thought the worst kind of fortune hunter, and will be frowned upon and ostracised. And the young lady, should she happen to permit his attentions, would be deemed weak in understanding and foolish, and will also be frowned upon and ostracised."

"And is no allowance to be made," she cried indignantly, "for the feelings of these people? It is uncharitable to assume there to be no affection in the second case."

His head jerked up, just for an instant, his eyes afire with some strong emotion. But just as quickly he lowered his gaze, and when he spoke again, his voice was quiet.

"Yet that is how society views the world, by surface characteristics only. Who can know what a man truly feels inside... or a woman? However much the young man—" Here his voice wobbled a little. "However much he might *wish* to court the second young lady, he had much better not do it, for the sake of both."

She could not speak, choked with misery as she was. Tears coursed down her cheeks unheeded. To be told, in the same breath, that he wanted to court her but he could not because of some nebulous fear of society's disapprobation was all too much. How could he be so foolish? If he cared anything for her, if her happiness was of the slightest importance to him, then he would set aside such fustian and offer for her at once. It was very necessary to tell him so.

"But Humphrey—" she began, leaning forward eagerly. He looked up sharply at the intimate use of his name, and suddenly his face was but an inch from hers. His lips were so close, so tantalisingly close. If she leaned forward just the tiniest bit—

"What is going on here!" came an angry voice. She groaned, and they sprang apart.

Humphrey jumped to his feet. "Julius, go away, will you? You are not wanted here."

"I can well believe it. How dare you steal Miss Quayle away to a secluded spot and make violent love to her? And look, you have made her cry! You are no gentleman, sir."

"For God's sake, Julius, have a care what you say to me, for I am in no mood to deal gently with you. Do not push me or I shall be forced to set you straight."

"Ha! Do you threaten me? But I see what your game is, Cousin. Kilbraith has cut you out, so now you think to look elsewhere, and of course you *would* make a mull of it. You have no delicacy of touch with the ladies. As if Miss Quayle could possibly prefer your heavy-handed—"

Hortensia jumped up and placed herself between them, brandishing her parasol. "Mr Whittleton, *do* go away. You are not needed in the least, I assure you."

"But he has made you cry!"

"We were speaking of... of my father," she said, improvising wildly. "His death is still fresh in my mind. Lord Humphrey was... was consoling me."

"You must think me very green if you expect me to fall for that faradiddle!"

"Are you calling me a liar?" Hortensia said hotly. "You are offensive, Mr Whittleton."

She turned away in disgust, but he grabbed her arm and pulled her back so sharply that she cried out in surprise. And to her inestimable delight, Humphrey drew back his arm, curled his right hand into a fist and landed a punch squarely on Mr Whittleton's nose.

14: A Picnic

"I really think you might stop laughing," Humphrey said, as he fished around in various pockets. "It is very distracting when I am trying so hard not to laugh at the poor fellow myself. Drat Billings! He fusses so over my cravat, but fails to put a handkerchief anywhere. Do you have anything to stop him bleeding? Oh, Julius, do stop yowling!"

"I fear my handkerchief would be inadequate for the task," she said, still chuckling. "Who would have imagined that one nose could bleed so much? Perhaps we might fetch a tablecloth from the pavilion?"

That set Humphrey off again, and so when more people started to appear, drawn by the shouts and Julius's cries of pain, they found Julius rolling on the ground, and Humphrey and Hortensia consumed with merriment.

The others seemed to be better provided with handkerchiefs than Humphrey was, and also took Julius's injuries with the seriousness he felt he deserved. "Shall we slip away while they are attending to the patient?" Humphrey whispered. "I shall be in the soup with Connie for spoiling her party, but there is no need to wait around to be scolded by everyone else, is there?"

Miss Quayle was agreeable, so they crept away through a gap in the wall, and then ran, still giggling, around the outside of the abbey ruins until they gained the lake again, and were visible once more from the pavilion.

"I had better take you back," he said, not quite able to keep the regret out of his voice.

"Must you?" She looked up at him with such a pleading expression that he was almost undone.

"I believe I must," he whispered.

"Oh." She hung her head and said not another word until they reached the pavilion, where she curtsied and thanked him politely for his company.

He bowed, and, before he could change his mind, walked swiftly away from her.

~~~~~

Hortensia did not watch him go, for it was too painful. She allowed herself to be directed to a seat, and took food from plates that were passed to her. She may even have eaten a little, although she hardly knew what. Someone set a glass of champagne before her, but she could not touch it.

After a while, she saw him creep into the other side of the pavilion and take a seat amongst the aunts. Julius did not reappear, so perhaps he had gone back to Drummoor to nurse his injuries. Good! If she never saw him again, she would be very well pleased. Such impudence, to interfere in that arrogant manner, as if he had any right! Humphrey had been quite justified in taking action. Her anger warmed her, and so, by degrees, she began to return to something approaching her normal equanimity. Not quite, for every time she caught a glimpse of Humphrey her heart somersaulted in the most alarming way, but at other times she even felt equal to a little conversation with her neighbours.

After all had eaten their fill, the tables were cleared except for dishes of sweetmeats and decanters of wine, and the servants were sent off to enjoy a rest. The party now began to merge into noisy larger groups, to chatter or to play cards or to stroll about the grounds. Rosemary walked away on Lord Kilbraith's arm, and Hortensia tried resolutely to be happy for her friend even as her own hopes had been dashed.

Her neighbours having moved away, Hortensia sat on her own, but she was so sunk in her own thoughts that she scarcely noticed. Besides, she was so accustomed to being ignored now that she saw nothing odd in it. It was only when a passing aunt sniffed and said loudly, "Disgusting! Trying her wiles on those far above her station!" and glared at her that she realised that she was the recipient of many curious looks, with much whispering behind fans. So she was to be blamed for the little set-to between Humphrey and Julius, was she? Of course, it must be her fault, for they were gentlemen and she was nobody, just a mere companion. That should have amused her, but somehow it did not. She was too listless to be angry, but she would not sit still to be so abused.

Rising, she walked away, head high, looking neither to right nor to left. She had no destination in mind, but her feet drew her again to the abbey. She walked through some parts that she had not seen on her previous visit, but eventually she came into the church again. This time she knew where she was bound, for the side chapel beckoned, even with all its painful memories. It was empty of prying eyes, and gratefully she sank again to her seat on the fallen stone, running over in her mind all that had been said. Was there any sliver of hope in his words? He had said, had he not, that he wished to court her—? Or had he? It was all couched in the most nebulous terms, if this, if that, with hypothetical young men and heiresses, so that she could no longer be certain what he had meant. Except that he was lost to her. Of that, there could be not the least shadow of uncertainty.

Humphrey filled her thoughts so entirely that somehow she was not surprised to see him enter the side chapel not long after her. When he sat down beside her, just as before, there was a rightness to it that pleased her, and she was neither shy nor distressed.

"Would you prefer to be left alone?" he said in that low voice that so thrilled her. "Because if so—"

"Oh no! I do not object to company." Not Humphrey's company, anyway. With some effort, she kept her tone light as she said, "Have you been much scolded?"

His lips quirked into a half smile. "A little. The aunts are deliciously shocked to be so close to a mill, and I have been required to describe every blood-drenched detail a dozen times, I swear. But it will be forgotten very soon, you may be sure. Just one more instance of rackety Humphrey disgracing the family name."

"Are you so rackety?" she said, entranced by this new idea of him. "You seem so upstanding a gentleman to me."

"I was used to be quite wild. Not like Gil, for he sets a new standard for disreputable Marfords, but I was always in trouble, yes. At school or at Oxford, if there was a mill in progress, I was bound to be in the centre of it. And I was game for any amusement. If there was some prank going on, I would be the one keeping the book and setting the odds."

"A gamester from the start. Your proposed career is well chosen." She hesitated, but she had never been timid, so she said boldly, "What is to become of your gaming house scheme now?"

He looked at her intently, but answered composedly, "I do not know. Perhaps it is time to abandon the idea, for it has caused nothing but trouble, and I have not the least idea where I might honourably find a hundred thousand pounds."

'From me!' her heart cried, and suddenly her pulse was racing. Perhaps there was another way... To give herself time to think, she said, "It is a large sum. Why so much?"

"Because I do not wish to set limits on wagers," he said at once, his face alight with enthusiasm. "I intend my house to be entirely honest, so although over time the odds will favour the house — the odds *always* favour the house — there will be occasions when the customers will win, and by large amounts. If I have not a sufficient reserve to cover such nights, then I shall be sunk — bankrupt and with gaming debts that would cripple me. Carrbridge would be obliged to step in, and then the entire family would be bankrupt. So I *must* have a large amount to hand when I establish my house. But it is devilish difficult to find such an amount, and although..." He stopped, and took a long breath. "Although I once thought to marry my way to such a fortune, my conscience would not permit me to use my wife's portion on such a risky venture. It is difficult to know what to do next."

So that was that. He would not marry her for love, and now he was telling her that he would not marry her for money either. She should be angry with him, but she was too gripped by her new idea.

"You need an investor, Humphrey," she said. "And I know of one."

"Where?" he said, his face filled with sudden hope. Then he took her meaning and the optimism collapsed. "No, no, no, that would not do at all."

"Why not? You need money, I have far more than enough, why not let me invest in your venture? Without... any other ties," she added, in case he thought she was talking about marriage.

"That would never do. You are all generosity and I thank you from the depths of my heart, but I could not possibly deprive you of half of your fortune. It would be unconscionable in me to do so. The world would question my motives and your good sense in such an arrangement, or they would wonder in what exact state we were to each other."

"The world, the world!" she said impatiently, rising to her feet, so that he was obliged to stand too. "You care too much about the world, Humphrey."

"And you care too little for it," he shot back. "Do not imagine that your fortune will protect you. If you wish to have a place in society, you must abide by its rules or risk having your reputation shredded."

"A place in society?" she said scornfully. "What place is open to me? As the daughter of a man who made his own fortune, I shall always be despised."

"Not by me," he said quietly.

"Even by you," she said, lifting her chin a little. "Have you not made it plain that my fortune defines me? My lack of fortune defined me in one way, and my possession of it defines me in another. You must do this or that, and you cannot do some other thing, and all because of my fortune. You are as shackled as any other of your class. Can you not step outside the constraints of propriety, and see me as a woman, as a *person?* I am your equal, Humphrey, in every way that matters. Not in the drawing room, for there you are a great nobleman and I am a rich nobody, but when we gallop together on the moors, there is no distinction between us. So treat with me now as an equal. I am prepared to stake half my fortune on this venture of yours. Will you not accept it in the spirit of the friendship we share? You are a gambler to your marrow, will you not take a chance now?"

She knew from his face that she had not convinced him. He licked his lips, shuffled his feet awkwardly, stared at the ground. "I cannot." The finality in his tone chilled her to the core. "It is impossible, and you must not think of it, I beg you. Your reputation—"

"My reputation!" she said contemptuously. "What has that to do with the matter?"

"Everything, do you not see? You must be so careful, and I cannot—" He stopped, closing his eyes as if overcome by strong emotion. "It is impossible for me—" He took a heaving breath. "You have no protection," he said, more calmly. "No father, no brother. No husband." A long pause. "It is for you alone to defend your own reputation — at least, for the moment. For a while. What you choose to do is for you to decide, but you do not understand the ways of the *ton*. I know it is presumptuous of me to speak so to you when I have not the least right, but you have no other to guide you. If you will be advised by me, you should proceed with the utmost caution and not deliberately set the world by the ears."

"When a matter is of importance to me," she said with dignity, "then I dare to take risks. I am not some timid shrinking debutante, terrified to open my mouth in case the great patronesses of Almacks should shun me. I am Hortensia Blythe, daughter of a gentleman, and I shall live my life as seems best to me, without reference to the arbitrary dictates of society."

And with that she spun on her heel and marched off.

~~~~~

Humphrey watched her go, heart-wrenched by her wilfulness, but stunned by her bravery. What a woman! She was everything that he admired and respected and adored. If she had stayed but a second or two longer, he might have simply swept her into his arms and carried her off, and let the world go hang itself. But she was gone and the moment was lost.

"That gaming house sounds like fun."

Humphrey jumped out of his skin. Spinning round, he saw a blond head peeping through the remains of a window.

"Charlie! Good heavens, man, you must not eavesdrop in that way. It is a very bad habit."

With a quick twist, Charlie jumped through the window and dusted himself down. "In London, eh? Where all the toffs live? That where it's going to be?"

"What is it to you?"

Charlie grinned, quite unabashed by the tone of censure in Humphrey's voice. "Can I work there? Not that I mind the stables, but indoor work would be better, and I know you don't want me as a footman at Drummoor."

"Can you imagine it, you and me in the same room?" Humphrey said. "It would confuse everyone horribly. They would expect me to serve the soup and you to eat it. And the same would be true if ever I contrive to establish this gaming house. Which seems unlikely at this stage, so you may forget all about it. In fact, you must forget everything you have heard here today, do you understand?"

The grin widened, and he put one finger to his nose. "Aha! Your secret is safe with me."

"Good, because there is a lady involved, and if you breathe so much as a single word to a soul, I shall tear your miserable head from your scrawny body, do I make myself clear?"

Charlie nodded, the grin wiped instantly from his face.

"Promise me!"

"I promise, I'll not breathe a word, I swear. Didn't understand half of what was said, anyway, 'cept that she's quite something, ain't she?"

"Yes, she is. Now surely you have work to do?"

With a flourishing bow, Charlie disappeared, and, very slowly, Humphrey followed. The rest of the afternoon, he diligently avoided Hortensia, spending his time as much with the Stoners as with his own family. In all that had happened, he had almost forgotten that the older Mr Stoner had the capability of unmasking the deception between Miss Quayle and Miss Blythe, but his casual questions elicited no worrying signs of suspicion. He discovered that Mr Stoner owned a small gaming establishment of his own in Newcastle, and the older man took a keen interest in his plans.

"If you send me a detailed list of your likely initial expenses, my lord, I should be delighted to cast an eye over it and advise on where improvements might be made. My little place is not so grand as yours will be, but I shall be able to make some comparisons."

"I should be very much obliged to you for any advice, sir," Humphrey said. "You are far more experienced in such matters than I, although it has to be confessed that I have spent a great deal of time in such places, over the years."

"It is not the same," Stoner said. "In the best-run of such establishments, the customer will never notice the servants moving about, replenishing wine glasses, remembering what each gentleman prefers to drink, producing a lady's favourite sweetmeat. It is like a play, where the audience is so absorbed in the performance, it is quite unconscious of the efforts behind the scenes. It takes a great deal of careful thought to produce the desired effect. Here — my card, my lord. You may write to me at any time."

But eventually, both parties began to drift away to the carriages, and the horses were attached. Humphrey found Hortensia standing disconsolately beside the curricle. She looked up hopefully at his approach.

"Do you need my assistance, Miss Quayle?" he said, attempting a smile.

Was that relief on her face? "Oh no, but I was not sure... I did not like to presume..."

"Well, up you go, then. Tom, pass the reins to Miss Quayle."

She stopped halfway between ground and seat. "Oh! I am to drive back?"

"Of course," he said, puzzled.

"I thought... oh, thank you, thank you!" Her smile this time was wide and sunny, the smile he so loved, and his heart jumped about painfully.

"Yes, yes, but on you go, and then slide across so that I may sit beside you." He knew his voice was gruff, but his throat was oddly tight.

They drove back dutifully in slow procession, and there was no banter between them this time. Too much had happened that day, too much had been said and done, for either to be comfortable attempting the morning's light tone. It was a bittersweet journey, Humphrey's pleasure in her company warring violently with his grief that she would soon be gone from his life. Six days — that was all the time they had left.

Yet he could not speak, it was impossible for him to say all he felt and desired. How could he? If he could not woo her openly, ardently as he would wish to do, he could not make any declaration at all. All he could do was to wait, miserably, until a suitable time had elapsed and his pursuit of Miss Blythe — no, Miss Quayle — had been forgotten. But by then Hortensia would be long gone, and he could not depend on her waiting for him, as he would wait for her. Why should she? How she must despise him now, for today he had as good as declared his love and yet still rejected her in every possible way.

When they reached Drummoor, he lifted her down from the curricle as before, and when he set her down, she lifted her eyes to his, those great, dark eyes that haunted his dreams. For several seconds they stood thus, their eyes locked, as if on the brink of some speech that would break the dam of constraint between them. His hands rested on her waist, and he would have stayed thus forever if he could, lost in admiration.

Then she stepped away from him and curtsied. "Thank you so much for allowing me to drive your curricle, Lord Humphrey."

And without a backward glance she disappeared into the house.

15: Storms

"It is such nonsense! Ridiculous man! How can he say such things!"

"Hortensia, dearest, do calm down a little," Rosemary said. "Will you not sit down? You are making me dizzy, pacing to and fro in that distracted manner."

Hortensia perched restlessly on the edge of a chair. The two women were in Rosemary's bedroom, still fully dressed despite the late hour.

"I wish I had never said anything," Hortensia said, her anger dissipating abruptly. "If I had not spoken, if we had just told Lord Kilbraith directly, everything would have gone on so comfortably. I had barely begun to have hopes of him, and now all my happiness is destroyed."

"You must not despair," Rosemary said. "Look how suddenly things can change." She blushed a little as she spoke.

"Oh yes!" Hortensia cried. "That is my only consolation, that your happiness is secure. Were it not for that, I might wish we had never come here. But how nonsensical it is!" She jumped to her feet once more, and strode across to the window and back. "We were getting along so agreeably, yet as soon as I told him who I was, he backed away from me as if I were on fire. And to say that he cannot approach me because society would see him as a fortune hunter — of all the foolish reasons!"

"But you must see how it would appear," Rosemary said. "Everyone knows we were invited here so that Lord Humphrey could marry a rich wife. His intentions towards me were very plain, and Lord and Lady Carrbridge have been so very kind, in the most particular way. I have been interrogated by all the aunts, you should know, as a possible bride of Drummoor. But once it is public knowledge that you have the fortune, not I, how can he suddenly turn his attentions to you? It would look so cold and mercenary."

"As if it is not cold and mercenary anyway! And Rosemary, if his attentions to you were calculated, his behaviour towards me must suggest a partiality, for he could not have known of the deception just at once, so surely—?" She sat down again abruptly. "It was mere kindness, was it not? He took pity on me, or perhaps he hoped to ingratiate himself with you, or—" A long pause, and then a sigh. Hanging her head, she went on, "It was no more than a light flirtation to him, I daresay. Something to amuse him, and give the plain companion some memories to warm her eternal spinsterhood."

"Oh no, dearest!" Rosemary said, shocked. "You are quite wrong, I am convinced of it, and Lord Kilbraith thinks so too. He is certain that Lord Humphrey likes you very much, that he has the greatest admiration for you. He let you drive his curricle, after all, and his wonderful matched pair, and what gentleman ever does *that* unless he is quite in love?"

"That only makes it worse," Hortensia said in a low voice. "If he loves me, then let him show it, instead of leaving me to wonder. Oh, how I hate these restrictions! A lady must never show her feelings, must always receive a gentleman's advances with cool politeness and must never, ever be forward. So I cannot get rid of Mr Whittleton and I cannot promote my cause with Humphrey."

"*Lord* Humphrey, dear."

"Oh, yes. *Lord* Humphrey," she said in a small voice. "Stand up, and I shall unfasten your gown, dearest. Let us go to our beds, and try to sleep."

~~~~~

Humphrey dismissed Billings, his nerves too jangled to listen to the valet's grumblings about the state of his attire after a mere few hours of wear. The man would be happiest if Humphrey stood to attention in a corner all evening, as motionless as a suit of armour, for only then would he return satisfactorily unrumpled.

Once the valet had left, radiating disapproval, Humphrey ripped off his coat and cravat, kicked off his shoes and shrugged himself into a robe. Moments later, even the robe was too much and was summarily tossed aside. He threw open the window, which Billings had closed, the night air being potentially injurious to his master's health. Even leaning out, however, the air felt close and sultry, and a few faint rumbles of thunder could be heard in the distance.

He wished there would be a storm, for it would suit his mood admirably. Such a tempestuous day, his emotions tossed about like a small boat bobbing on a wild ocean. And then the awkward drive home, and the even more awkward apology to Julius for breaking his nose. Not for hitting him, though. He could not apologise for hitting a man who was annoying a lady. And after that, the whole dreary evening to be got through, with Hortensia pale but composed, not meeting his eye, and the family either chiding him for getting into a mill, or teasing him unmercifully. And one or two, hearing the tale, had said, "Miss Quayle, eh?" and looked at him curiously, and then at her, as if wondering what anyone might see in the mouse of a companion.

All of it set him on edge, and the lingering heat was oppressive. There was nothing for it but to find a cooler spot, somewhere he could rest his troubled mind and consider what might be done. He padded through the dark corridors of the house, the shadows jumping about as his candle wavered. Then up into the gallery attics and up again, onto the roof above the library wing. The library itself had a pitched roof, but most of the central part of the house had a flat roof, the crenellated battlements lending themselves to many a secret tryst by night, while by day they were the scene of childish games involving imagined siege engines, trebuchets, bows and arrows and invading hordes of armoured knights from France or terrifying clansmen from Scotland.

At this hour, however, the stout defending warriors were tucked up in their beds in the nursery wing, and even the trysting housemaids and footmen were sleeping before rising with the dawn. Humphrey was alone.

At first he walked aimlessly about, first looking down into the fountain court, and then out over the main entrance, but eventually his steps let him to a point above the kitchen court, and here he halted. He knew where her room was, of course. There was a board below stairs with every guest's room, and the maid or valet assigned to them, and he had just happened to be passing one day and had just happened to see her name. The rose room. Her friend was in the larger, more luxurious jasmine room with a view over the gardens, but Hortensia's room looked out into the more prosaic kitchen court, and if he positioned himself just so, he could see her window...

She was there. The window was wide open, and she had her arms resting on the sill. The moon was full on her, making her upturned face a pale ghost of the orb above, whitening her bare arms and her slender throat. Her dark hair tumbled about her face, and something glittered on her cheeks — was she crying? His heart twisted in sudden pain. Was this his fault? Had he distressed her so much that she, his strong, magnificent Hortensia, was reduced to tears again? He blinked away tears of his own.

When he could see clearly again, she was gone.

He strode about the roof, too agitated to care if he were seen. It was intolerable! He was miserable, she was miserable too — why should they not pursue their own happiness, like rational people? Why must they be bound by the petty constraints of society's whims? What had she said? *'I am your equal, Humphrey, in every way that matters.'* And so she was, and not merely his equal, for she was stronger, more daring even than he was. *'I shall live my life as seems best to me.'* Such a grand philosophy. And perhaps with her two hundred thousand pounds, she could afford to cock a snook at the *ton* and live an independent life — a free life. How glorious that would be!

Was it possible...? Did he dare to follow her lead and step outside the tight clasp of society's arms? What would it be like to be free, not to care what anyone thought? He could not imagine it. But with every circuit of the roof, he grew more certain that he had to try. If he could just secure her hand — how happy they should be! What did anything else matter? Yes! He would do it! Tomorrow, he would dare to court Hortensia.

The rumbles of thunder were drifting nearer, and the first fat drops of summer rain began to fall around him, kicking up the dust. He laughed out loud, and broke into a trot, and then a run. Before long, the rain was falling in earnest, a steady downpour that bubbled across the roof and gurgled into the drains. He ran faster, laughing, rain dripping down his face, his clothes clinging to him, until he was soaked and exhilarated and breathless. Then, still smiling, he dripped his way back to his room.

~~~~~

This happy state of affairs lasted for precisely one night. Humphrey woke the next morning to all the same doubts that had assailed him the previous evening. How could he speak? Could he even be sure that she would welcome his advances? Had she really been crying? Perhaps they were tears of rage, not sorrow, or perhaps they arose from some other cause that had nothing to do with him. It was arrogant of him to presume that a lady's happiness might depend solely on him.

And then there was Carrbridge. As soon as he had heard of the deception, he had sought out Kilbraith to express his outrage at the ladies' behaviour, and to apologise, as host, for allowing a guest to draw him in. Kilbraith had just laughed at him, and said that he had guessed it all long since, and could not find it in his heart to condemn Miss Blythe or Miss Quayle. But Carrbridge could and did, and when he got Humphrey on his own, had ranted about how lucky they were that he had not yet made an offer.

"For it would be the most shameful thing to have such a deceitful person in the family. Kilbraith may not care, but he is Scottish and I daresay they have not the sensibilities of the English. For our own family, I could not countenance such a marriage. It would bring the greatest discredit to the Marford name, Humphrey, and I will not have us dragged through the mire, and people whispering about us. We have had our share of scandals, it is true, but always the most *respectable* sort — gambling and duels and mistresses and so forth. Nothing alarming in any of that. But I will not have anyone saying that this family was taken in by two trumpery girls from abroad and fooled into marriage."

"Would it be as dreadful as all that?" Humphrey said miserably. "Might it not be that the Marford name is strong enough to wipe away any stain?"

"Do not even think about it," Carrbridge had said sternly. "You are to keep well away from Miss Quayle... Miss Blythe..." He huffed in annoyance. "You see how awkward it is? One does not even know what to call either of them. Promise me, Humphrey... give me your word that you will not do anything foolish."

"Carrbridge..." He hesitated, then decided he had nothing to lose by being honest. "Carrbridge, would you keep me from the love of my life because of family pride?"

His brother paused, looking at him intently. "Is that how it is? But if that is so, it will still be so in six months' time, or a year. Let all this business die down, and then we will see, for I should not like you to be unhappy, you know. Give it a year, and Connie will bring her into society and if the lady behaves in a properly demure manner, as one new to society should do, then it will all be forgot. Then you may marry her with my goodwill, if you still wish it."

And Humphrey had had no option but to agree, and having given his word, he could not break it without deeply disappointing his brother. And yet... what of Hortensia? He was torn in two ways, his desire to be with her warring with his determination to follow his brother's wishes.

It was a most unaccustomed state for him. Humphrey Marford the gambler, the man who cast his stake instantly on the turn of a card, who set his horse at the highest wall or the widest ditch and never flinched from his course — yet now he dithered like a spinster, quite unable to see his way forward. If he followed his heart, he brought distress to his brother and shame to the family name. If he kept to his brother's wishes, he might lose his one chance for happiness. Whatever was he to do?

As he dressed, letting Billings' scoldings about his sodden clothes rumble round his head without attending much, he reminded himself that he must endure only a few more days of this agony.

When he was finally deemed sufficiently of credit to his valet to be released upon the world and allowed to go downstairs, he found Connie in a lather of excitement.

"What do you think?" she said triumphantly. "Lord Kilbraith has written to his father, and the earl wishes him to take Miss Blythe directly to Scotland. No, Miss Quayle. Ah, but no, she must be Miss Blythe a little longer. But *both* the ladies are to go to Scotland, in fact." She lowered her voice to a whisper. "But now you must get to the point with *your* lady, Humphrey. You have not much time left, unless you plan to chase after her all the way across the border."

"Connie, I—"

"Never mind Lord Carrbridge, you know," she whispered conspiratorially, smoothing the skirt of her riding habit. "He thinks only of honour, but love is much more important, so you must not have qualms. Faint heart never won fair lady and so forth. Who said that, was it Shakespeare?"

"I do not think so. Connie, you must not—"

"But you get on so well with her, Humphrey! And she is the one with the fortune, so you must see— Yes, yes, my dear, I am coming," she said to the marquess, who was trying to urge her towards the stables for their morning ride. "Are you busy today, Humphrey? Will you call at Tambray Hall?"

He pulled a face. "Must I? The Melthwaites are so dull."

"I know, but they are my aunt and uncle, you know, and they ask after you so pointedly whenever Lord Carrbridge and I call, and you know that Lady Melthwaite cannot go out now. Everyone else has paid a call, except you. Yes, yes, my dear, I shall be there directly! Please, Humphrey. Take Harriet with you, then it will not be so bad."

Humphrey was cast into even deeper gloom. The Melthwaites were possibly the most boring people he had ever had the misfortune to encounter. Once upon a time, he had managed very successfully to evade them, for despite being close neighbours, the Marfords had seldom visited and never dined there, inviting them once or twice a year to one of the larger entertainments at Drummoor so that their dreariness might be diluted in merrier company. In London it was possible to escape them almost entirely, or do no more than nod when passing on the stairs at a ball.

But when Connie had burst onto the family, she had insisted on raising the Melthwaites' status to that of cherished family, and so she and Lord Carrbridge visited often and issued regular invitations to dine at Drummoor, although thankfully they never came. The worst of it was that she insisted on the rest of the Marfords calling too, and so once or twice each summer Humphrey found himself press-ganged into a visit.

He made his way to the tapestry room, where he might reasonably hope for some seclusion to think about Hortensia and consider his predicament. Instead, he found his brother Reggie there, rifling through newspapers and journals.

"You have not seen last week's *Sagborough Chronicle,* have you? There was an advertisement— Good Lord, Humphrey, you look as miserable as a month of wet Sundays. Whatever is the matter?"

Humphrey sagged into a chair, and the whole story tumbled out, the words pouring out of him like water from a tap. "Tell me there is a way out of this, Reggie, for God's sake, for I have not the least idea what I should do."

"Have you not?" Reggie said gently.

"Can it really be as bad as all that? Surely the family's honour can survive the addition of one daughter of a nabob?"

"Oh, if that were all! Such things happen all the time, and so long as the daughter is also a lady and knows how to behave in society, with not the least whiff of trade about her, she will be tolerated, at least. But she must be beyond reproach, Humphrey, and this business of changing places... it makes us look foolish, and you know how Carrbridge stands on his dignity. He does not like to be made a fool of, and now we have Sharp doing whatever he wants, and these by-blows of Father's turning up... no, I can see why he would not like it."

"But the *ton* will not care about such a trivial matter, surely?"

Reggie shook his head. "Perhaps. Perhaps not. But you must see how it would look. One lady comes here as an heiress and secures Lord Kilbraith. Immediately the other lady reveals herself as the true heiress and secures *you*. They would look like the worst kind of society climbers, scrambling their way to the upper branches of the nobility by deception, and *you* would look like the world's most gullible fool. The whole family would be tainted by association. You know how these things work, Humphrey."

"Then what am I to do?" Humphrey whispered.

"You know the answer to that," Reggie said calmly. "You are a gentleman, Humphrey, you *know* what you must do. Stand aside and let her go to Scotland for a while until the fuss has died down. Then in the spring—"

Humphrey made a convulsive groan of dismay.

"—in the spring," Reggie went on relentlessly, "she will come to London, and the *ton* will see how charming and amiable she is, and not at all a grasping hussy, and you may make your approach then."

The prospect was unbearable. "Perhaps if I were to explain all this to her?" he said hopefully. "So that she understands that I will speak in the spring? Do you think?"

Reggie sighed. "You cannot possibly declare yourself now, and yet not offer for her formally. That is not the behaviour of a gentleman, Humphrey. Or do you plan to enter into a secret engagement with her? More deception?" His voice softened as he went on, "Sometimes one has to wait for happiness, brother."

"As you did," Humphrey said, remembering. "You left town to spare Miss Chamberlain from gossip."

"A lady's reputation is so vulnerable," Reggie said softly. "We must do everything within our power to protect the ladies we love."

"Truly spoken," Humphrey said sorrowfully. "And I have given my word to Carrbridge, so I am bound by that, and cannot speak, no matter how much it pains me."

"But there is always satisfaction in behaving as one ought," Reggie said. "Come, can you not take pleasure in that?"

Humphrey managed a small smile. "No, for I am bidden by Connie to visit the Melthwaites, and therefore to Tambray Hall I must go. There is no pleasure to be had in that."

Reggie laughed. "If you can postpone the Melthwaites until another day, then Merton is looking for one of us to accompany him to Silsby Vale House. He wishes to visit this Mrs Cecil Andrews to find out more about the house, and requires support from one of the family. That would be a more congenial outing for you, would it not?"

Humphrey perked up at once. The air would be so clear after the overnight rain, and a ride over the moors would be just the thing. He jumped up at once and went to find Merton. At least he could put his aching heart to one side for a while.

16: Mrs Cecil Andrews

The stable court was rain-washed to sparkling cleanliness, the air was clear and Humphrey's spirits rose immeasurably as his horse clip-clopped briskly out into the park. He had looked wistfully at Ganymede, who whickered hopefully at him, but instead took one of Gus's long-limbed beauties. Ganymede must wait for Miss Quayle's attention. Merton rode one of the estate's general hacks, often ridden by the grooms, but still a decent ride, and as soon as they were clear of the pleasure grounds, they both unleashed their mounts. Humphrey reached the woods first, but Merton was not far behind, his grin matching Humphrey's own.

"I should do this more often," Merton said, laughing. "Which I say every time, of course."

"Why do you not? You could ride whenever you want."

"I do not like to take advantage of Lord Carrbridge's generosity," Merton said, as they entered the woods, walking the horses to rest them. "When there is good cause for me to go visiting, then I jump at the chance. It will not be long before my own stable is established, and then I shall ride every day, I assure you."

Humphrey looked at him curiously. "There is no need to be so determinedly independent, Merton. We have any number of horses sitting in the stable eating their heads off which you might ride whenever you wish."

"Which is an unnecessary expense, as I point out often to his lordship. There are three times as many horses here as are needed, not to mention the grooms. I have no wish at all to add to the burden."

"Are we still in the suds, Merton? I had hoped our finances were on a sounder footing now."

"The process is very slow, my lord. It is a matter of looking at every holding or expense or investment individually, and determining how best the income may be improved or the expenditure reduced, and then there is the need to wait for leases to terminate and contracts to expire. Certainly his lordship's financial position is healthier than it was, and by next Lady's Day, it will be much improved, and I shall be in a position to eliminate many of the debts altogether."

"And will reducing the stables help a great deal? I suppose it must, for some of those horses are never put to the least use, yet they still eat just as much. Are oats expensive, Merton?"

He smiled. "It is not just the cost of oats, my lord. There is the farrier to be paid, and stabling in town, and the duty, too. Not to mention the duty on the many carriages, and the grooms — the cost of manservants is very high. And there are so many footmen, too."

"You would not have us let all the footmen go, Merton? In a house the size of Drummoor—"

"No, no! Footmen reflect the marquess's station. But I should like to reduce the size of the stables, and perhaps dispose of some of the carriages that no longer see any use. That should save two or three hundred pounds a year."

"That is rather a small amount," Humphrey said.

"But that small amount may be combined with a number of other small amounts saved elsewhere to add up to rather large amounts. There is always waste in a large household, and for those prepared to examine every expense, no matter how small, there are great economies to be made which do not inconvenience anyone. Indeed they may not even be noticed. For instance, have you observed any diminution in the quality or quantity of wine consumed?"

"Not at all. If anything, I would say the quality is somewhat improved."

"That is because the amount of wine purchased has remained unchanged for some thirty years, a time when, I must suppose, the marquess of that time entertained rather lavishly. The wine cellars, large as they may be, are quite full. I have reduced the wine bill by three quarters, and yet the wine served is somewhat better quality because it is drawn from mature stocks."

"That is very ingenious," Humphrey said. "And this is what you were accustomed to do for Sir Osborne Hardy when you worked for him?"

"Indeed, and over many years my modest amendments had the happy effect of doubling his income, while also reducing his expenditure by half."

"You are a clever man, Merton. I am very sorry indeed that Sir Osborne is dead, but it has been a fortunate circumstance for us, in sending you to straighten us out. But tell me, what would your advice be in my own case? How should I proceed if I wish to obtain the one hundred thousand pounds to establish my gaming house?"

"My advice would be look for a number of investors each willing to contribute a small amount to the venture, and then to marry Miss Blythe. The real Miss Blythe, that is."

"Ah... you know about that? Naturally you do. You are quick-witted and observant, so you worked it out."

"Thanks to Mr Julius Whittleton, and a letter I wrote on behalf of the marquess, a reply to which was, most surprisingly, not received. You understand me, I take it? My suspicions were confirmed by talking to Mr Percival Stoner at Branksford Abbey. He was very helpful, and agreed to say nothing at all about the matter."

"So that was your doing! It seemed likely that the whole deception would be unmasked in the most embarrassing way possible, so it was a great relief when my fears in that direction came to nothing. It will all be public soon enough and then… but you suggest an array of investors, so why then would I need to marry Miss Blythe?"

"Why, for your own happiness, my lord. And hers, of course."

Humphrey pulled his horse up sharply, causing the creature to toss his elegant head in protest. "You can say that with surety? That her happiness is at stake?"

"With surety? No man may be sure of a lady's heart until he puts it to the test. But it is my opinion, and also that of Lady Hardy, that Miss Blythe holds you in the greatest affection."

"And yet how can I speak?" Humphrey cried in frustration. "To court one lady openly, and then transfer my attentions the instant it is revealed that she has no fortune — it would be despicable, and would put me on a level footing with Julius, which I do *not* want. It would be of all things improper, and insulting to both ladies. Do you not agree that it would be improper?"

"My lord, I cannot advise you on such a subject. Sir Osborne was wont to say that if one doubts the propriety of an action, one had much better not do it, and especially where a lady is concerned. He was always most solicitous of Lady Hardy, and guarded her good name jealously. But he was a second generation baronet, which is not to be compared with the son of a marquess of long lineage. Much is forgiven those of high rank."

Much might be forgiven him, as the son of a marquess, but how much would be forgiven Hortensia, a woman of no particular family, her fortune arising from trade? She could not afford to put a foot wrong. And then, when her deception was uncovered... If he were to marry Hortensia, he wanted her to be accepted into good society, just as he was, and not snubbed or sneered at or disdained as a vulgar mushroom. He was not convinced that even the Marford name was sufficient to overcome such a history. Even Carrbridge disdained her. What was he to do? His mind was no nearer to a resolution. His heart drew him strongly in one direction, but his head disagreed.

Humphrey fell silent, and they rode on without further conversation.

~~~~~

Silsby Vale House dozed in the noon sunshine, with no sign of gardeners or grooms. But when they rode round to the stables, the same groom appeared that Humphrey had seen before.

"We meet again, Robert! But tell me, is it safe to leave my horse with you? For the last time I did so, the walk home was most unpleasant."

The man looked shamefaced. "Beg pardon, milord, but I didn't know. I were just following orders."

"Very well, then. Take good care of this fellow, for he belongs to Lord Augustus Marford, and he will rip your guts out and feed them to the crows if any harm befalls a horse of his."

The man blanched. "I'll look after him, milord, I swear it."

"Good. I am glad we understand each other. Is your mistress at home?"

"Aye, milord. She never goes out."

"What, not even to church?"

"Parson won't have her."

"A fine example of Christian charity," Humphrey muttered, as he dismounted.

The housekeeper admitted them without demur, albeit with a sour expression on her face. They were shown into the same sitting room as before, where Mrs Andrews received them warily. Refreshments were sent for, although Humphrey had no wish for any, and while they waited for the tray to arrive, and then for the lady to pour tea and cut slices of cake, nothing was said that did not relate to the weather, the ease of their journey there and the likelihood of a good harvest. After a while, it fell upon Humphrey to maintain this conversation, for Merton was busy eating cherry cake, and the lady, having exhausted her repertoire of small talk, said little beyond "Oh indeed, my lord" and "Certainly, my lord" and "Is that so, my lord?".

Having finished his cake, and no more being forthcoming, Merton at last commenced to explain the reason for the visit. Mrs Andrews looked from one to the other, and then said, faintly, "I can tell you nothing."

"You may speak freely, Mrs Andrews," Merton said. "I am Lord Carrbridge's secretary and have his full confidence, and Lord Humphrey is his lordship's brother. We stand here in place of his lordship, so we have the authority to ask these questions."

"Oh, I do not doubt it," she said. "But I do not have the authority to answer them."

"Because of Sharp?" Humphrey said impatiently. "You need not regard him."

She paled, her hand fluttering tremulously at her throat. "Mr Sharp is master here, my lord. I *must* regard him."

"By what right does he rule here?" Humphrey said. "He does not own this house, nor is he your husband. Is he related to you, madam?"

She shook her head, but answered firmly, "He is master here."

Humphrey set his tea cup down carefully on a side table and leaned back in his chair, scrutinising her. She lowered her head under his gaze. "You are afraid of him. He has some hold over you, perhaps?"

"Financial?" Merton hazarded. "Do you owe him money?"

She licked her lips, her fingers smoothing her gown over and over, although it bore no creases. "I can tell you nothing."

Merton frowned, and began in severe tones, "Then we must—" but Humphrey waved him to silence.

"Mrs Andrews," he said gently, "whatever your history with Sharp, you are dealing now with the Marquess of Carrbridge, who owns this house. Sharp is the marquess's land agent, an employee, and acts only under his authority, so he cannot compel you to do or not do anything."

"That's what *you* think!" she said, with a grimace.

"No, it is what the law thinks, and it is also what the marquess thinks, and you may be very sure, madam, that the marquess and the law together are far, far more powerful than Sharp. You need not fear him." Still she hesitated, so he went on, "But no one can help you unless you speak of your dealings with my father and with Sharp."

She looked down at her fingers still smoothing imaginary creases in her skirt, but when she looked up again, Humphrey saw resolve in her face. "Very well. I will trust you, my lord, and in truth, it would be a relief to tell someone all that has happened to me. Mr Merton, would you be so good as to look in that cupboard over there... no, the one to the right. Yes, that one. You will find a bottle of brandy and some glasses. Please pour me some brandy. A little more, if you please. And do take some yourselves. No? As you please." She sipped and almost purred with satisfaction.

171

"Let me begin at the very beginning," she said, settling back in her chair, the brandy glass in her hand. "We moved here, Cecil and I, not long after we were married, when his father died. At first, we lived modestly enough. Being neighbours to Drummoor, we were invited there occasionally — a dinner, or a ball, or one of the famous summer garden parties of those days. But then Cecil inherited a little money from an uncle, and nothing would do but he must go to London for the season and move in the same circles as the Marfords. And of course, he was drawn into the gambling. He loved it, and nothing I said would dissuade him. Needless to say, for the man was a fool, he was soon in too deep, losing money everywhere. But would he quit? Of course not! And eventually, as I had told him would happen, he lost everything he had — the money, the house, everything — to your father. Charles Marford."

She took a long draught of brandy, and sighed, although whether on account of the sadness of the tale or satisfaction at drinking brandy in the middle of the day was more than Humphrey could tell.

"Charles was very kind," she went on. "Such a charming man, and so handsome. You look so like him, my lord — goodness, it quite takes me back! He allowed us to stay on here without paying rent, which was generous of him. But Cecil resented it so. Almost I think he would have preferred it if we had been thrown out on our ears and left to rot in a ditch. Three months later, he took a gun out rabbiting, and never came home. He was found with half his head blown off in the western spinney. An accident, the coroner said. Self-inflicted, the parson and half the county said." Again the brandy glass was raised and she took a long swallow.

"It was a relief, to be truthful, for poor Cecil was not the man he had been, not a man I could respect. Charles was very understanding. I could stay on under the same terms, he said. I think he felt some guilt, for he often brought a haunch of venison or beef when he came over. He had an interest in one of the housemaids at the time, so he was here a great deal. He would have his dinner with me, and stay the night, and I suppose the housemaid crept into his room. There was a child—"

"Charlie," Humphrey said.

She smiled. "Charlie, yes. Very like his father, as you are, my lord, although very light-fingered. Always stealing. We had to send him away in the end. But the time I speak of was before Charlie was even born. Your father liked to talk to me. I think he was lonely, for there had been some great tragedy in his life, a woman he had loved and lost — something of the sort. Then he had been forced into a society marriage, and he chafed rather at the restrictions. He was so unhappy."

Humphrey listened in silent astonishment to this description of his father, a man who, whatever his other failings, had always behaved with great tenderness towards his wife. Had he really been unhappy? Or was it mere words to charm a gullible widow into his bed? Perhaps he had really disliked his marriage, and had come to love his wife despite that. It was a puzzle. Humphrey asked no questions, but vowed to relate the whole of it to Carrbridge, who, being the eldest, might remember something of their father in these long-ago times.

Mrs Andrews sighed. "He was so generous, so charming... it was almost inevitable that he should turn to me. For two years he came to me, although less often at the end. Then one day he told me he would come no more. He gave me this to look after, to keep things private, he said..."

She rose gracefully and went to a small desk at one end of the room. Unlocking it with a key she kept hidden beneath a vase, she produced a small roll of papers tied with ribbon. This she passed to Merton, who swiftly untied and unrolled the pages.

"The title documents," he said with a satisfied smile. "Also, some lesser papers relating to the estate. Thank you, madam. These prove the marquess's ownership."

She nodded. "That was the last I ever saw of him. I missed him, of course, but I understood. He was the heir to the title, a man of importance, and I had been merely a passing dalliance to him. These great men — they take whatever they want, is it not so? I was not resentful, and my life was peaceful. But then, about six months after Charles had left me, Mr Sharp came. It had been decided that I must pay rent after all, he said. Of course I could not. I lived the most frugal life as it was, for all I had was my jointure, too hedged about with restrictions for Cecil to gamble away. So then he suggested—"

She broke off and frowned into the brandy glass, as if surprised to find it empty. Silently Merton rose and refilled it.

"He did not say it in so many words, you understand, for he never spoke in a straightforward way, but it was clear enough. If I were to... *accommodate* him, then the payment of rent need not trouble me."

"That is despicable," Merton said, in shocked tones.

She shrugged. "It is the way of the world. I had no protection, no husband or brother or son to stand up for me. It seemed preferable to me rather than destitution, and perhaps the workhouse. And it was not so bad, so long as I did exactly as he wished, and the servants too. He had a great temper if he was thwarted, although he never hit *me*. But I could not bear the upset, when he was cross. So we all did whatever he wanted, and he was satisfied."

"Have you no family at all?" Humphrey said.

"A brother who washed his hands of me when Cecil died. A sister who washed her hands of me when I took Charles into my bed. Even the parson has washed his hands of me," she said, with a sudden smile that gave some indication of how pretty she must have been in her youth.

"Well, you have protection now," Humphrey said, standing abruptly, for he was too angry to sit still. "I shall ensure that Sharp does not come here again, and just to make absolutely certain of it, I shall send over one of the footmen to act as butler and make sure you are not troubled again."

"Oh!" Her eyes widened. "My lord, thank you! That would be wonderful, for the housekeeper is in Mr Sharp's pocket, you know. She reports everything to him, and intercepts all the mail, and prevents anyone from calling on me. At least she could not deny *you*, my lord! It is so difficult, and I sit in here, day after day, seeing no one, not able to go out except for a monthly shopping trip to York, and even then she accompanies me."

"Mrs Andrews, you are a prisoner no longer," Humphrey said gently.

They left her in tears of gratitude, and rode home slowly, rather overwhelmed.

"What is to be done about Sharp?" Merton said.

"Nothing," Humphrey said shortly. "There is nothing that *can* be done. If you put all this to him, he will protest his innocence. He put no pressure on the lady, she simply offered herself. Of course she is not a prisoner, it is all in her mind. And it is all her word against his. He is the most slippery snake in the world."

"There must be *something* we can do," Merton said.

"I should like to smash his smug face to pulp, but that would put *me* in the wrong," Humphrey growled. "It is not right, not right at all, but at least we have put a stop to it. Mrs Andrews will not be troubled by Sharp again."

"It is contemptible, taking advantage of a lady in that way," Merton said. "Sharp is the very devil."

Humphrey said nothing, wondering about his own father, who had also taken advantage of the lady, and the housemaid, too. What had Mrs Andrews said? *'These great men — they take whatever they want'* and he could not deny it. His own father had been scarcely less despicable than Sharp. Selfish, careless, cruel — thinking only of his own pleasure, and heedless of the path of destruction left in his wake. And if his father had not used Mrs Andrews, would Sharp have dared to do so? He was very much to blame. One could not act as one pleased and ignore the consequences, not if one were a gentleman.

The more he thought about it, the more he knew that his own path was plain — he could not blindly follow his own wishes and pursue Hortensia. He must be circumspect, abide by his brothers wishes and do all as he ought. He must keep away from her for now, no matter how difficult.

17: An Audacious Plan

Hortensia woke to another dreary day, her spirits quite downcast. Her anger had long since given way to despondency. What now was there to look forward to? No rides with Humphrey, no close-fought games of piquet, no quiet conversation before dinner. And no Rosemary, either, for she was entirely absorbed in her new-found love, and had eyes for no one but Lord Kilbraith.

Rising early, Hortensia ordered a tray in her room, for breakfast was too public for her bruised nerves just now. What if she should meet Humphrey there? And there was Lady Carrbridge, too, who was bound to try to throw them together. No, she would keep out of the way, until everyone had gone off on their various schemes. Lord Reginald and the Chamberlains were bound for York to see about wedding clothes. Lady Carrbridge was to accompany the aunts to the Dunborough's strawberry-picking party. The younger guests were to go to Harkwell for the village's midsummer feast. Before long, the house would be quiet and then she could slink out of her room in safety.

As soon as she dared, she donned her riding habit and crept away to the stables. Oh, the joy of having a decent horse to ride! As soon as she was settled somewhere, she would set up her stable. But not snooty London, or stuffy Bath. No, she knew where she wanted to live, and it was just a matter of finding the right estate to buy. There was a property for sale beyond Harkwell... but would Humphrey be angry if— No, she need not regard his wishes. He took no account of her feelings, so why should she consider his? She may live wherever she chose, for it was no concern of his.

As Tom was saddling Ganymede, a familiar face peeped out from one of the stalls further down. It always made her smile to see him, with his features so like Humphrey's.

"Hello there, Charlie! How are you?"

"Very well, ma'am," he said, coming boldly down to stroke Ganymede's nose.

"Keeping yourself out of trouble, are you?"

He laughed. "Good as gold, I am! Aren't I, Tom?"

"Mister Tom to you, if you don't mind," Tom said equably. "He's got the cheek of Old Nick himself, that lad has, and you don't want to go encouraging him, madam. But he hasn't put a foot wrong lately, I have to say."

"I am very glad to hear it," Hortensia said. "I am sure Lord Humphrey will be pleased." She was not at all sure why she mentioned Humphrey, except for the pleasure of hearing his name spoken, although there was a little stab of pain, too.

"Hope so," Charlie said, although a shadow crossed his face as he spoke. "He's been right good to me, speakin' up for me an' all. An' I hope he knows I'd do *anything* for him."

"I am sure he does," Hortensia said, absentmindedly, her thoughts already away on the moors, planning her first gallop. "Towards Mishmere today, Tom?"

The cloudless blue sky and the freshness of the air alone could not have lifted her spirits, but Ganymede's power and strength could and did. As she reined him in after their first gallop, she was laughing in delight, Humphrey almost banished from her thoughts.

But by the time she had returned to her room, all her gloom was back in full force. An hour or two of riding every day was not enough to relieve her dismals. There was nothing to be done but endure, and count the days until she could leave this place forever. Except, of course, that she would also be leaving Humphrey forever, and that brought the tears very close to the surface.

She had just changed into her morning gown and was about to dismiss the maid, when a scream echoed through the house, then another, followed by much shouting and the thumping of running feet. The maid's eyes were wide.

"Oh, Lor', now what?" she said.

"Let us go and see who is being murdered, shall we?" Hortensia said bracingly.

Upon opening the door, the yelling was louder, and emanating from further down the corridor.

"Leggo of me! Leggo!" a male voice shouted.

"Hold him! Don't let him escape! Letitia, grab his legs." Female voices, followed by more screaming.

Hortensia set off at a fast pace, rounding a corner only to run full pelt into a crowd of women in the sombre attire of lady's maids. On the ground, pinned down by two solidly built women of at least sixty, was Charlie. A younger woman was crying, and another had a bloody nose. They were all so busy shouting instructions and urging each other on, that no one took the slightest notice of Hortensia's arrival.

"What is going on?" she cried. Then, louder, "Stop all this caterwauling at once!"

Silence fell, punctuated by sniffles, and an occasional wriggle from Charlie.

"Oh! Miss Quayle! Beg pardon, madam, but we was just apprehending this 'ere thief."

"It's one of the grooms, by 'is uniform," another said. "Shouldn't even be in the 'ouse."

That was true enough. It was going to be difficult to explain away Charlie's behaviour, yet it had to be done. He was family, and if he were to be hauled off to the constables, or, even worse, transported to Australia, it would be a dreadful thing for the marquess and marchioness. Could one be hanged for stealing? She could not say for certain.

"Yes, but do get off him," Hortensia said. "He will suffocate, you know, if you sit on his head."

"But if we do, he might escape!"

"If you do not, he will die and you will likely be charged with murder, but the choice is yours. Have you some rope or some such? Strong ribbons? Good. Fetch some and we shall bind his hands. And feet, to be safe."

Cautiously, the two women moved off Charlie, while another of their number, perhaps more sensible, tied Charlie's hands and feet with strong twine. He gazed at them with wary eyes, but made no further attempts to escape.

"There now, he is quite safe, and you may tell me what has happened here," Hortensia said.

"Why, I caught him in the very act of thieving, ma'am. Caught him in Lady Patience's room, with the jewellery box open."

"He had the stolen item in his hand?"

"Well... no, madam, but I'm sure he put something in his pocket — that pocket there."

Hortensia's heart plummeted. If Charlie had been doing no more than snooping about it would have been possible to explain it away, but actual stealing was another matter. But there was no help for it. "Charlie, I must look in your pocket. You understand, I am sure." She gave him her most meaningful glance, but she could not speak more explicitly and could only hope that he understood she was on his side.

He raised fearful eyes to her, but gave a quick nod of acknowledgement.

She knelt beside him. Gingerly, she put her hand in his pocket... and drew out a dazzling necklace encrusted with emeralds. The assembled ladies all gasped. Hortensia rocked back on her heels. A brooch could be explained away, even a diamond pendant, if it were small, but this... it was worth a fortune. What on earth had he been thinking? But there was no possibility of explaining it away.

Two footmen had now appeared at a run, and, to Hortensia's relief, Mr Merton. He, at least, would appreciate the delicacy of the problem. She drew him aside, and in a few quick sentences, told him what had happened.

"He will have to go to the constables," Mr Merton said in the same quiet tone. "I see no help for it. Nor can we expect leniency from the magistrate, not for a groom, whoever his father may be."

But that gave Hortensia the glimmering of an idea. "Mr Merton, can you contrive to get me two minutes alone with him? Or with no one but you? I need to talk to him privately."

He asked no questions. "Basset, Gaffney, we will take him down to the blue room for now. Ladies, you may return to your duties. Miss Quayle and I will see this fellow on his way to the constables in Sagborough. Miss Cartwright, this is your mistress's necklace, I believe? Pray see it safely stowed away. Miss Quayle?"

Almost, he got away with it. His tone was so authoritative, in his quiet way, that the younger lady's maids began to drift away. But the two stout older women who had been sitting on Charlie were not so easily deterred.

"I need to go with him," Miss Cartright said, pursing her lips. "I have to bear witness against him. Saw him with my own eyes, so I did."

"You may bear witness at his trial," Mr Merton said in his mild way.

"I shall tell my tale to the constables," she said determinedly. "And Miss Wilde here will come with me, to bear witness to his attempts to escape, which speaks forcibly of his guilt. I know my duty, Mr Merton."

"Very well," he said, giving no sign of alarm. "Miss Cartwright and Miss Wilde may accompany him to Sagborough. Pray fetch your bonnets, ladies. The rest of you — about your duties, if you please."

"Bring a Bible, ladies," Hortensia said. "You may instil a degree of penitence in the prisoner on the journey by reading him improving verses."

Charlie rolled his eyes, but Hortensia merely glowered at him. The ladies disappeared, and the two footmen hauled Charlie to his feet, and assisted him towards the stairs. Mr Merton and Hortensia followed at a little distance.

"Do you have a plan?" Mr Merton whispered. She nodded, and he gave a very slight smile. "It had better be a good one," he said.

She was not sure whether it was good or not, but it was certainly audacious, as it must necessarily be, given the tight spot that Charlie was in.

The blue room was a small, unwelcoming room beside the main entrance. She guessed it was a place where unexpected visitors might be deposited while the butler determined what to do with them. There was no fire, no tray of decanters, nothing but a ring of firmly padded chairs and a few undistinguished paintings on the walls. Charlie was plopped unceremoniously on a chair. He said nothing, but he was white-faced and his eyes were huge with fear.

Again, Mr Merton took charge of the situation. "Basset, pray order the carriage brought round for a journey to Sagborough. The smaller chaise. Gaffney, fetch some brandy. The prisoner looks like to swoon, and I could use some myself."

The two footmen left the room without questioning the orders, but Hortensia was puzzled.

"You sent the senior man to order the carriage, and the junior for brandy?"

"It takes longer that way — Gaffney will have to go to Crabbe for the brandy. Say what you have to say, Miss Quayle, for we have but little time."

She nodded. "Charlie," she began, "believe me when I say I intend to get you out of this mess, if only for Lord Carrbridge's sake. You are family, so exertions must be made. I have no idea what made you do this, but—"

"Why, for Lord Humphrey!" he said, in surprised tones. "So he can have this gaming house he wants. He's been so good to me, that—"

"You are an idiot, Charlie," she said briskly. "Now, listen carefully. When you get to Sagborough, let them arrest you and lock you up. Then, and only then, you will tell them that you are Lord Humphrey Marford. You had a bet with Mr Merton here to get yourself arrested for... how much would you wager, Mr Merton?"

"That will never work," Mr Merton said with alarm. "He may *look* like Lord Humphrey, but—"

"Nonsense!" Charlie said, in his plummiest accent. "I assure you, my dear fellow, I shall have not the least difficulty in persuading the constables that I am Lord Humphrey."

Mr Merton's eyes widened, but with only the merest hesitation, he said, "Five hundred. That would be about Lord Humphrey's level."

"Very well. The bet was for a monkey, do you understand, Charlie? And you must pretend to be Lord Humphrey, and not let up for a moment, no matter what happens, understood?"

His eyes gleamed. "Oh, yes! A monkey, a wager to get myself arrested, keep up the accent. I can do that."

"They will not release him," Mr Merton said, urgently. "Not just because he says he is Lord Humphrey, no matter how convincing."

"No, the case will have to go to the magistrate. But you need not worry, Charlie. Just remember, you are Lord Humphrey Marford. You are the son of a marquess, remember?"

"Aye, and I really am," he said, grinning. "You're very clever, miss."

"We shall see," she said. "Do not let me down. Mr Merton, may I trouble you for a note detailing the bet? To convince the magistrate."

He nodded, understanding. Hortensia exhaled slowly. It was a relief to have Mr Merton involved, for he was very quick on the uptake, and entirely to be relied upon.

Just then, Gaffney returned with the brandy, with Crabbe and another couple of footmen in attendance, and there was no more opportunity for private talk. Hortensia could only hope it had been enough. Mr Merton slipped away, and returned soon after, pushing a piece of paper into her hand. Shortly after that Miss Cartwright and Miss Wilde appeared, one holding a Bible and the other the book of common prayer, so it was to be supposed that Charlie would have a dull time of it on his journey to Sagborough.

The carriage was brought round, Charlie and the two ladies were disposed within it, and, after some discussion, Mr Merton and Gaffney, the largest footman in the house, were squeezed in also, and the carriage rolled on its ponderous way.

Then Hortensia turned, and fled through the house to the stables.

"Tom! Tom, where are you? *Tom!*" She raced up one side of the stables, then back down the other. "*Tom!*"

"Here, madam."

"Oh, thank God! Where is Lord Humphrey, do you know?"

"Aye, he went off to Tambray Hall with Lady Harriet in her carriage not half an hour ago."

She made rapid calculations in her head. "Yes, that is possible — just. But there is no time to be lost. Tom, I need the curricle, right now. Please have the greys harnessed at once."

"Lord Humphrey's curricle, madam?"

"Yes, of course! At once! It is imperative!"

To her enormous relief, he did not quibble, but instantly nodded once. "Twenty minutes, madam."

"Make it fifteen. I shall be back directly."

She ran again, first to the attics, and then to her own room for a pelisse and bonnet and gloves, and a small portmanteau. Then another race back to the stables, where the greys were already waiting. She tossed the portmanteau onto the rumble seat, and jumped up onto the driving seat.

"Tom, you are wonderful. Pray get us moving while I fasten these wretched buttons."

"Aye, madam."

They clattered over the cobbles and out under the arch, Tom expertly deploying the whip, while Hortensia fastened the tiny pearl buttons on her pelisse, and then tied the ribbons on her bonnet.

"Oh, the devil take it! I forgot my gloves. Never mind, I daresay I may drive well enough without them. Let me have the reins now, Tom, and hold tight, for I am going to spring them."

Tom blew the horn to alert the lodge to open the gates, and they tore through as if on fire, and then on through the village, the horn again in use to ensure no one stepped inadvertently in front of them. Hortensia hardly noticed, being fully occupied in controlling the spirited horses, who were well pleased to be allowed to proceed at such a pace, and most unwilling to slow down for the least obstacle. They passed within an inch of the parson's gig, startling the two ladies it conveyed, and then neatly dived through a curricle-sized gap between a cart full of carrots and a carriage that looked familiar.

"Oh, well done!" Tom cried. "A fine piece of driving, Miss Quayle!"

"Thank you, but was that a Drummoor outfit?" she said.

"Lady Moorfield and Lady Patience," he said. "Don't worry, we went past so quick, I'll wager they never saw a thing."

"It cannot be helped if they did," she said. "Which way to Tambray Hall, Tom?"

"Next left, madam. It's a tight corner, with a mile post on the inside. After that, you should have a clear road until close to Camnay Farm, where the hay wains will be out for scything the two big meadows."

They drove in almost total silence, Hortensia concentrating on the horses, and Tom making only the occasional remark to warn of turns and possible hazards. In not much more than half an hour, therefore, they came to the neat stone wall that marked the southern perimeter of Tambray Hall. Approaching them in the opposite direction was Lady Harriet's neat carriage.

"Devil take it!" Hortensia said, pulling the curricle to a halt in the very centre of the lane so that carriage would be forced to stop. "I had hoped to reach him before they even arrived here. Now we have a problem."

Two heads peered out of either side of the carriage as it slowed to a halt. Even before the wheels had stopped turning, one door flew open and Humphrey descended in a lather of indignation.

"Tom, what the devil are you about—? Oh! Miss Quayle? What is going on?"

"I must take you to Sagborough, Humphrey, but you have quite spoilt my devious plan, for you have already called at Tambray Hall and now — good day to you, Lady Harriet! — and now Lord and Lady Melthwaite have seen you, and it is imperative that no one should know where you are. But it is too late and I am very cross with you."

He smiled up at her, not in the least disconcerted. "I would by no means spoil any plan of yours, Miss Quayle, devious or otherwise. But pray explain it all to me, and perhaps we may contrive some amendment which will make you less cross."

And her stomach fluttered at the affection in his voice, and the warmth of his smile. She could not help herself from smiling back just as warmly.

Beside them, Lady Harriet looked from one to the other, and murmured, "Well, well, well. So that is how it is."

Quickly, Hortensia explained about the stolen necklace, and how Charlie had been hauled off to the constables. "So you see, we must help him! You do understand, do you not?"

Humphrey laughed. "Oh, yes! And how are we to do that? Are we going to spring him from prison?"

"Of course!" she said. "At least — *you* are, Humphrey."

18: Sagborough

Humphrey could not help laughing, partly from exhilaration, for what could be better than breaking into the prison at Sagborough and snaffling a prisoner from under the noses of the constables? But partly, it was the excitement on Hortensia's face, which so exactly matched his own. What a woman she was! No weeping or wailing or hand-wringing for her. Instead, she formulated a plan and carried it out. Although...

He frowned. "I am not quite sure how it is to be done. The prison is moderately secure, you know. How are we to break in?"

"Oh, no necessity for breaking in. You will walk in through the front door."

His frown deepened. "But—"

"And he will walk out of it. Do you not see? I have told him to tell the constables that he is you."

"But that will not work! If I go into the prison, the constables will see at once that there are two of us who look exactly the same."

"Really, Humphrey!" she cried. "You are very slow today. Naturally you will not walk in looking as you do now. You will be a parson — I have brought some clothes from the play attic, although I hope they fit, for you are very large, it must be said. I even have a Bible for you, but you must think up a name for yourself and a reason why you have been asked to go there, for I cannot think of every little detail. Then, when you go in, you must ask to be alone with the prisoner, you know — so that he might confess, or some such. Then you switch clothes, and Charlie walks out as the parson."

Humphrey was laughing so hard by this time that he could form no coherent sentences. It was Harriet who began to object.

"But that just puts Humphrey in prison instead of Charlie, so it seems to me that he is in just the same difficulty."

"No, no!" Humphrey said, trying to stop laughing and not quite succeeding. "Do you not see? If Charlie is caught stealing, he will be hanged for it, or at best transported. But Lord Humphrey Marford pretending to be a groom and stealing a necklace for a wager?"

"Oh, I see," Harriet said. "A slapped wrist, perhaps, or a few days in prison, depending on the magistrate."

That set Humphrey off again. "Oh yes, depending on the magistrate!"

"But there is a difficulty," Hortensia said. "I had hoped to intercept you before you called on Lord and Lady Melthwaite, but now they know that you were here this morning, so you could not be in the carriage on your way to Sagborough at the same time."

"A great many people know where Humphrey was bound," Harriet said. "His valet, several grooms, my coachman, although he will say nothing of it."

"They are all servants," Hortensia said. "But if Lord Melthwaite tells everyone that you were here—"

"But I was not," Humphrey said. "Obviously, I cannot be here, since I am busy stealing a necklace and being hauled off to Sagborough. However, someone impersonating me might possibly have been here."

"Ohhh!" breathed Hortensia. "How splendidly ingenious! Naturally you bribed Charlie to take your place on the visit to Tambray Hall."

Harriet laughed, but shook her head also. "You are both insane, and possibly even brazen enough to pull it off. You may be assured of my secrecy, and Merton is discretion itself, so you need have no fears there. Good luck, Humphrey, and congratulations, Miss Quayle."

"Erm, thank you, but—?"

"I never thought Humphrey would ever find his equal in daring, but it seems he has. You are very well matched, and will be very happy together, I daresay, if you can avoid being hanged first. Good day to you both, and enjoy your stay in prison, Humphrey. I shall tell Connie not to wait dinner on your account."

And with that she climbed back into her carriage, the impassive coachman manoeuvred past the curricle and the equipage disappeared towards Drummoor in a cloud of dust.

Tom scrambled into the rumble seat while Humphrey climbed into the curricle. "Shall you drive, my lord?" Hortensia said in a small voice.

"You seems to be doing perfectly well," he said. "Pray continue, Miss Quayle."

They drove on for some miles, rehearsing the story again, but Humphrey cursed Harriet for her foolish clumsiness. If she had said nothing, they would have gone on in the highest spirits. Hortensia had called him by name, in the most delightful manner, and he had had the most tremendous difficulty in not calling her by name, too. Now the casual mention of them being *'well matched'* had set a damper on the spirits of both. There was a constraint between them, and how he hated it! In the two days since the outing to Branksford Abbey, they had hardly spoken a word to each other, apart from polite greetings and requests to pass the buttered prawns. She still wore her drably unadorned greys and lilacs, and still passed almost unnoticed amongst the company as the mousy companion, Miss Quayle. No one appreciated her but Humphrey, for even Julius had been routed, yet they were as strangers to each other.

But as they neared Sagborough, and the leafy lanes and golden fields gave way to cottages and then houses and finally the many-storeyed buildings of the town, gradually she began to relax and even smile a little, as the excitement of the venture could not be suppressed. He directed her off the main road into small, quiet back lanes and they drove to a secluded spot at the rear of the prison, shielded from view by a wing of the building and some overgrown pear trees. Here Humphrey donned the greatcoat, wig and hat of a clergyman.

"You forgot a plain neckcloth," he said, struggling into the coat with Tom's laughing assistance, for it was several sizes too small.

"I packed a scarf," she said. "That will have to do to hide your magnificently arranged cravat. Oh dear! That coat has surely not been in fashion these thirty years. "

"Poor Billings!" he said, shaking spiders from the wig. "If he could see me now, he would give notice on the spot."

"No, he would not, for you are not Lord Humphrey Marford at this moment," she retorted. "Who are you, in point of fact?"

"I am Mr Nathanial Hay, the parson of St Simeon's Church in the parish of Mishcombe," he said at once, in the quavering voice of a septuagenarian. "I was summoned by... someone, I shall think who it might be presently... and informed that Lord Humphrey was in trouble and— Lady Hester, of course! No one would question the wishes of such a sweet old lady. Lady Hester sent me to talk sense into her foolish great-nephew. There, will I do?"

She giggled. "Poor Mr Hay! Such a dapper little man. I dare swear he never in his life looked so disreputable as you do now. Let us hope no one in Sagborough knows the real Mr Hay. But you will carry it off admirably, Humphrey. Good luck! Oh, I almost forgot." She fished the rumpled note from Mr Merton out of her pocket. "You will need this for the magistrate. Go on now."

He stood beside the curricle, and took one of her hands. "Thank you, Hortensia. I hope Charlie is suitably grateful for all this. Oh — but what are you planning to do with him?"

She was blushing furiously at the use of her name, and when she answered her voice was not quite even. "Why, take him straight back to Drummoor. Where else should he go?"

"I am not sure, but not there. If any of the maids should see him—"

"Oh. Yes, of course. What about the inn where you met him?"

"I have a better idea. Take him to Silsby Vale House, where his mother is cook. She can knock some sense into his skull, if anybody can. Tom knows the way to Silsby Vale, then Charlie can direct you from there. I must go, but... Hortensia, do not wait here too long for Charlie. If this goes wrong, neither of us will be coming out tonight. When the church clock next strikes the hour, you must go, understand?"

She nodded. "You will be all right? I mean — you will not be transported or anything of the sort? I should not like that at all!"

"Neither should I," he said, smiling up at her suddenly anxious face. "Have no fear, the magistrate will treat gently with me."

"Of course, for you will know him well, I daresay. You probably dine with him."

Humphrey laughed. "Most assuredly, and I shall not even have to suffer the rigours of prison for very long. The court is in session tomorrow, so I shall be home in time for dinner and we shall drink champagne and toast the success of our little adventure. Good bye for now."

"God be with you," she said quietly.

Reluctantly he released her hand and strode away. At the corner, he looked back to see her white face watching him. She gave him a tremulous smile, and he responded with a little wave. Then he turned the corner, walked along to the entrance to the constables' house, and pushed open the door, remembering to stoop a little, since he was an elderly parson now.

It was a dispiriting place, the constables' house, just a few rooms squeezed between the courthouse and the cells. There were only two public rooms, one an office and the other fitted with benches for those awaiting the release of a prisoner. Since both had a propensity to be filled to overflowing with argumentative drunken farm labourers on market and festival days, the furnishings had the tired air of battle-hardened survivors, covered with dents and scratches, and not a chair or table in the place with four solid legs.

All was quiet today, and one of the constables bustled out from the rear rooms, where he had no doubt been enjoying his dinner, judging by the spot of gravy on his chin. He was a well-rounded man, who would undoubtedly enjoy his meal, and not be happy to have it interrupted. But he understood the significance of the parson's hat and the Bible, and made a passable effort at a smile.

"Good day to you, sir. How may I be of service to you?"

"I am Mr Nathanial Hay, parson of St Simeon's Church in the parish of Mishcombe, by Drummoor," Humphrey began, in his querulous voice. "I understand you have one of my parishioners in your care just now, my good sir. Lord Humphrey Marford."

The constable's eyebrows rose. "Well, he *says* he's Lord Humphrey, sir, but he ain't no gentleman, by his manner o' dress, sir."

"Ah, the foolish boy! These nobles, they will have their little jests! And their little wagers. Has he not explained how it came about?"

"Oh, yes, sir, but... so he really *is* Lord Humphrey? Lor' love me, I'd never have guessed it! But a charge has been laid, sir, and he'll have to go up before the magistrate tomorrow."

"Of course, of course! I expect nothing less of you, my good man. You carry out your duties in the most exemplary manner. The citizens of Sagborough must sleep easier in their beds at night knowing that the splendid men of the constabulary are protecting them."

The constable's chest puffed out a little. "Why, thank'ee, sir! It's right grand to be appreciated, like."

"No, Lord Humphrey has made his bed, and now he must lie on it, eh? He will see how the magistrate likes his little joke. But his great-aunt, Lady Hester, is most concerned for his immortal soul, and has asked me if I might visit him in his rough cell and induce him to pray with me."

"Ah, Lady Hester!" the constable said, his face softening. "Such a beauty she was, in her day. My old da', he danced with her once, at the harvest ball at the assembly rooms. They don't come to the harvest ball no more, the Marfords, but in those days they did, and danced with anyone who asked 'em. I remember her well. Anything to oblige poor Lady Hester. How is she, the dear, sweet lady?"

"Very frail, but in good spirits, as always."

"Tell her we've not forgot her here in Sagborough. This way, sir, and mind that beam or you'll crack your skull, a great, tall gentleman like yourself. Down this way — watch that flag, sir, it's a bit uneven. Here he is, sir, the prisoner." He rattled his keys, the lock creaked and a heavily studded door was flung open. "I'll just wait out here, sir."

"No need, my good man. You may lock me in with him, so that you need not fear he will escape, while you have a few minutes to finish your dinner. Let us have... oh, twenty minutes for quiet prayer and reflection."

"Well, now, I'm not sure..."

"You would not want to deprive a man of his chance to talk privily with a man of God, I am certain."

"Oh no, not at all, sir. Twenty minutes, then."

The keys rattled, the lock clanked, and the constable's ponderous footsteps echoed into the distance. Then silence fell. The cell was a gloomy place, lit by one barred window high up on the wall. Apart from a bucket and a wooden shelf against the wall, to act as both seat and bed, the room was unfurnished.

Humphrey turned to Charlie, who was sitting on the bench watching him with a bemused expression on his face.

"I say, who are you?" Charlie said, in the polished voice of a nobleman. "I did not send for you."

"Well done, Charlie! Very impressive, but you can drop that voice now."

"Milord?"

"Well spotted. Can you do my parson's accent, do you think?"

"Of course I can, my good man," Charlie said at once, in quavering tones.

Humphrey grinned. "Excellent. Get your clothes off and put these on, and you will walk out of here a free man in under twenty minutes."

"What? Not a chance," Charlie said. "I'll not let you do this for me."

"But I will not have to," Humphrey said. "No one is going to hang the brother of the Marquess of Carrbridge."

"Which is me, just now. I can do it, you know I can — convince everyone I'm you, like."

"Only by perjuring yourself in court." Charlie looked at him blankly. "Only by lying. Whereas I really am the marquess's brother. No lies needed. Well, not many. The magistrate will waggle a finger at me and tell me not to do it again. No time for arguments, Charlie, just swap clothes quickly otherwise you will get me into hot water too."

"Oh. Don't want to do that, milord. I'd do anything for you, you know that. Don't never want to get you into trouble." And he began shrugging out of his clothes.

They both had a little difficulty with their new attire. Humphrey had trouble squeezing himself into Charlie's tight-fitting uniform, and Charlie could do nothing with Humphrey's cravat. In the end, Humphrey tied it for him in a simple knot, trying to suppress Billings' anguished countenance from his mind, and hoping that the scarf and greatcoat would cover the mess.

The constable's heavy tread was already approaching, when Humphrey grabbed the Bible and slammed Charlie's hand onto it. "Swear to me right now that you will never do anything like this again."

"I swear it. And... thank you, milord. Thank you."

Then the keys rattled, the lock creaked and the door swung open. "You finished, Mr Hay, sir?"

"I am, my good fellow," said Charlie, in such an authentically querulous voice that Humphrey was lost in admiration. "We have prayed together, and I must hope that his lordship is in a more penitent frame of mind. Good day to you, my lord."

"Good day, Mr Hay," Humphrey said in his own voice. "Thank you for visiting me. Pray give my regards to Miss Hay and Miss Agnes."

"I shall do so. May God forgive you your sins, my lord."

And so saying, Charlie swept out, head high, the Bible under his arm.

The door clanged shut, and Humphrey started to laugh. Then, he settled himself on the bench as comfortably as he could, and prepared for a long, uncomfortable night.

19: *Repose And Reparations*

Hortensia had twice to walk the greys about while she waited, to prevent them from getting cold. Three times she sent Tom out into the square to read the time from the church clock. But before the hour struck, a tall figure in greatcoat, wig and hat came round the corner. Her heart lurched, but then she saw at once that it was not Humphrey. Something about the set of the shoulders was all wrong. Charlie had almost as much height as Humphrey, but he had not the same breadth of shoulders.

She should have been pleased that their little scheme had succeeded but instead she was rather downcast. Humphrey was in prison, and there was no knowing how that would end. Oh, if only he were there beside her, smiling up at her in that heart-stopping way of his, holding her hand—

No, this would never do. She needed to pull herself together. Charlie climbed nimbly into the curricle without a word, and Hortensia set the horses in motion at once. Tom, who had been holding their heads, jumped up behind them. They clattered through the cobbled streets of Sagborough at a sedate pace, so as not to attract too much attention, but they were an odd grouping altogether — a rich gentleman's curricle being driven by a lady and with a seemingly elderly and ill-dressed parson as a passenger.

Turning onto the York road, they passed some fine old buildings clustered around a market square and then a range of working yards for a barrel-maker, an ironmonger, a glass-blower and a brewer, before the town abruptly ended with two or three larger properties ringed by walls and high railings. Almost at once, they plunged into woodland. After a mile or so, they turned again onto a smaller road following a lively stream dotted with small mills and their clusters of cottages. Then more woodland, followed by good farm land, the fields studded with cattle. The hedgerows rose on either side of them, the great heads of cow parsley nodding gently. Bees hummed in the afternoon sun, and every mile, every new vista of splendid English countryside raised Hortensia's spirits a notch.

They crossed another road from York, and then dropped down into a broad valley.

"Wait a minute," Charlie said. "This ain't the way to the marquess's house. This is Silsby Vale."

"Indeed it is," Hortensia said. "Lord Humphrey felt it would be safer for you if you do not return to Drummoor for a while. If any of the ladies' maids who saw you today were to recognise you in the stables, there could be some very awkward questions asked. I am taking you to stay with your mother for a while."

"Oh." He was silent for a while. "'is lordship said I was to go there?"

"He did."

"Then I will, although I don't know as anyone there'll be very 'appy to see me, like."

Hortensia noted the sudden lapse into the local vernacular, and Charlie's left foot tap-tap-tapping nervously. "If you are not content to stay there, Charlie, I shall take you somewhere else," she said, although she had no idea where that might be.

"You're very kind," he said, and almost his voice seemed to be breaking. "Don't know why you'd do anything for me."

"Because you are half-brother to the Marquess of Carrbridge," she said gently. "For his part, he wishes to take care of you and see you respectably established. I hope you wish also to do him credit, and to do nothing to bring dishonour on the family."

"I do!" he cried. "I do wish that... not bringing dishonour... everything you said. But it's difficult sometimes to know what to do. I'd like to help Lord Humphrey, but I seem to make a mess of it. I only wanted to help him get his gaming house, and I thought those rich ladies wouldn't miss a few bits and pieces."

"A few!" she said in alarm. "Did you take anything else, Charlie?"

He hesitated, and she could almost hear him considering lying. But then the shoulders slumped. "A couple of things."

"Where are they? Not in your room, I hope?"

"Nah, not that stupid! There's a big jug thing with birds on it near the top of the stairs by the long room with all the paintings. They're in there."

Hortensia interpreted this to be the Chinese vase near the gallery. "I shall retrieve them, if I can. But Charlie, you must never do anything like this again, do you understand?"

"Aye. So 'is lordship said. Made me swear on the Bible, miss."

He sounded so indignant that she could not help laughing. "Never mind, Charlie. A blameless life may be dull, but at least it will not be cut short by the hangman."

"But what's going to happen to me now, miss? I s'pose I can't go back to Drummoor."

"Probably not. It is too confusing having two of you looking so alike, when you can imitate each other so well. One would never know whether one was talking to Lord Humphrey or you. I expect we shall find you some honest employment somewhere. Although…"

"Yes, miss?" he said hopefully.

"With your talents, a life on the boards would be a possibility. Acting, Charlie, in a theatre. Would you like that?"

"Not sure, miss — madam. Never been to a theatre."

"We must take you to one, then you could decide whether it might suit you. Ah, we are coming into the village. Direct me to Silsby Vale House, Charlie."

The village straggled in a listless way along both sides of the stream. About a mile beyond the last house, they came to palings and, before long, an entrance, the gate standing wide open. Hortensia turned the curricle between the gateposts and up a short drive to the house. There she stopped, breathed an 'Ohhh!' of delight and gazed about her.

The house drowsed in the afternoon sun, its stone walls a delicate pink that was both warm and elegant. Roses and summer jasmine mingled over the front door, filling the air with heady perfume. Insects hummed and buzzed, and vivid orange butterflies fluttered in profusion over many-coloured beds of flowers. Beyond the house, a willow whispered over a small pond.

Hortensia was mesmerised, quite unable to move. The house was so quintessentially English, its comforting serenity as familiar as a favourite shawl, that she felt, for some unfathomable reason, that she had come home.

Then the front door opened, and down the steps came one of the footmen from Drummoor.

"Fitch? Goodness, what are you doing here?"

"I was sent to help out, madam. May I assist you to alight?"

"Oh — no, thank you, Fitch. I can manage." Lightly, she jumped down onto the gravel drive, still gazing around, breathing deeply to absorb the intoxicating air. It was a place of enchantment, which left her feeling as if she had stepped into a painting.

"The mistress is in the garden," Fitch said. "May I take you to her? Tom can see to the horses. And... the other person." He gazed with disfavour on Charlie, still in his parson's disguise.

Dreamily, Hortensia followed him round the side of the house, past the pond, to a lawn surrounded by a semi-circle of towering rhododendrons, their great flower heads a fiery red. In the centre of the lawn, a lady sat at her ease on a comfortable chair. Perhaps she had been sleeping, for there were pillows at her back and a footstool at her feet, but she sat alertly now, looking eagerly towards Hortensia crossing the lawn, then rising to greet her.

"Miss Quayle, madam," Fitch said.

"Oh! How do you do?" her hostess said with a tremulous smile, holding out her hand in a delightfully informal manner. "I am Maria Andrews, widow of Mr Cecil Andrews. How charming of you to call, although I do not believe we have met?"

Hortensia curtsied, shook the proffered hand and returned the smile. Mrs Andrews was an amply endowed lady of middle years, her gown a good, if home-stitched, effort at fashionable style. The chair she had risen from was worn, and in need of recovering. At a guess, Mrs Andrews was struggling to survive on a widow's stipend.

"I beg your pardon for descending on you so unexpectedly. I am from Drummoor—"

"Oh!" Mrs Andrews raised a hand to her mouth. "Oh dear! Is it... is it about Mr Sharp?"

"Mr Sharp? No, I know nothing about a Mr Sharp. It is about Charlie, your cook's son."

"Oh, *Charlie*. Oh, thank goodness!" She laughed. "Please, will you not sit and tell me all about it?"

Another chair was brought out, tea and cake ordered and Hortensia explained briefly about Charlie, before launching into her paean of praise for the house. Within half an hour, Mrs Andrews had told her the whole history of it, and her own unhappy tale. Within an hour, Hortensia, in her turn, had unburdened herself to her new acquaintance, who instantly sympathised with the difficulties of sudden wealth and switching places and attractive young men. They both cried a little, and Hortensia felt immeasurably better.

"Oh, this house is so restful!" she cried. "How lucky you are to live here."

"True enough," Mrs Andrews said. "Now that Mr Sharp comes here no more, the place is just as it ought to be — a peaceful haven. At least, I do *hope* he comes here no more. Lord Humphrey said... but I cannot be quite easy about it, all the same. For if he *should* return, he would be very cross to see me sitting outside like this, and entertaining in this way. But if anybody calls on me, I cannot turn them away, can I? It is only polite to receive callers. And I do so enjoy company, and sitting in my garden and being at peace. I *am* very fortunate, am I not? But I daresay I shall be obliged to leave here soon."

"Oh no! But why so?"

"Why, because his lordship will want to get full value for it, either by selling it, or finding a tenant willing to pay rent, which I cannot afford to do."

Hortensia stared at her, suddenly unable to breathe. "No, but I can! I can afford rent, or — I could even buy it, if Lord Carrbridge would sell. Mrs Andrews, how would you like to live here forever, as my companion?"

~~~~~

Hortensia returned to Drummoor too late to do more than throw on the gown chosen at random by her maid, thread a ribbon through her hair and rush down to dinner. No one noticed her arrival. The company was agog with excitement at the news that Lord Humphrey had been arrested, and Lady Patience, whose necklace had been stolen, was for once the focus of everyone's attention. No one mentioned the loss of any other jewellery, thank goodness! If the other two items had not yet been missed, there was still time to return them to their owners.

She had planned to slip away after dinner to retrieve them from the vase, but she was called upon to play the pianoforte to accompany one of the Whittleton ladies on the harp, and then to turn the pages for Rosemary. After that, she was immediately drawn into a game of whist, and the evening wore away without an opportunity. Her expedition to the vase would have to wait.

So it was after midnight before she crept from her room and through the night-darkened corridors. Twice she was almost caught out, once by a footman conveying a decanter of brandy to some sleepless soul, and once by a trysting couple whispering in a window embrasure, half hidden by the curtains. Was the gentleman Mr Merton? She rather thought it was. But eventually, by means of circuitous detours, she reached her destination.

There was no moon, but just enough light filtered through the window as to silhouette the Chinese vase. She slipped her hand inside, and pulled out two items, a hideous diamond choker and a massive ruby-studded ring. She could not imagine any person of fashion wearing either of them. Nor, more to the point, could she remember ever seeing either of them before. How on earth was she to replace them unnoticed if she had no idea who owned them?

She heard males voices coming up the gallery stairs and saw the wavering lights of a couple of candles, and her heart leapt into her mouth. And at that point, her courage failed her. It had been a long, trying day, she was exhausted and this was too difficult a problem for such an hour. She had no idea what to do with the jewellery, and she could not for the life of her bring herself to care about it. If only she had someone to talk it over with, someone to help her. She had never felt lonelier in her life.

Tears prickled at her eyelids. Sliding the jewellery soundlessly back into the vase, she slipped away into the night. Tomorrow, when Humphrey came home, she would ask him about it. He would know what to do! Humphrey always knew what to do. And perhaps, her heart whispered, he would look at her in that magical way and hold her hand. Perhaps he would call her Hortensia again… But she cried herself to sleep all the same.

~~~~~

It must have been the longest night in Christendom, or at least it seemed so to Humphrey. The constables called him *'milord',* and fed him bread and soup and ale at regular intervals, but he was very glad when he was led out of his small cell, allowed to wash and then taken to another cell below the courtroom. Then another interminable wait before he was taken up narrow stairs and into the close atmosphere of the courtroom, crowded with noisy spectators and the overpowering smell of unwashed humanity crushed together. And there facing him above the heads of the lawyers and court officials was the magistrate.

"Name," that gentleman said, not looking up from the paper he was reading.

"Lord Humphrey Marford," said Humphrey in ringing tones.

Heads turned, conversations died away, mouths dropped open. And then the entire courtroom burst into laughter. Even the magistrate quirked an eyebrow and gave a small, resigned sigh.

"Really, Humphrey," Lord Carrbridge said. "I do not expect to see my own brother brought before me."

"No, my lord. Quite so, my lord. Beg pardon, my lord," Humphrey said meekly.

That brought more gales of laughter. But they had to go through the formalities, and so the constable read the charges, and Humphrey agreed that, yes, he had stolen the necklace, but only for a bet. The details of the wager were discussed, Mr Merton, who was conveniently in the gallery, agreed that he had made the bet with Lord Humphrey, and the note was produced for Lord Carrbridge to inspect.

"You are very foolish, Humphrey," he said in his best peer of the realm voice. "You have caused a great deal of trouble and upset, and I cannot be seen to condone such behaviour. You will apologise to the ladies concerned, and recompense the constables with a barrel of ale. You are hereby fined five hundred pounds and bound over to keep the peace for a period of one year. Now go away and stop cluttering up my court."

"Yes, my lord. Thank you, my lord."

As he was released from the prisoner's box, he saw Miss Cartwright and Miss Wilde, their expressions a mixture of relief that it was only a mischievous prank and nothing more serious, and disappointment that they had not, after all, had their glorious moment in the witness box. He bowed and said all that was proper and invited them to the Carrbridge Arms across the road for refreshments, and after a glass or two of port, they declared him a silly boy, and *so* like his father, who was also a betting man and forever in one scrape or another. He listened politely while they regaled him with some very boring tales of the eighth marquess, and felt at the end of it that, whatever his crimes, he had been amply punished.

20: The Summer Ball

Hortensia waited in vain for Humphrey to return from Sagborough. The morning dragged on, and he did not come, leaving her in the most dreadful suspense. But shortly after noon, Mr Merton returned and sought her out, sending a message for her to attend him in the library. She found Lady Hardy there, too, with her piles of books for cataloguing, an endless task which Hortensia could not decide was a worthy enterprise or merely an excuse to linger a little longer in the hospitable shelter of Drummoor. Or perhaps the lingering was driven more by Mr Merton, for where one was, there the other generally seemed to be. And Hortensia wondered then about the midnight tryst that she had thought involved Mr Merton. Was the other party Lady Hardy? How interesting.

"Lord Humphrey was brought before Lord Carrbridge, and was merely fined, and bound over to keep the peace," Mr Merton said. "I felt sure you would wish to know at the earliest opportunity."

"Oh yes! Thank you! Will he be returning soon, do you suppose?"

"As to that, I left him doing penance with the two ladies' maids at the Carrbridge Arms. I imagine he will return with Lord Carrbridge later today, when court proceedings are suspended."

"Oh. Of course." The thought of the jewellery secreted in the Chinese vase niggled at her, like a persistent gnat. It was not of the greatest importance, but it was a matter which she could not resolve herself. So she explained the problem to Mr Merton, who at once grasped the significance.

"Indeed, these pieces must be returned to their owners as soon as possible, but the one person who knows whence they came is not here. However, if you will entrust me with the commission, Miss Quayle, I shall consult with Lord Humphrey when he returns and see if he is able to find a solution. It is not, I feel, a matter with which you should concern yourself."

"Oh, certainly not!" said Lady Hardy. "It is much better to leave all to Lord Humphrey. He has, after all, taken upon himself the role of thief, so it is for him to return the stolen items, in whatever manner seems good to him. Your involvement is not suspected, Miss Quayle, and so it should remain."

"On that point we are agreed," Mr Merton said. "You will excuse me, Lady Hardy, Miss Quayle, I am sure, if I return to my desk before we are overwhelmed by the evening's entertainments." He bowed and made his departure.

Lady Hardy shook her head and laughed. "Oh, this ball tonight! Connie does love to entertain. She was such a flighty little thing when she was younger, you know, but now look at her! A leader of society, and quite at home in the great houses of London or the shires. And such a matchmaker. She has you paired off with Lord Humphrey, as I am sure you are aware."

"I do not think that will work," Hortensia said, trying not to blush, but failing.

"There are difficulties, it is true," said Lady Hardy. "The position is awkward, and one cannot be too provocative without doing penance. But in time, if you are both patient, all will be well, I am sure of it. Wait but a few more months."

A few months! Hideous thought. Hortensia's head hung low. "Waiting is very trying."

Lady Hardy went on gently, "My dear, some things are well worth waiting for. Indeed, if an outcome is sufficiently desirable, one may wait for years in great contentment."

"May one?" Hortensia lifted her head a little, and saw that Lady Hardy was looking conscious. Was it possible that she was blushing? She was such a composed lady that it was hard to be sure, but it certainly seemed— Had she been waiting years for Mr Merton? Then they must have become attached while she was still married to Sir Osborne Hardy, and waited patiently through his long illness. Were still waiting, during her year of mourning. But then...

Could Hortensia wait so long for Humphrey? Yes of course, if it were necessary, but it was *not* necessary. There was no reason for him not to court her, and no reason for them not to marry. They were both of age, there was no insuperable gulf of situation that had not been bridged a thousand times before. A man of rank and a woman of fortune — it was an old story, which the world could hardly object to. And yet... he would not bridge that gulf, nor reach across it to claim her. Foolish, foolish man! They could be so happy, if only... Yet he was determined to make her miserable. And now she had a ball to endure.

A ball at Drummoor did not quite merit the extravagance it would require in London during the season, but it was still a spectacular event. There would be flowers, musicians and vast numbers of candles within the house and lanterns without. One hundred and twenty would sit down to dinner in the great hall, followed by a musical recital from two Italian opera singers in the long gallery, and then back to the great hall, the servants having by that time cleared the floor for dancing. And — a great excitement —

there were to be German waltzes, which threw all the young ladies into a flurry of giggling anticipation.

Except Hortensia. She could see no pleasure in the evening, for the dinner was to be preceded by an announcement from Lord Carrbridge, informing the world that Miss Hortensia Blythe and Miss Rosemary Quayle were not the people to whom those names had previously applied. That they were, in short, scheming deceivers. Even if he made light of it, and expressed the opinion that it was a very good joke, and how amusing that everyone had been taken in, she and Rosemary would still be sunk in the estimation of almost all the company.

She dressed with unusual care, selecting one of her finest ball gowns for the occasion, in a green silk so pale it was almost translucent, with a darker overtunic. For the first time, she opened her jewellery box and selected a simple diamond pendant that her father had given her for her sixteenth birthday. She allowed her maid to dress her hair with greater elaboration, with ribbons and feathers and a bejewelled bandeau. And then she went downstairs to meet her fate.

~~~~~

Humphrey had it all worked out in his mind. He would allow himself just one dance with Hortensia, and it must be a waltz, so that he could hold her hands and gaze into her eyes as they twirled about. That would have to be enough to sustain him through the next few months. He would need to leave Drummoor, of course, until she herself had quit it. Impossible to remain under the same roof without speaking, for he would be driven mad. So tonight he would dance with her, for his own sake, and tomorrow he would go away, for his brother's.

But the prospect made him desperately unhappy. How was he to go on without seeing her every day? Even when they passed whole evenings without speaking, he could still look at her, still see those beautiful eyes, and the little curls that fell against her soft cheeks, and bounced when she shook her head. And what would she do once he had left? Perhaps she would forget about him, and meet someone else she liked better and be lost to him for ever. Such was the fear that roiled constantly inside him.

If only he could simply scoop her up and ride off with her perched on his saddle bow, as the heroes of old did, or fly with her to the stars, like mythical gods. But there were no heroes or gods any more, only mortals bound by society's laws, and by God's.

The drawing room was already full before her arrival. With his greater height, Humphrey could look over the heads of the throng and so saw her slink inside surreptitiously as if to escape notice. His breath caught in his throat — this was how she should always look, with diamonds in her hair and around her neck, in a gown that made her look every inch the lady she was. The mousy companion was gone for good. But she did not see his admiration, for she kept her head down.

Without conscious thought, he found himself drawn towards her, gradually inching through the sea of feathered turbans towards her. But then dinner was announced and there was a general movement towards the doors and he lost sight of her. He found himself alongside one of the Miss Ellesmeres, who was smiling and bobbing her head at him in the most distracting way, like a hen. Eventually, he got the point, and offered her his arm. So there was his dinner companion chosen, and no possibility of finding his way to Hortensia's side.

Once he was seated, he looked around for her again but could not see her anywhere. It was only when Carrbridge stood to make his announcement that he realised that his brother must have led

Hortensia in, for there she was at the very head of the table beside him, and Miss Blythe — no, Miss Quayle — on his other side.

The butler banged his staff for silence, and Carrbridge began to speak.

"My lords, ladies and gentlemen, pray indulge me for a few moments to reveal to you a very clever joke which has been played on us all. For a month now, we have enjoyed the charming company of Miss Blythe and Miss Quayle, newly arrived on our shores from India, and we have come to know them both well. Now, it seems, we must adjust our ideas, for these two ladies have been teasing us. The lady we know as Miss Blythe..." He smiled at her and she rose to her feet, blushing. "...is in fact Miss Quayle. And the lady we have been addressing as Miss Quayle..." Hortensia rose, her face blank. Was that insouciance or terror? "...is actually Miss Blythe. Tonight, however, they reveal their secret to you all and take their places amongst you under their true names once more. Is it not a good joke?"

In what was clearly a rehearsed movement, the two swapped places, and Humphrey saw that Hortensia must have been led in by Lord Kilbraith, for he now had Miss Quayle's blonde head beside him, while Hortensia was between Carrbridge and Sir Richard Frimble.

There was some laughter, but most of the audience registered astonishment, rapidly succeeded by whispered disapproval, which lasted for most of the first course. Only when the wine had begun to flow freely, with the usual effect upon those imbibing, did the whispers give way to the customary levity of such occasions.

When the ladies had withdrawn, Humphrey found himself sought out by Kilbraith.

"I am glad it is all in the open at last," Kilbraith said in satisfaction. "Not that it makes the slightest difference to me, but it is best to have everything above board, and now we may... move forward."

"What will your father say when he finds out?" Humphrey said.

"He already knows, or at least, I had already conveyed to him my own suspicions on the matter. He assured me he would not regard it in the slightest, so long as Miss Quayle freely confesses all, as she has now done."

"Still, it will not go down well amongst the sticklers for propriety."

"I think we have fewer of that nature in Scotland than elsewhere," Kilbraith said, eyes twinkling. "None of the family ever go to London, preferring to seek our jollity in Edinburgh, so we need not mind our manners quite so much. But it is awkward for *you*. There will be those who sneer at Miss Blythe, and consider her quite beyond the pale on this account."

Humphrey grimaced in rueful agreement. "It would have been difficult enough overcoming the stigma of money from trade, nor does she have any connections of note, but this little game is most unfortunate. I had hoped that Carrbridge's treatment of it as a joke might have helped, but it seems that Miss Blythe is to be subjected to a great deal of disapprobation."

"It is a setback, certainly," Kilbraith said. "Still, you will not let that weigh with you, surely? From what Miss Quayle tells me, her friend already has a great affection for you."

"I wish I could be sure of that," Humphrey said gloomily. "Affection or no, she thinks me a very poor-spirited creature, too timid for words."

"Surely not! After your bet with Mr Merton, and your daring in carrying out the enterprise?"

"I can be daring enough in such games," Humphrey said sorrowfully. "But I cannot aspire to equal Hortensia Blythe. She expects me to be as daring as she is, regardless of the consequences, and I fall woefully short. She is the bravest woman I ever met, Kilbraith, and I admire and respect her more than I can say, yet if I approach her, I set myself against the express wishes of my brother in the matter."

"Ah, that is awkward indeed. We are all of us bound by family loyalty and the bonds of blood before all else. And yet, would you set your own happiness and the lady's below your brother's? It may be that he does not appreciate the strength of your feelings."

"I have told him of it, but he expects me to wait a year, until any scandal has died down," Humphrey said.

"Well, that is perhaps sensible," Kilbraith said. "One does not like to take undue risks with a lady's reputation. Ah, we are moving already. Carrbridge is keen to hear the opera singers, it appears."

The musical recital was every bit as tedious as Humphrey had anticipated. Although some of the gentlemen slipped away to play cards in the tapestry room, the male retreat in times of great stress, such as a ball, he did not feel Connie would be best pleased if one of her brothers-in-law did the same. So he dutifully made his way there, fixed a smile of bland interest on his face and stood discreetly at the back, just below the portrait Great-Uncle Christopher, a high court judge with a fearsome reputation for hanging any man he took in dislike, regardless of the facts of the case or the supposed crime.

Humphrey's virtue was rewarded, however, for from his post beneath the judge's huge curled periwig and bushy eyebrows, he was able to watch Hortensia unobserved. She was worryingly pale, he saw, and although she had chosen an unobtrusive seat in a far corner of the gallery, she was surrounded by young men. They whispered in her ear, and smiled and preened and pointed to the printed order of songs, perhaps explaining the meaning of the Italian to her, while she shook her head repeatedly and returned them monosyllabic answers.

He had not previously appreciated the dramatic effect that the inheritance of two hundred thousand pounds might have on a young lady. Here was one who had been virtually ignored for a whole month, because she was only a companion, and therefore nobody of consequence. Who would bother to take notice of such a lowly person? Having neither wealth nor rank, and her beauty hidden behind unadorned attire and a retiring demeanour, not one man had thought to expend any effort in her direction. Only Humphrey had seen something more to her.

Yet now, not two hours since her true state had been revealed to the world, she was under siege. Julius had taken his broken nose away from Drummoor in high dudgeon, but two other Whittletons were in Hortensia's court, together with two Marford cousins, the Dunborough twins, a nephew of Sir Richard Frimble's and even Mr Dunshaw, the apothecary, who must be fifty if he was a day. Poor Hortensia! It was absolutely necessary to rescue her, and at once. But he could not get near her, for the room was crowded with chairs and people standing about.

As the recital ended and everyone was streaming out, he waited for her, but somewhere in the crowds, he missed her, and made his way alone down to the great hall. The tables had been cleared away to the sides of the room, and the empty floor awaited the dancers, as the musicians tuned their instruments. During dinner, a small number of them had played in the minstrels' gallery behind the carved wooden screen, but for the dancing greater numbers were required and they had abandoned the gallery in favour of a dais at one end of the hall.

The room was abuzz with excitement, feathers and fans waving, silk skirts shimmering and jewellery twinkling in the light of a myriad of candelabra. Humphrey walked slowly round the room, looking for a certain pale green gown and a bejewelled bandeau, but he could see no sign of her. When he eventually recognised the remnants of her court standing in a disconsolate cluster, he realised that she had slipped her leash and run away, and he could not blame her one bit. Yet that was so like her! She had not needed his help to escape her suitors after all. What a splendid woman she was.

But now she was gone and he would not, after all, be able to dance with her, and that was the end of any possibility of pleasure in the evening. The hours stretched dark and drear before him. No amount of candles could light the room when she was not in it. But then his eye caught a flash of green behind the screen of the minstrels' gallery. So that was where she was hiding herself! Well, it was a good spot, where she could watch the dancing, if she were so minded, without having to fend off her unwanted coterie of admirers. Somehow it lifted his spirits to know that she was there, close to him but safely hidden away, enjoying her solitude.

He stood moodily in a corner, supposedly watching the dancing, but in reality trying to detect the merest hint of green silk in the gallery above. Was she still there? He thought she was, but—

"Humphrey! Just the person I want."

"Connie," he said warily.

"If you are not dancing, then I have a commission for you."

"You have only to ask." But he was still wary. Usually such a request meant dancing with some half-grown miss who had not yet learnt the steps of the dance, but was very happy to bruise Humphrey's toes while she practised.

"I see that Miss Blythe is not yet dancing. Would you be so good as to find her, and see if you cannot persuade her to step onto the floor?"

"Connie, no!" His anguish was perfectly genuine. "I am not persuaded she would welcome such interference. If she wished to dance, then she would be here now. Do not ask it of me, for you know I cannot."

"I know no such thing, and if you are going to talk about some mysterious male code of conduct, you know I have no time for such foolishness. At least go and talk to her like a rational being instead of lurking about like a wet day in November, and putting a damper on everything."

He was torn, for the necessity to keep his distance from her was beyond question in his mind. Yet the prospect of seeing her, talking to her again was almost irresistible.

He sighed. "It will not hurt to talk to her, perhaps, but it will be entirely her choice whether she dances."

"Of course!" Connie said brightly. "Off you go."

21: The Minstrels' Gallery

Obediently, he crept out of the great hall and trod slowly, oh so slowly, up the chapel stairs, which were the nearest to the minstrels' gallery, then stood irresolutely just outside it. His heart hammered in his chest so hard that he felt as if he were shaking. Meeting her in public, in the crowded great hall — yes, he could have managed that with equanimity. He could even, he felt sure, have danced with her without making a co mplete fool of himself. But to seek her out privately, when she had deliberately secreted herself away... Connie should not have asked it of him. Such a romantic, Connie! She was certain that five minutes in each other's company would resolve all differences and enable them to live happily ever after. Would that it were so simple.

But it had to be done, so, taking a deep breath and then another, just to be sure, he entered the minstrels' gallery.

It was gloomy, the many lights from the hall below barely penetrating the heavily carved wooden screen. At first he could see nothing, but as his eyes adjusted to the reduced light, he caught a hint of green from the far end of the gallery.

"Miss Blythe?" he said, as he made his way towards her.

She was sitting on the bare wooden floor, her back to the wall, gloves and fan discarded. Her knees were drawn up, with her face resting on them. At the sound of his voice, her head shot up, and the sight of her tear-stained face tore at him in the most painful manner. His poor Hortensia! All he wanted to do was to sweep her into his arms and hug her tightly, kissing away all her grief. But somehow seven and twenty years of gentlemanly restraint held him in check.

"Do you wish me to go away? Should you prefer to be alone?"

She shook her head so decisively that he was heartened. Sitting down beside her, he stretched out his long legs and took her hand in his. Without gloves, the contact was extraordinarily intimate, the warmth of her fingers under his making it hard for him to speak. Yet she made no protest.

With an effort, he said, "I am so very sorry. This evening must be difficult for you." She nodded, not looking at him. "The fuss will die down, in time," he went on. "It will be a great wonder for a while, as the word spreads of your little deception, but it will be forgotten eventually when some new scandal erupts."

"Oh, that. I do not regard *that* in the least," she said, sounding surprised. "It is a relief to set it all behind me, and it will not change anything between Rosemary and Lord Kilbraith, so I cannot but be happy about it."

"Oh. Then perhaps it is the unwanted attention from suitors that distresses you?"

"That is tedious, certainly, but I do not cry because I am suddenly popular."

"Then... why?"

She looked him full in the face. "You said we would drink champagne together."

Pain washed through him. So that was why she was so upset! He had been so lost in his own misery, he had quite forgotten his promise. Stupid, stupid, stupid! How could he have been so thoughtless? "So I did! How unforgivable of me not to honour my promise. Miss Blythe, may I fetch you a glass of champagne?"

She nodded, and he jumped up and rushed away to find a footman in the hall below. The man went off ponderously to find champagne, while Humphrey hopped from foot to foot in impatience. What if she were gone when he returned? She could take off in any of a dozen different directions, and he would never find her again in that great maze of a house. The footman returned bearing an opened bottle of champagne and two glasses on a tray. Humphrey almost snatched it from his hands and raced off. Had he asked for two glasses? He thought not, but Gaffney would understand the implication of a gentleman in a tearing hurry for champagne so late in the evening. Well, it was not quite that kind of assignation, for Miss Blythe was a lady through and through, but still, he supposed it was an assignation of a sort.

She was still there. Thank God! She even gave him a tremulous smile, and had stretched her legs out in a more relaxed pose instead of huddling against the wall, all curled up in her anguish.

He sat beside her and they sipped champagne together, and there was a pleasing rightness to it. It was not quite proper for them to be alone in this way, but they could hear the music of the dance, the stamp of feet and buzz of conversation, with an occasional burst of laughter, and it was almost as if they were in the great hall. Safely hidden away behind their screen, yet they were still part of the joyful festivities going on below.

"Can you forgive me?" he said. "In all that has happened, my words went out of my head."

"It is of no consequence!" she cried. "There is nothing to forgive. It is entirely my own foolishness, because I was so worried about you last night, wondering how you were going on and what would happen to you in court. I did not understand just at first that

Lord Carrbridge was to be the magistrate. And then you were late back and there was no opportunity to talk to you, or even to see you, so I did not know— And I so looked forward to it, the champagne, that is! Knowing it was all over and you were safely home again, you see. But it does not matter in the least, for here you are now. Did Mr Merton inform you of the other pieces that Charlie had taken?"

She seldom chattered in quite that rattling way, but he guessed she was nervous and that was what made her talk more than usual.

"He did, and I was able to retrieve them, although I had no more idea than you where they might have belonged. Such hideous things! I should certainly have remembered if I had ever seen them before. I gave them to Aunt Patience, telling her that I had no idea where they had come from, which was quite true. And she apologised for her maid sitting on my head, to which I replied that I had no memory of any such event, which is also true, although she thought it merely a polite form of words. Then she smacked my wrist with her fan and told me I was a naughty boy who ought to know better. So all ends well, except that I have to think of a way to return Merton's five hundred pounds to him."

"He has not paid you!"

"Indeed he has, for it was a debt of honour, and Merton is the most honourable of men. But I shall find a way to repay him. A couple of decent horses and a groom — that should do it. More champagne?"

She agreed to it, and they sipped and chatted and it was as if there had never been any constraint between them. Her expression relaxed — not quite smiling, but composed, her tears quite fled. When the musicians struck up for the waltz, he remembered his plan from earlier in the evening.

Jumping to his feet, he bowed to her. "Miss Blythe, may I have the very great honour of this dance?"

Immediately her face changed, a mask of wariness descending. "I am not going down there!"

"No, no! There is room enough here, if we are careful."

"The waltz?"

"Do you object to it on principle?"

"Oh no, but— I am not a very good dancer, Humphrey."

His heart lurched to hear her speak his name. "Neither am I. Shall we try anyway?" He held out his hand for her, and she grasped it without hesitation, allowing him to pull her to her feet. "We start side by side, like this."

"I know how it goes. I watched you practise with Rosemary, remember?"

He did not, in fact, remember any such thing. Had she been there during Connie's wet-weather lessons? If so, he had not noticed her. It was not until he had seen her ride Ganymede that he had become so attuned to her presence or absence in a room. It was hard to remember a time when he had not been helplessly in love with her, yet he had only known her a few short weeks. Such a brief time, yet now his life was incomplete without her.

Slowly they moved in time to the music lilting up from the great hall below. Humphrey had to concentrate on his steps, for although it was not a complicated dance like the quadrille, her nearness and her ungloved hands resting in his turned his brain to blancmange. With each shift in the arms or spin around he was more out of his depth, like a boat that has broken its moorings and at any moment might be swept away downstream and out to sea. Yet he could not stop. When another change in position brought his arm around her waist, he was lost, pulling her tightly to him and burying his face in her hair. Ah, her soft hair, mercifully free of the dreadful cap. He could smell her perfume, feel the warmth of her hand in his, and the cool smoothness of silk beneath his other hand. But still they were dancing, swirling around with the music. Still restraint held him.

Then she lifted her face to his, and he was entirely swept away. He leaned nearer, brushed his lips softly across her forehead, her cheeks, her closed eyes... As softly as a butterfly's wing, his lips touched hers. Then again. And yet again. Each time he pulled away, the return was sweeter, less tentative, more ardent. She made a little sound, like a whimper, then her hand crept to his cheek, and around to the back of his head, pressing him closer to her. He closed his eyes and gave himself utterly to the moment, lost in bliss.

It seemed like hours later when they finally came to themselves. To his astonishment, the waltz was still going on in the hall below, although faster now, punctuated by squeals. In the great hall, the dancers were spinning, spinning, all violent movement. In the minstrels' gallery, the two dancers stood motionless, clinging together, gazing into each other's eyes, dizzy with enchantment.

She sighed, and he smiled, moving away from her just a fraction.

At once there was a shift in her expressive face, and she tipped her head to one side. "Well?"

He looked at her, puzzled.

"Humphrey, you cannot do that and not say anything, you know."

"I... no?"

"No!" she cried, wriggling free of his embrace and pushing him away. "If you kiss me that way, at least speak to me afterwards. Say *something*. Oh, you are hopeless!" She stamped her foot in

frustration. "I suppose you still have some fustian in your mind about my reputation."

He knew what she wanted. A declaration of love, perhaps even an offer of marriage, and it was true, a passionate kiss could only be a prelude to something more. He could not walk away from her, not after that. Yet what could he say? The same difficulties still held sway in his mind. But he need not now assume indifference, for their kisses had swept away all pretence between them. He could at last be honest with her.

"Hortensia…" She stilled at the use of her name. He cupped her face in his hands, and said gently, "I cannot speak yet. I *cannot*, and indeed it is your reputation which is at the forefront of my mind. So we must be patient for a while—"

"How long?" she said breathlessly.

"It would be best to wait a year—"

"A *year!*"

She spun away from him again, and rested her forehead on the wall. From the way her body shuddered he guessed she was crying again. Damnation, but this was hard on both of them.

"Hush," he said, wrapping his arms around her waist and kissing the top of her head. "You must not cry. It will pass in no time—"

"No!" she cried. "You cannot expect me to wait so long. I cannot! I *will* not!"

"Hortensia…"

She spun round to face him. "You do not know what you ask. When one has to wait, everything changes. I waited once before for a man to come back to me, but he never did."

"Who was he? Someone you met in India?"

"Captain James Quayle, of the East India Company's Madras Army."

"Miss Quayle's father? He must have been a lot older than you."

"A few years. You remind me of him — he was big, too, and blond." She reached up with one hand to run her fingers through Humphrey's hair, and his breath was suddenly ragged. "One *noticed* when he entered a room. I fell very much in love with him when I was fourteen, and by the time I was sixteen he was in love with me, too. But I was too young to marry, he and my father both said. We must wait. So I waited, and he went away to do army things, and still I waited, while his letters became less and less frequent. And then he put himself in front of a bullet, idiotic man, and that was that. So you see why the idea of waiting holds no appeal for me. Waiting is just another way to say no."

"Not to me," he said quietly. "I should never abandon you."

"You would not mean to," she said bleakly. "Sometimes it happens anyway. Life is uncertain, Humphrey, and who knows what may happen in a year? We are all in God's hands. And it seems to me that if a man says it is imperative to wait a year, perhaps he is not so keen anyway, for if two people are of age and there are no other obstacles, why should they wait?"

"But there *are* other obstacles," he said quietly. "Must I enumerate them? There is your lack of rank or connection to any family of consequence. There is your fortune, made by trade. And there is my status as a confirmed fortune hunter. Any one of these individually might be readily overcome, but now there is the matter of your concealed identity. For myself, I care nothing about it, but for others... like my brother..."

"Lord Carrbridge? What has he to say to it? He cannot prevent you from marrying where you please. We are both of age, after all."

He took a long breath. This was so difficult. "Your reputation is... damaged, and Carrbridge feels that the family would also be damaged if... I do not believe it, myself, but it is important to him and I cannot... I *cannot* go against his wishes in this matter. He has supported me for years, and asked very little in return, so I owe him my loyalty. You must see that. He feels that if nothing precipitate is done to draw attention to ourselves, then the scandal will die down. If we are patient and discreet, and allow Connie to introduce you to the *ton* next season, then all may be well, and you will have London at your feet, as you deserve."

"But I do not want London at my feet," she burst out. "I cannot imagine a worse fate than to be forced to endure London, and the season. Rosemary and I spent a month there, solely to replenish our wardrobes, and I could not wait to leave it."

"That is because you knew no one and moved only on the fringes of society," he said. "London is very comfortable if one moves in the first circles. I cannot wait to take you to Almacks and Carlton House."

"Can you not understand?" she cried, one clenched fist thumping his chest in frustration. "I have not the least desire to go to Almacks or Carlton House. I should hate it! Even staying here has been torture to me — so much time sitting in drawing rooms and morning rooms, pretending to be engrossed in my stitchery, or exchanging mindless conversation on suitable topics. If you had not been kind to me and lent me Ganymede I should have run mad, I swear it. I do not care if I never go to Almacks!"

"Easy to say, yet you do not know what you would be giving up."

"Humphrey, I am six and twenty years of age. I understand enough of the world and of myself to know what I want, and now I have the money to live my life as I choose. London holds no appeal for me. People everywhere live and die without ever setting foot in London, and enjoy contented, fulfilling lives. I intend to make my home here in Yorkshire, where I can ride on the moor every day and breathe clean air and not be *caged*. Lord Carrbridge is to sell Silsby Vale House to me, and it is my intention to live there with Mrs Andrews as my chaperon and—"

"What?"

"—companion, and if I have my way, then I shall never go to London again."

"Mrs Andrews? As *chaperon*? Do you know her history? *She* will not increase your consequence!"

"I know all about her, and if you think I care about my consequence, you have not been listening to a word I have said."

"Hortensia..." He stopped, unable to grasp the magnitude of her rejection. It was not just him she abjured, but his family, his rank and his whole way of life. How could he marry a woman who rejected everything he was? He slid down the wall to sit, knees drawn up, head bowed.

"Humphrey?" She plopped to the ground beside him in a froth of pale green silk. "Can you accept me as I am? Because this will never work if you cannot."

He lifted his head, not looking at her but comforted by her nearness. Surely there was a way past this? "I feel I do not know you at all," he said, his voice choked with emotion.

"I am not sure that I know you, either," she said, wrapping her arms around one of his, and resting her cheek on his shoulder. "You appeared to me to be everything I have dreamed of — a man who was happy to step outside the bounds of propriety, who had the courage to be different. But you are no more than a fly caught in propriety's web after all, afraid to take any chance. Afraid to defy your brother. Afraid to take a chance on *me*. Do you not want to risk it?"

"I do not know what I want," he said slowly. "I cannot see a way forward."

"What does your heart say?"

But he could only shake his head and repeat, "I do not know."

22: A Gamble

They stayed for hours in the minstrels' gallery, drinking champagne but not talking very much, not kissing, and both of them reluctant to leave, it seemed to him. But when the music had finally stopped and the great hall below them had emptied, the only sounds the chink of glasses and scrape of table legs as the servants righted the room, they could no longer avoid the parting. They kissed again, and then, separately, made their way to their rooms.

Billings was dozing beside the fire, but he had waited up much later than this for Humphrey on his heavy gaming nights, so the valet was not reproachful. Humphrey silently suffered himself to be undressed and prepared for bed. Then, as soon as the door had closed behind Billings, Humphrey threw back the bed curtains and got up again. He shrugged into a robe, then sat himself in the window gazing unseeingly at the gardens, pondering his dilemma.

It had seemed so simple. He had planned to say nothing to Hortensia, leaving the next day without declaring himself, for it would hardly be honourable to speak, knowing they would have to wait. They would meet again in the spring, when the season began, and then he would court her in good earnest. Or perhaps Connie might invite her for another visit before then. But now... everything was upside down. She would not go to London. She was not prepared to wait. She cared nothing for the good opinion of the *ton*. He could not but admire her spirit, but it was so foolish!

Or was it...? His indecisive mind flip-flopped about. What if they were to marry anyway? What dreadful harm could come of it, except that the patronesses of Almacks might not send them vouchers? Would that be the end of the world? If he had been looking for a well-bred wife, then Almack's would be the very place to meet one, but—

The click of the door alerted him. Before he had time to wonder where his pistols were, or even to move, a face peeped round the door, framed in an abundance of unrestrained dark hair .

"Oh, thank goodness!" Hortensia said, shutting the door behind her softly. "I was afraid I had got the wrong room, and just think how awkward that would be."

He felt he ought to be shocked, but somehow it was typical of her. "Hortensia, what on earth are you doing here?"

"Why, I came to see you, of course. We cannot have things left in this unsatisfactory manner, so I have decided that we shall settle everything once and for all. Do you have a small table? Ah, this one will do. Help me carry it over here, will you? And now some chairs. Yes, that one, and the one from the window. Do you have some more candles? Mine is burning very low."

He did as he was bid, trying not to laugh at her bustling about arranging chairs in the middle of the night in a man's bedroom, as if it were a perfectly ordinary thing to be doing.

"There now, we may sit comfortably and have a talk."

"Do you want some brandy? Or I might have some port..."

"Oh no, I am still full of champagne. I am a little hungry, since we missed supper, but I daresay you have nothing to eat, and one cannot ring for a servant under the circumstances, can one?"

"Probably not," he said. "Hortensia, we had much better leave any further discussion until the morning. We have both been overwrought this evening, not to mention drinking a whole bottle of champagne between us, and I do not think this is the ideal time for rational thought. Or place," he added, eyeing his bed not five paces away.

"No, no, this is precisely the right time. The place, I grant you, is unconventional, but I could not think where else we might go at this time of night."

"Each to our own beds, to sleep," he said, but he could not help smiling. He knew her well enough to understand that she was talking so much because she was nervous.

"Perchance to dream? No, not yet. Humphrey, we must get this settled, and it must be done now because in a few hours I shall be leaving here to go to Silsby Vale House and—"

"So soon!" he cried, shocked.

"I must, because Maria is terrified that Mr Sharp will turn up on the doorstep. Who *is* Mr Sharp, by the way?"

"The agent here, who abused his position rather."

"Indeed! He sounds like a dreadful man. So, I shall be gone, and it will be much more difficult to find an opportunity to talk, and I am determined not to let everything drift on for week after week. Humphrey, I need you to be honest with me. Will you?"

"Of course."

"I have to know what you want from me."

He sucked in his breath. What did he want. *Her.* Of that much he was certain, but how? How was it possible? "Hortensia, you want me to make a commitment that I am not yet ready to make."

"Very well, then. I will make it simple for you," she said, her chin rising defiantly. "There are only three options. I could become your wife, or your mistress, or we could part for ever."

He could not speak. This was too blunt, too plain-spoken! Surely there must be other ways?

"Choose," she said. "Choose one of the three, and then we may move forward."

"This is… impossible!" he cried. "I cannot make such a decision, not without careful thought."

"No," she said quietly. "No more careful thought. You have had time enough for careful thought. I want to know what is in your heart, Humphrey, not your mind. Do not weigh the options, one against another, as you might when buying a new horse. This is not a matter for rational thought, it is a matter of passion, of desire, whether it be for me, or my fortune, or for your position in society. One of them will be pre-eminent, and if you set aside logic, you will know which it is. What do you want most?"

"Do not ask it of me," he cried in anguish. "I cannot decide, not like this."

"Very well," she said. "We will let chance decide." From a pocket in her robe, she produced a dice cup and a single ivory die. "You may throw for your future, like the gambler you are."

"No, Hortensia," he whispered. "I cannot do this."

"If you throw a one or a two," she went on relentlessly, "then we part for ever. If you throw a three or a four, I shall be your mistress, and you may have whatever life you wish for otherwise. If you throw a five or a six, then you marry me and we work out our differences together. But Humphrey — you will be bound by the outcome. However the die falls, that will decide our lives, whether together or apart."

"No," he whispered. "This is madness."

She set the dice cup on the table. "Throw."

"No."

"Throw."

"You cannot make me."

"Very well, then I shall throw in your stead." She snatched up the dice cup and shook it.

"No!" he cried, and lunged forward to grab it from her. She jerked it high to keep it out of his reach, but the sharp movement shook the die free, and it sailed through the air. With a cry of despair he leapt after it. It fell on the floor, bounced out of his grasp, fell, bounced again. He dropped to his knees and stretched for it, missed, cried out in terror. It settled...

It was a six.

"Oh, thank God!" he whispered, his head lowering until it almost touched the floor. "Thank God, thank God, thank God!"

From the table behind him, he heard a low chuckle.

"Now you know what you want," she said.

He was too shaken to see the humour in the situation. If the die had fallen some other way—! It was unthinkable. He could not let her go, nor could he take her as his mistress. There was only one future for them, and that was marriage. Yet what a way to find that out!

"Hortensia, you will be the death of me," he said. Scrambling to his feet, he picked up the die and tossed it onto the table. It settled with the six upwards. "Oh, wait..." He threw again. Another six. Then another. Slowly he began to laugh. "You devious little hussy! This is loaded!"

"Well, you did not really suppose I would leave all to chance, did you? *You* may not have known what you wanted, but I did."

He sat down in a rush on his chair, rolling the die between his fingers. "You must think me such a fool."

"Not a fool, no. Too clever by half, in point of fact. You spend too much time trying to reason everything out, the way you do at piquet — if I have this card and this other one, then I discard that one. But love is not susceptible to reason, Humphrey dear. Love is closing your eyes and taking a deep breath and leaping into the darkness. There is no knowing how it will end, but you believe it will end *well* because you have this other person leaping alongside you, holding your hand and not letting go, no matter what happens. Love is about faith and trust and taking a chance without stopping to weigh the risks. Will you take a chance with me, Humphrey Marford?"

And without hesitation he answered, "Yes. Yes, I will, Hortensia Blythe, because I love you and need you and you matter more to me than anything else in the world. And a great deal more than Almacks." She giggled at that. "We will work something out, I daresay, about London and all that business. If we get married in the autumn—"

"No."

"No?"

"We will get married straight away. I imagine you will be able to get a special licence—"

"And in the time it would take me to get to London and back with it, we could have the banns read."

"A common licence?" she said wistfully. "One could be had from York, I daresay."

"I have a much better plan," he said. "We will do as Marfords have done for generations, which is to have the banns read in the church at Mishcombe, and then walk in procession to our wedding so that the villagers may shower you with rose petals and have their fête afterwards. We always provide a big feast on the village green for family weddings, and there hasn't been one here for years."

She tipped her head on one side, thinking. "If we see Mr Hay tomorrow, the first banns could be read on Sunday, and then we may be married two weeks on Monday."

"Why the rush?" he said gently. "Most ladies like to savour the time of courtship. What about wedding clothes and the like?"

"Because I am terrified you will start *thinking* again, and find all sorts of reasons to delay. Marry me at once, Humphrey, or I shall go mad." He hesitated, and she said. "You know, I really feel you *ought* to marry me as soon as may be, for the sake of my reputation. After all, here I am in your bedroom, in my nightgown."

"If you creep back to your room—"

"But I have no intention of creeping back to my room, Humphrey dear. Not until the morning, anyway."

"Oh."

He could have argued with her. He could even have carried her back to her own room, although he suspected she was quite capable of screaming all the way. Instead he laughed.

"You are an outrageous, wanton woman, Miss Blythe, and I utterly adore you."

He blew out the candles.

~~~~~

Hortensia wore one of her new morning gowns, purchased in London but never worn while she was pretending to be a companion. Her maid, a dour Yorkshire woman whose highest praise was *'You'll do, ma'am'*, actually smiled as she dressed her. Even so, Hortensia insisted her hair be left in a simple coil on her crown, with just the two soft curls either side of her face. But she left off the spinster's cap. She would be wearing caps again soon enough, but they would be delicate lace confections, not the monstrous plain cambric affair she had assumed as part of her disguise.

"There, ma'am," said the maid. "You'll do very well."

Seeing herself in the mirror, Hortensia doubted it. The gown was a glorious statement of fashion, expensive, elegant and very flattering to her figure, but there was no hiding her plain face or excessive height. She would never be a beauty, and it was a miracle that not one but two men had fallen in love with her in her life. She could hardly believe her luck. One had slipped from her grasp, but she was determined not to lose Humphrey.

Breakfast was an awkward affair, Connie crying in delight at the news of the betrothal, and the men smiling, slapping Humphrey heartily on the shoulder or pumping his hand in congratulations.

Only Carrbridge looked balefully at him. "You could not wait, then," he said sorrowfully.

"I could have done, but she could not," he said. "And you may blame your wife for it, sending me to find Miss Blythe last night. And now we are to be married in two weeks, and it is all Connie's fault."

"Two weeks!" Connie cried, aghast. "Why such haste? Three months is the usual time, if you are to have any hope of the carriage being ready, and all your wedding clothes. And Humphrey, you will want your brothers here for the occasion."

"I believe we must keep to our plan," Humphrey said, paying studious attention to his plate.

"But—" Connie began.

"My dear," Carrbridge said, resting one hand on hers, "it is best to leave such matters to Humphrey and Miss Blythe."

"But—" She looked from Hortensia, trying not to blush but failing, and Humphrey, still staring at his plate, and said, "Oh!" in surprise. "Oh, I see. Yes, of course."

After breakfast, Hortensia and Humphrey walked through the village to the parsonage to arrange for the banns, with Lady Hardy and Mr Merton as chaperons. There they were congratulated again, offered elderberry wine and plum cake, and thoroughly fussed over by Mr Hay and his two spinster sisters. Hortensia could not help comparing Mr Hay, so tidily and sensibly attired, with Humphrey's ramshackle appearance in his disguise, and it was as much as she could do not to laugh. She dared not catch Humphrey's eye in case that set her off.

When they were sufficiently stuffed full of plum cake to satisfy the Miss Hays and were allowed to leave, Humphrey raised the matter of Mr Sharp, the agent, with Mr Merton.

"Mrs Andrews is in fear of his return, and I should like to be able to reassure the lady, but I have not seen hide nor hair of the man for some time."

"No one has seen him," Mr Merton said. "According to Mrs Sharp, he has been back twice, but only to change his clothes and take a fresh horse. Then he is away again. He has written twice to inform his lordship of his whereabouts, as he was asked to do, and he is apparently inspecting some far-flung properties in Northumberland and Cumberland, but naturally he is not specific. He never says more than he is obliged to."

"What is he up to, Merton? It is nothing good, I am sure."

"He has had the sole management of all the marquess's estates and holdings for some years now," Mr Merton said thoughtfully. "A certain carelessness might be understandable, and certainly his record-keeping leaves a great deal to be desired. He has behaved reprehensibly towards Mrs Andrews, too. And the money...

there is something amiss with the money. Whenever his lordship has asked, Mr Sharp has produced the necessary funds, but where those funds are kept is a mystery. I have not yet found him out in any wrongdoing, but I have my suspicions. If Mr Sharp does not soon present himself at Drummoor, I believe his lordship will have no option but to begin investigating his financial affairs."

"At least Miss Blythe will be able to offer Mrs Andrews some support," Lady Hardy said. "The poor lady must be very distressed."

"I am not sure how much support a young lady may provide against a man like Mr Sharp," Mr Merton said.

Hortensia smiled. "Oh, I shall keep my pistols loaded."

Humphrey laughed. "You have pistols? Of course you do!"

"Even so," Mr Merton said, "I shall ask his lordship if another footman may be sent there temporarily, and perhaps one of the burlier grooms. Several solid young men may be as effective a deterrent as loaded pistols, in their way."

"You think Miss Blythe would not dare to shoot a man," Humphrey said. "You are quite mistaken. My betrothed is perfectly capable of shooting anyone."

"I do not doubt it," Mr Merton said. "I should prefer it if Miss Blythe were not required to do so."

"Yes, indeed!" said Lady Hardy. "Miss Blythe and Mrs Andrews must be protected. It is as well you are to marry so soon, Lord Humphrey, for then you will be on hand to protect the ladies."

Hortensia smiled and said nothing. Let them protect her if they wished, she did not care, for she had Humphrey. Soon she would be Lady Humphrey Marford and the world would be a wonderful place.

23: Tigers, Elephants And Snakes

Humphrey was to escort Hortensia to Silsby Vale House that afternoon. Her boxes had already been packed up and sent around by road, together with the maid, a footman and a groom, who were to stay until she had her own staff in place, but Hortensia wanted to ride and Humphrey was not minded to deny her any pleasure.

She rode Ganymede and he rode Titan, and after the initial gallop, they walked the horses companionably side by side.

"I shall miss Ganymede," she said with a sigh. "May I borrow him sometimes, after we are married?"

"You may not," he said. She looked so shocked that he smiled. "But I may ask that favour of you sometimes. He is yours, my betrothal present to you."

"Oh, Humphrey!" she said, her eyes sparkling with tears. "You are so good to me. But what may I give you?"

"You have already given me everything I desired, my love, in bestowing your hand upon me. What more could I wish for?"

"One hundred thousand pounds, perhaps, to start your gaming house?"

"Not that, no. I shall not take your inheritance from you. Once your lawyers arrive to discuss the marriage settlements, I shall suggest that they wrap it all up in trust for our children."

She reined Ganymede to a halt, and waved Tom to go on ahead. "No, that is not how it is supposed to be. What is mine will be yours when we are wed, for you to do with as you please."

"Your lawyers will point out that I am a known gambler, and likely to lose your fortune at faro or dice. They will recommend that you give me a modest allowance, and keep the rest out of my reach. And they would be right to so advise you."

"And I would be right to tell them that you are no reckless gamester. Besides, I want you to have your gaming house. That is how we met, after all, because you wanted a rich wife to fund it. Now you will have one, so please, let me give you a hundred thousand, at least. The rest may be tied up however you wish, but let me do this for you, Humphrey, please."

"I have been discussing my plans with Mr Stoner — do you remember him, from the abbey? We must have him to stay once we are settled, by the way, for he is such an interesting man and you can talk about India with him. Anyway, he has been advising me on the gaming house, and he and a few of his business associates are prepared to invest in the venture. I do not think I can raise a hundred thousand, but enough for something a little more modest, in York, perhaps, so that I should not need to go to London."

"Do you... not want to go to London?"

"Not if it takes me away from you, no."

"Oh." Again he saw tears in her eyes. "So you are not marrying me for my money after all."

"Of course not! I am glad that you have it, for otherwise I could never marry you, since I could hardly expect you to live in poverty for my sake, but for myself, I do not want it. All I want is *you*, Hortensia."

"Oh," she said again.

"I thought you understood," he said gently. "I love you, my darling. I adore everything about you, my brave, beautiful Hortensia."

"Beautiful?" she whispered. "No one has ever called me beautiful before."

"But you are! Yours is not a milk-and-honey prettiness, like Miss Quayle's, but the radiance that comes from within, from strength and a quick wit and the sureness of good sense and a delight in life. When you allow that radiance to spill forth, it lights your whole being and you are utterly magnificent."

They walked on in silence as she contemplated this new idea. Humphrey wondered what she saw when she looked in her mirror — the ordinary, rather severe features, no doubt, and the overlarge eyes and mouth. She never saw herself engrossed in a card game, or exhilarated from a fast ride, as he did. She never saw her own beauty. But she would, for he would make her so happy that she would walk about all day with such a smile on her face as could not be disguised, even when she looked in her mirror.

Lost in their own thoughts, they reached Silsby Vale House and turned in through the gates.

She stopped, looking up at the mellow walls of the house. "I shall give you this place, then," she said. "This will be my wedding gift to you, and with all the tenant farmers who pay rent, you will have a useful income of your own. A man should be master in his own house, do you not— Wait, why is the front door open?"

Humphrey was wondering that himself. Yet no one emerged. Then shouts were heard from the stables. Kicking their horses into motion, they raced round the corner, gravel spraying, Tom just behind them.

Sharp. Even in a melee of grooms and gardeners and a couple of maids, that tricorn hat could not be mistaken. He had hold of Mrs Andrews by one arm and his whip was raised.

"Stop that at once!" Humphrey yelled, kicking aside the stirrups and leaping from Titan's back.

Sharp stopped, lowered the whip and shifted his angry scowl to a more conciliatory expression, although he did not release Mrs Andrews' arm. "Why, my lord, good day to you, but this does not concern you. A man may chastise his mistress if she misbehaves, the law will support me on that."

"But—"

"Release her or I shoot," came an implacable voice from above.

Humphrey turned to see Hortensia, still mounted on Ganymede, pointing a pistol at Sharp.

Sharp laughed. "Lady, put that thing away or you—"

She fired, the shot echoing off the walls, and Sharp's hat spun away. Ganymede whickered and half reared, but even with one hand, she held him in check and quietened him. Then, tossing the used pistol to Humphrey, she pulled another from her saddle bag and cocked it.

"The next one is for your heart unless you leave immediately."

Sharp looked about him, then, defeated, he started to walk past them. She turned the horse to watch him walk down the drive, step by slow step. He reached Tom, who was holding Titan and his own horse, and suddenly lunged for Titan, grabbing the reins from Tom's hands. With an agility surprising in a man of his age, he leapt into the saddle, and kicked the horse into motion.

"Shall I kill him?" Hortensia said conversationally.

"Best not to," Humphrey said.

She fired. Sharp yelled, Titan reared and Sharp fell neatly from the saddle, with blood pouring from one shoulder.

Humphrey began to laugh. "Lucky you had all these men here to protect you, Miss Blythe. Whatever would you have done without us?"

~~~~~

Despite Connie's fears, most of Humphrey's brothers were at Drummoor for the wedding, Reggie and Miss Chamberlain rather surprised to be beaten to the altar, Gus breaking his journey on his way to Northumberland, and Monty newly ordained. Only Gil was absent, busy with his Hussar regiment preparing to take ship for the Peninsula.

Gus was engaged on a mission for Tattersall's, to value and bring to auction the stables of the recently deceased son of a duke. He was accompanied by another man, a very small man, swaddled in a greatcoat adorned with a vast number of capes, and the garish blue and yellow striped waistcoat of the Four-Horse Club.

"This is another Tattersall's man, Captain Michael Edgerton, formerly of the East India Company Army," said Gus to the group assembled in the entrance hall to receive them.

"The East India Company Army?" Connie said. "Do you know Miss Blythe, Humphrey's betrothed? Her father was in the East India Company."

"It is a very large company," Hortensia murmured. "Delighted to meet you, Captain."

"Miss Blythe? Miss Blythe?" he said, raising a quizzing glass to one eye. "Not... oh, surely not? Do I have the honour of addressing *Tiger* Blythe?"

"Good heavens, I have not been called that for years!" Hortensia said, laughing.

"My dear Miss Blythe, permit me to shake your hand!" Edgerton said, suiting the action to the words. "It is too great a privilege to meet you, after hearing so much about you."

"May I show you to your room, Captain Edgerton?" Connie said, brightly.

"No, no, no, do not whisk him away like that," Gus said. "We need to know all about Tiger Blythe."

"It is quite all right, Lady Carrbridge," Hortensia said. "It is nothing terribly disreputable."

"Disreputable! Disreputable! I should think not," said the captain. "Miss Blythe once shot a tiger at point-blank range that had got into the kitchen."

"Oh!" said Connie faintly.

"It was going to eat the cook's youngest boy, and I could not allow that, could I?" Hortensia said.

"What was your total tally?" the captain said.

"Seven," she answered. "It should have been eight, but General Westfield claimed the final one, and one does not quite like to argue with a general. Not when he has an entire army at his command. But it should have been mine, all the same."

"Seven tigers," the captain breathed. "And the elephant, of course. A bull elephant was bearing down on her, Lady Carrbridge, but she stood her ground and took the thing down with a single shot. Magnificent. Quite magnificent."

"Goodness," Connie said, hand to mouth.

"It was not quite so dramatic as it sounds," Hortensia said, laughing. "The tale has grown in the telling, as such tales always do.

Another year or two, and it will be a whole herd of elephants, I daresay."

"How does one shoot an elephant?" Humphrey said.

"With a steady hand, and right at the mid-point between the ears. So I was taught, and since I am here to tell the tale, I can vouch for its effectiveness."

"Well," Connie said. "Good gracious. You are full of surprises, Miss Blythe. Captain, do let me show you to your room. You will want to refresh yourself after your journey. Were the roads tolerable, would you say?"

Most of the group drifted away to their various activities, and Connie's voice could be heard diminishing into the distance. The brothers stayed in a loose group around Hortensia.

"No wonder you were so calm in winging Sharp," Humphrey said.

"Oh yes, that was nothing at all in comparison to tigers and elephants. Although snakes — I do not like snakes, Humphrey, so you will have to deal with any spitting cobras we encounter in Silsby Vale."

"You winged Sharp?" Gus said in tones of wonderment.

"She did," Humphrey said proudly. "Although the devil has run off again. Only lingered long enough for the ball to be dug out of him, then he was gone. Not sure we shall see him again, this time."

"What a lady!" Gus said. "Tiger Blythe — you will be the toast of London, Miss Blythe, once this gets around."

"Will I? I am a very disreputable person altogether, you know — the daughter of a nabob, and no society manners to speak of. The patronesses of Almacks will never approve me."

"Ah, now that is where you are wrong, for although you would not be good *ton* in the ordinary way, you are an original. So maybe not at first, but you will get your vouchers for Almacks, Miss Blythe."

"How much will you bet on it?" she said.

Gus laughed out loud. "Name your price, Miss Blythe."

"Five hundred," she said at once. "Five hundred says you are wrong, Lord Augustus."

"Done," he said, eyes twinkling. "By all that is wonderful, Humphrey, where did you find her? Because if ever a couple were well-matched, it is you two."

"I know," Humphrey said smugly. "She is magnificent, is she not?"

And they all agreed that, indeed, she was.

~~~~~

Hortensia walked to her wedding in a shower of rose petals and good wishes from the villagers of Mishcombe, to the accompaniment of several fiddle players, the beat of hand drums and the mournful whine of bagpipes, although she secretly felt the latter would be better suited to funerals. The church was packed, Lord Carrbridge gave her away and Lady Carrbridge cried copiously. Afterwards, everyone streamed out of church to eat and drink, the nobility and gentry at a decorous wedding breakfast at Drummoor and the villagers to feast, drink and dance until midnight, or longer if there were still ale to be had.

Her only sadness was in parting from Rosemary. She and Lord Kilbraith had stayed on to see her wed, and although Rosemary smiled and hugged her and wished her every imaginable felicity, the tears she shed were not just the result of happiness. They had been friends for ten years, sharing all the joys and sorrows of their lives. They had wept together when Captain James Quayle had died,

Rosemary's grief at losing her father matched by Hortensia's in losing her great love. And they had wept together again when Hortensia's father had died. They had supported and comforted each other on the long journey from India, and giggled together at the curiosities of English society. And now each was to begin a new chapter of her life, with a man who loved her and a family ready to welcome her into its embrace. Even though they stepped willingly onto their new paths, still it was hard to part.

"Might you come to Scotland one day?" Rosemary said, her great blue eyes filled with tears.

"We will come," Humphrey said gravely. "We will dance at your wedding as you have danced at ours."

That afternoon, Lady Carrbridge's own carriage conveyed the newly married pair to their home at Silsby Vale House, where Mrs Andrews and their entire staff, enlarged with the help of an agent in York, waited to welcome them. Then unpacking and dinner, after which Mrs Andrews announced that she was very tired and would go to bed.

The newly married couple looked at each other.

"Shall we go up too?" Hortensia said, suddenly shy.

"Not yet. Come and sit on my lap, Lady Humphrey, and let me kiss you."

She was more than happy to oblige him, and for a while there was no sound in the room, except for the steady tick of the clock on the mantel.

When they finally broke apart, he sighed and said, "I am so glad we did not wait. Look at poor Reggie, with this delight still weeks away. I wonder if he has even kissed Miss Chamberlain, let alone had her sitting on his lap in this delicious manner."

She snuggled closer to him. "It *is* delicious, is it not? But they are proceeding in the way that feels comfortable for them. Not everyone is like us, or would want to be. You are not sorry, then? That we rushed into this?"

"How could I possibly be sorry?"

"Because you are giving up a lot for me. No matter what Gus says, you will be ostracised in London. You might even receive the cut direct, and you would feel dreadful if that were to happen. You have always been good *ton* and now you will not be."

"Ah, but I have such compensations as to make me not repine in the least, for I have you, my darling, and what more could any man need?"

She buried her face in his broad shoulder. "You are so good to me, Humphrey, and I love you so, so much. I am not sure what I should have done if that die had fallen wrong."

"It could not have fallen wrong," he said softly. "However it had fallen, it would have brought me to realise what I wanted... what I *needed*. You, Hortensia. Tiger Blythe. The bravest, most magnificent woman in the world."

She sighed with contentment, and allowed her new husband to carry her up to bed.

Thanks for reading!

If you have enjoyed reading this book, please consider writing a short review on Amazon. You can find out the latest news and sign up for the mailing list at my website: http://marykingswood.co.uk/

A note on historical accuracy - and an apology!: I have endeavoured to stay true to the spirit of Regency times, and have avoided taking too many liberties or imposing modern sensibilities on my characters. The book is not one of historical record, but I've tried to make it reasonably accurate. However, I'm not perfect! If you spot a historical error, I'd very much appreciate knowing about it so that I can correct it and learn from it. Thank you!

One area where I have taken some liberties is geographical. In *The Daughters of Allamont Hall*, I squeezed the mythical county of Brinshire into a non-existent space between Staffordshire and Shropshire. In *Sons of the Marquess*, however, Drummoor is firmly set in the (very real) county of Yorkshire, the West Riding to be precise, and not too far away from York itself. I haven't attempted to place it precisely, to give myself the freedom to add estates and towns and villages of my own invention. In the interests of such creation, several very real towns have been wiped off the map. To the good people of Yorkshire, I apologise.

About Sons of the Marquess: *the Ninth Marquess of Carrbridge is happily married to the former Miss Constance Allamont, he has an heir and a spare in the nursery, and all seems set fair for a life of perfect bliss. His five younger brothers are a bit of a handful, but young men like to spread their wings a bit. If only they weren't so expensive! And whatever happened to that huge income his father used to boast about? It seems to have vanished in a generation. And now there's the unknown son of his father's who claims to be the legitimate heir to the Marquessate. It's a bit much for a Marquess to deal with. Fortunately, his wife has some ideas about recovering their position...*

Book 0: The Earl of Deveron (a novella, free to mailing list subscribers)
Book 1: Lord Reginald
Book 2: Lord Humphrey
Book 3: Lord Augustus
Book 4: Lord Montague
Book 5: Lord Gilbert

About the author

I write traditional Regency romances under the pen name Mary Kingswood, and epic fantasy as Pauline M Ross. I live in the beautiful Highlands of Scotland with my husband. I like chocolate, whisky, my Kindle, massed pipe bands, long leisurely lunches, chocolate, going places in my campervan, eating pizza in Italy, summer nights that never get dark, wood fires in winter, chocolate, the view from the study window looking out over the Moray Firth and the Black Isle to the mountains beyond. And chocolate. I dislike driving on motorways, cooking, shopping, hospitals.

Acknowledgements

Thanks go to:

My mother, who first introduced me to the wonderful world of Jane Austen.

Shayne Rutherford of Darkmoon Graphics for the cover design.

My beta readers: Mary Burnett, Graham of Fading Street.

Last, but definitely not least, my first reader: Amy Ross.

Sneak Preview of Lord Augustus: Chapter 1: The Cherry Tree Inn

Lord Augustus Marford knew all the foremost inns on every major road in England. The foremost inns, naturally, being those which would best attend to the needs of his precious horses. If they served edible food and a decent claret, and provided beds with clean linen, well, that was an added benefit, but not, in his view, essential. He was happy to eat and drink whatever was put in front of him, and could sleep on the floor if the situation demanded it, as he had proved on more than one occasion. But allow his beloved animals to be tended by half-drunk ostlers and careless grooms? No, it was inconceivable.

So it was that Gus and his travelling companion, Captain Edgerton, found themselves at the Cherry Tree Inn at Kelthwaite, even though the White Hart opposite and the George and Dragon just down the road looked more salubrious and had more patrons.

"You sure about this, Marford?" Edgerton said, looking up at the peeling paint on the sign over the door.

"Have I led you astray yet?" Gus said genially. "You are free to stay elsewhere if you wish, but I shall not entrust Jupiter to anyone else."

And as soon as their little party had clattered under the arch to the yard, ostlers scurried out from all sides to attend to them, and led the horses into well-appointed stables. Gus stayed long enough to ensure that Jupiter was receiving lavish attention from his own two grooms, and that the other horses were being cared for to an acceptable standard, then he made his way at a leisurely pace into the inn.

The pained tones of Captain Edgerton echoed about the low-beamed taproom. "No parlour? No parlour? Whatever sort of an establishment is this, to be so deficient in accommodation, and when you have the brother of a marquess condescending to stay here, too. It is excessively disappointing."

Gus could not hear the innkeeper's replies beyond a gentle murmur at intervals, but this was not a place where bluster and rank would have much effect. If he had wanted flunkeys bowing low enough to sweep the floor with their noses, he would have gone elsewhere.

"Edgerton, it is not the innkeeper's fault if his rooms are all taken. There are only two parlours here, after all, and the taproom will serve us very well."

"Your lordship is most understanding," the innkeeper said, a little dumpling of a man, as innkeepers often were. "My humblest apologies, but one of my parlours is under new paint, and the other is already taken by a lady."

"But only the daughter of an earl," Edgerton protested. "I believe Lord Augustus takes priority."

Gus laughter. "No, no, no, that will never do! Turn a lady out to sit in the taproom? Where is your chivalry, Captain? Do you have chambers enough for us to sleep in, my friend? Two would do it, if the grooms sleep in the hay store, but if you have only one, then the valets must have it, and the captain and I will take the hay, too, for I owe it to my cravat to ensure that Willett enjoys perfect repose."

"We have rooms, my lord, but— Ah, my lady, one moment, if you please."

"One moment? We have waited a great many moments already, and— Gus? Gus Marford, as I live and breathe!"

"Erm…" Gus was never good with names. So many ladies drifted into his view at balls and dinners and theatres, and he was usually thinking about something else and not paying much attention. Now he gazed at the statuesque lady with pale blue eyes, a mouth overfilled with teeth and a mountain of frizzy fair hair topped with a froth of lace, and scrambled to recall who on earth she was.

She gave a throaty chuckle. "How mortifying! You do not remember me at all, do you? Lady Emma Frensham. Heavens, Gus, we played spillikins as children often enough, and you pushed me into a pond once."

He laughed. "Emma! Of course. Where are you bound?"

"To Maria's place, at Carlisle, to comfort her in her grief." She rolled her eyes. "Prostrate, she is, as you can imagine. Hated the man when he was alive, but is inconsolable in widowhood, apparently. Oh, let us not stand about in this foolish manner. Come and share our parlour with us. There is only the one, so there is no running off and hiding, as you are wont to do, Gus. Do come in. Yes, bring your handsome friend with the Four Horse Club waistcoat. We have a splendid blaze going."

"In August?"

"You know what Aunt Prudence is like."

"Ah, Lady Prudence. Now *her* I remember," Gus murmured. Emma only laughed.

There was indeed a splendid fire going, so splendid that the room seemed hot enough to bake bread. Gus felt his shirt collars wilting as soon as he stepped into the room. Beside the fire, an elderly lady sat ramrod straight in a wing chair. Her hair was as white as snow, although mostly covered by a voluminous black crepe cap. Her gown was black bombazine, and she wore black gloves and a great quantity of jet beading. She turned small, intent eyes on them, then raised a lorgnette to examine them more closely.

Emma waved the two men through, and whispered, "As soon as she has her claret, she will nod off and we can let the fire die down." Then in a raised voice, she turned to the old lady. "Aunt Prudence, look who is here! It is Gus Marford, Carrbridge's brother, do you remember him? He used to play at the hall when I was a girl."

"Of course I remember him, you silly girl. Just because I am a little hard of hearing does not mean I am in my dotage. Well, m'boy, not seen you for an age. Daresay you turned out ramshackle. All you young men are ramshackle these days. Still, better ramshackle than silly, like this niece of mine. Who is your friend? Military man, by his bearing, although the waistcoat is a trifle overpowering."

"Lady Prudence, Lady Emma, may I present Captain Edgerton, formerly of the East India Company Army, but presently engaged at Tattersall's, as am I."

"Your sense of direction is failing you, Marford," Lady Prudence said. "Tattersall's is in London." She cackled, hugely amused at her own wit. Gus raised a dutiful smile, and Edgerton tittered almost convincingly.

The innkeeper entered, ushering in a servant with a tray bearing two wine bottles and four glasses. Lady Prudence brightened perceptibly.

"Over here!" she called out. "Whatever took you so long? We have been waiting forever, and what could be simpler than claret? Every half-decent inn in the country has such a thing to hand. Yes, yes, just put it down. I shall pour my own, since you would undoubtedly spill some. Cannot do the simplest thing, you people."

The servant rushed to oblige, setting one bottle and a glass on a small table beside her. Lady Prudence poured herself a large measure of wine, and drank it without pausing. Then a second, which she consumed in two draughts. The third took a little longer. Then, with a heavy sigh, she set down the glass, leaned back in her chair and closed her eyes.

"She will be asleep soon," Lady Emma whispered. "Poor dear, the carriage *will* bump her about so, and she does like her sleep in the afternoon."

And before long, gentle snores emanated from the wing chair, and then, as the lady's mouth fell open, rather louder rumbles.

"Do not mind her," Lady Emma said in her normal voice. "We may be comfortable now and enjoy an excellent coze before dinner. Captain Edgerton, may I trouble you to pour the wine? So tell me all the news of Drummoor, Gus. Lady Carrbridge is increasing again, I hear, and what is this about Humphrey? I heard a whisper that he is to be wed soon."

"Done already," Gus said.

"Oh, a hasty business. You know what will be said of *that*, I am sure. But she is quite something, my spies tell me. Rides as hard as a man, and shoots tigers before breakfast."

Gus laughed. "Not before breakfast, perhaps, but she certainly shot our land agent one afternoon."

Emma sat bolt upright in her chair, mouth wide open. "No! Intentionally?"

"Oh, very. He was harassing a lady, so Miss Blythe — Lady Humphrey now, of course — shot his hat from his head, and then, when he tried to make good his escape, asked Humphrey if she might kill him. *'No, better not,'* says he, so she hit him in the shoulder instead. As fine a shot as he had ever seen, Humphrey said. They will deal very well together, for she is every bit as insane as he is. More so, perhaps."

"She sounds gloriously original. Oh, I do hope he will bring her to Melton this autumn. I should so like to meet her. And what of the agent? He survived, I take it?"

"Oh, certainly, which is more than he deserved. A great deal of havey-cavey goings on are suspected, and as soon as the surgeon had dealt with him, he disappeared. Even his wife has no idea where he is."

"With Lady Humphrey taking pot-shots at me, I might be inclined to disappear myself," she said, laughing. "But tell me, what brings you so far north? I do not often agree with Aunt Prudence but she is quite right on one point — it is novel to meet two Tattersall's men so far from London. You are on Tattersall's business, I take it?"

"Indeed. We are to catalogue and value the stable of the late Marquess of Darrowstone, and arrange for the transportation of anything of unusual interest."

"Oh, poor Darrowstone, God rest his soul! And his poor father! The duchess gave him three sons who all survived to adulthood, and all of them dead now. The poor duke!"

Gus shrugged, not much interested in the Duke of Dunmorton's sons. Edgerton was interested, however.

"That is most unfortunate. What happened to them?" he said.

"George, the youngest, smashed his head in falling from his horse. Edward, the middle one, died on the Peninsula, as so many of our brave young men have done. And now Henry, the eldest, has gone out in a boat and drowned himself. It is a dangerous business, getting into a boat. I have never dared to do it myself. And now the duke's heir is some paltry third cousin from Cheshire, who is an attorney or some such. Dreadful business. But Gus, if you are going to Castle Morton, you must be sure to tell the duke that I am still unwed, and would be very happy to provide him with a lusty heir or two."

"Emma! You cannot be serious! Why, Dunmorton must be sixty if he is a day."

"And what is that to the point?" she said, looking rather pink about the cheeks. "He was one and sixty last spring, and, I make no doubt, still a fine looking man. He used to stay with us sometimes when he was younger, for he and Papa were at school together. I always liked him, and I think we should rub along very well together. Far better than that evil witch of a wife of his, may she burn in Hell for tormenting him so. And let us be honest, Gus, who else would have me but a man with failing eyesight? I am one and thirty years old, with a face more like a horse than a woman. My own mother used to weep when she looked at me, and Papa did not want to spend a penny on my come-out, for what could be a greater waste of time, he said? And he was quite right about that. All of my sisters took at once and are countesses now, but I shall end up an old maid like Aunt Prudence and be required to chaperon my nieces about. One glare from my frightful gaze and all their unsuitable suitors will shrink away in horror. But I should so like to be a duchess and outrank my sisters. So will you tell him? Please?"

She was so earnest that Gus dared not laugh at her, but he thought it a foolish notion all the same. If a man of more than sixty years were to take a wife, and that man a duke, he would hardly look at a tired spinster like Emma Frensham. He would pick up a pretty little debutante and put a smile on his face for his declining years. But he said all that was proper, and soon after the servants arrived to prepare the table for their dinner, Lady Prudence woke with a snort, and all sensible conversation was at an end.

The dinner was indifferent, the service slow and the taproom noisy enough to penetrate even to the parlour. Lady Prudence kept up a continuous monologue of grumbles, which only Captain Edgerton attempted to respond to, by upbraiding the servants whenever they put in an appearance. However, by the time the third bottle of claret was getting low, and only the cheese and nuts remained on the table, she retreated to her chair to sleep away the hours until it was time to go to bed.

Edgerton then turned his attention on Lady Emma, engaging her in a light flirtation that had her giggling and blushing like a debutante. But when Gus went out to check on the horses, Edgerton followed him out.

"She is quite something, your Lady Emma," he said.

"Not mine, nor ever like to be," Gus said. "If you are going to ask about her dowry, I have not the least idea, but if she could lay claim to anything substantial, I make no doubt she would have been snapped up years ago. Huntsmere is not a man to flaunt his wealth, which usually means he has none. Mind you, Landry runs expensive, by the look of it."

"Huntsmere? Landry?"

"Your pardon, Edgerton, I forget you have not grown up with these people. The Earl of Huntsmere, father to the Lady Emma. Viscount Landry, only son and heir to the earl, and Emma's brother."

"Right. So not much money, and the heir is running through what there is of it, if I understand you correctly."

Gus laughed. "You are not serious, Edgerton? About Emma?"

"A titled wife? That would suit me very well, if she has a reasonable dowry."

"You must have a good income, surely? You hardly need to look for a rich wife."

"I do not *need* to, no. I have fifteen hundred a year, few expenses and an expectation from a great-uncle. But a little more would make me very comfortable. I should like a snug little hunting lodge and a string of hunters like yours, Marford."

"I can see the attraction in *that*, to be sure, but marriage is a high price to pay for the pleasure, I should have thought. I have my hunting without the need to become leg-shackled first."

"You are a queer fish, Marford. You think more of your horses than of any woman."

"Of course I do! Look at Jupiter — such a splendid creature, and see the intelligence in those eyes! And no need to have any conversation, or dance with him, or bring him posies of flowers. Horses are far superior to humankind, Edgerton."

"Hmm. I wager you will find yourself leg-shackled eventually, nevertheless. Bound to happen."

"Not if I can help it," Gus said firmly.

END OF SAMPLE CHAPTER OF *Lord Augustus*

Made in the USA
Coppell, TX
08 July 2022

79702616R00152